Fion

Fiona's Fate

FREDRICA ALLEYN

BLACK
lace

First published in 1994 by
Black Lace
332 Ladbroke Grove
London
W10 5AH

Copyright © Fredrica Alleyn 1994

Typeset by CentraCet Limited, Cambridge
Printed and bound by Cox & Wyman Ltd, Reading,
Berks

ISBN 0 352 32913 0

Black Lace novels are sexual fantasies.
In real life, make sure you practise safe sex.

Chapter One

*F*iona Sheldon surveyed the long, mahogany dining-room table, now set for tonight's dinner party for twenty guests, and wondered where on earth her husband, Duncan, could be. Not that she was particularly anxious to see him. Ever since her friend Bethany had arrived to stay, Duncan had spent most of the time trying to persuade Fiona to suggest a threesome to her friend. Last night he had become particularly insistent, and in the face of her continuing refusal the violent sex between them – she couldn't possible call it lovemaking any more – had left her physically and mentally bruised.

No, it wasn't that she wanted to see him for herself, it was just that he always insisted on making a final check of dinner-party arrangements himself, and tonight he was running out of time. The invitations had clearly stated eight-thirty for nine and it was already seven forty-five. She wondered where on earth he could be, and what was important enough to take precedence over a dinner party specifically designed to appease the growing antagonism between Duncan and the powerful Trimarchi family.

Checking her watch, Fiona decided that she couldn't wait for him any longer. She told the housekeeper that

1

everything looked spelendid, then went upstairs to her bedroom to change. She only hoped that when Duncan did finally arrive he wouldn't be in one of his increasingly frequent bad moods. Dinner parties like this were difficult enough without that added complication.

Even as Fiona was making her way upstairs, her head buzzing with worries about the state of her marriage and the evening that lay ahead, Duncan was kneeling naked on the double bed in the main guest room, his hands round the deliciously curved waist of Bethany Morris, Fiona's closest friend. He was lunging fiercely into her from behind as she lay face down on the bed with her waist-length red hair spread out over the ivory-coloured silk sheets.

A little under six feet tall with grey hair and very pale blue eyes, Duncan was still, at fifty years of age, an attractive man. He took care of his figure and was immensely proud of his physical stamina. At this moment he was thrusting into Bethany, his hands gripping her waist more tightly than was strictly necessary and every time he drove into her he took pleasure in her gasps.

Bethany felt warm and moist and as his rhythm increased in power, her face was pressed hard into the bed, muffling her cries of pleasure and making the bed shake. Her breathing was rapid, and the muffled moans became more frantic as her climax approached. Duncan remembered Fiona's tight-lipped acceptance of him last night; her ice-cool response to his furious, rough taking of her, and compared it to the buxom, animal-like responses of her friend. The thought spurred him on.

It was no longer Bethany he was taking; it was Fiona. He slammed into her harder and harder, punishing her for refusing to accept his way of life, his desires and wishes, while beneath him Bethany squirmed and cried out as her body responded. She felt the wonderful, gathering tension deep within her; the ache low down in her stomach that heralded her ultimate satisfaction and, totally unaware that Duncan didn't even remember who she was any more, she waited for the final trigger to bring her to her climax.

Duncan didn't disappoint her. As she waited, poised on the edge of satisfaction, his right hand moved from her waist and up to her right breast which he grasped so tightly that even Bethany was taken by surprise. Then he bent his fingers so that his hand became a claw and he raked his nails from the outside of her swollen breast inwards to the rigid nipple, leaving five livid streaks of red on the creamy flesh.

At exactly the same moment as his nails marked her breast, he pulled her body hard against his and the tightening of her vaginal walls as she went into a fierce orgasmic spasm triggered his climax so that he ejaculated within seconds of Bethany's own climax.

The violence of his orgasm took him by surprise. He realised that it must be because he'd been thinking of Fiona, and how different her response would have been. Collapsing onto the bed next to his mistress he smiled to himself. However much his wife tried to distance herself from him, he knew that in the end he could always get pleasure from her. Either like this, by having an affair with her best friend, or by bringing about his favourite fantasy. He could always force Fiona into doing what he wanted because of her ridiculously outdated loyalty to her parents, and the belief that it was her duty to try and please her husband. Well, it would please both him and Bethany to have Fiona join them in this very bed and before Bethany left he would make sure that it came about.

Bethany lay quietly beside him. She'd rather hoped that the sex would go on for longer. She was quite capable of more than one orgasm, as Duncan well knew, but it looked as though this time she was going to be unlucky. She took hold of Duncan's right hand and put it between her thighs, but he simply laughed and removed it.

3

'No time for that this evening, Beth. It's the big dinner party in half an hour, remember?'

Bethany pouted and rolled onto her side. As though she could forget. She'd spent most of the day helping Fiona get everything organised, and as running a house held no attraction for her at all, it had been an incredibly boring day. All that had kept her going had been the thought of sex with Duncan later, and now that had ended far too quickly.

They'd been lovers for nearly a year. Her friendship with Fiona, which went back over ten years, long before Fiona's marriage, had provided them both with numerous opportunities to meet but this was the first time they'd actually been able to have sex under the same roof as Fiona and it had certainly added to Bethany's excitement; Duncan's as well she thought.

'What did my wonderful wife have to say about me today?' he asked, idly running a well-manicured hand down Bethany's spine.

'She was complaining that you're not nearly as thoughtful as when you were first married!' laughed Bethany. 'I pretended to sympathise, but she didn't give me any interesting details.'

'The trouble with Fiona is that she behaves exactly the way she looks, like a well-bred lady. It's what I wanted on my arm and at my table, but it certainly isn't what I want in my bed!' laughed Duncan. 'Still, it's stimulating trying to change her.'

Bethany sighed. 'You'll never change her. Fiona's surprisingly strong-willed over things that she really believes in. That's probably the only reason she stays with you,' Bethany added with a touch of malice.

'She stays with me because I provided her bankrupt parents with a home and her useless father with a place on one of my company's boards, which makes him feel a useful member of society again. To Fiona's way of thinking, that means she has to fulfil her side of the bargain and be a "good wife".'

'What a shame you'd rather have a bad one!' laughed Bethany, wriggling on top of Duncan and rubbing her body the length of his. 'What did she say about a threesome?'

Duncan pushed Bethany away none too gently and began to pull on his office clothes. 'She said no, of course. I'd probably have been disappointed if she'd said yes. After all, most of the pleasure will come from her reluctance. I like bending her to my will.'

'I shall have to pretend I don't like it either,' said Bethany quickly. 'Otherwise it will be the end of our friendship, which will make it more difficult for us to meet.'

'Wonderful, you can play the outraged guest, Fiona will be the hysterical wife and I shall be the villain of the piece and have the time of my life. I can hardly wait. However, for now, duty – and more importantly Alessandro Trimarchi – calls.'

'What's so special about him?' asked Bethany, her body still tight with unsatisfied desire. She resented anyone who took her lover away from her before she was finished with him.

'I owe him a hell of a lot of money,' retorted Duncan, his usually urbane tone somewhat brittle. 'I'm relying on Fiona to be extra nice to him. He's bound to find her attractive. All men do.'

Privately Bethany thought it was highly unlikely that Fiona, in the kind of mood she'd been in all day, would agree to being 'nice' to anyone just to please Duncan, but she kept a diplomatic silence. If Duncan was let down by his wife then he would almost certainly make sure that they had their threesome once the dinner party was over, and that was something Bethany could hardly wait to experience.

'What shall I wear tonight?' she asked, sensuously running her hands over her full breasts.

'Whatever you like. Fiona's the one who matters tonight,' Duncan retorted.

5

When he'd gone, Bethany threw a slipper at the door to relieve her temper and frustration.

Duncan walked into his wife's bedroom just as one of the maids was helping her dress for the evening. He dismissed the maid with a brief wave of the hand, then strolled across the room to stand behind Fiona, who was sitting in front of her dressing-table mirror.

She had chosen a crimson off-the-shoulder dress and her shoulder-length chestnut coloured hair was hanging in loose curls. Her dark brown eyes were flecked with green, he noticed, something that only happened when she was nervous or excited. Tonight he guessed that it was nerves. Early in their marriage it had amused him to arouse her just enough to see the green flecks appear and then lose interest in her. Watching the green lights vanish gave him a glow of sexual power that was almost as good as a climax, and no matter how much Fiona tried to disguise her disappointment she never realised that her eyes gave her away. It had been a good game, but he had tired of it quickly, as he tired of most things.

Fiona eyed him carefully in the mirror. He looked amiable enough, but she knew that was meaningless. His moods could change with terrifying swiftness. 'You're later than usual,' she said softly.

'I was held up at the office. Everything under control?'

Fiona nodded. 'Of course.'

He stood over her, his hands resting on her naked shoulders. 'There's a small bruise behind your shoulder bone at the back here that shows. Have you any concealer stick?' he asked.

They both knew that the bruise had happened last night, but Fiona's eyes dropped from where they had been holding his in the mirror. She didn't want to remember last night.

Silently she handed him the concealer stick, and then glanced into the mirror again. Duncan licked a finger, rubbed the stick against it and softly spread the flesh-coloured cream over the purple bruise. His finger was featherlight, almost caressing, and yet Fiona shivered. For a moment more he stood there, letting the other fingers of his hand play across her skin and feeling the tension grown in her body, a tension born out of a mixture of sexual excitement that she desperately wanted to stamp out, and fear of whatever other pain he might inflict on her.

He found it amusing to watch her like this, but there was no time for mind games right now. Quickly, he opened the jewel case that he'd brought with him and drew out a necklace of rubies and diamonds, complete with matching earrings.

'You chose the right dress, Fiona. These will go perfectly with it.'

Fiona, her body still burning from the touch of his fingers on her exposed back, stared expressionlessly at him in the mirror. There was always a catch to Duncan's presents. This time she had no doubt that it was a bribe directed once again at his desire for a threesome with her and Bethany. It was a waste of his money she thought with a brief flash of pleasure. She'd never let him humiliate her best friend like that.

'All you have to do, Fiona,' he said flatly, 'is be nice to Alessandro Trimarchi tonight. You've done that sort of thing for me before, only tonight it's even more important. If you fail, I may well end up as bankrupt as your precious father, and then where will we all be?'

Fiona shuddered. The memory of various elderly plump fingers straying over her arms and neck and generally being intimate with her during long, hot evenings while his husband watched her ensnare his opponents made her feel sick, but the reminder of what would happen to her elderly parents if she didn't do as he asked was the only spur necessary to make her co-operate.

'Well?' he asked impatiently.

Fiona nodded. 'Don't I always do what you want?' she asked shortly.

'In our public life yes, but in private you're sometimes a great disappointment to me,' he retorted.

'I've no intention of living my private life to suit you in order to protect my parents. If it's business it's different,' she said shortly.

'I suppose you're protecting Bethany when you refuse my request for a threesome?'

'Yes, I am. Bethany and I have been friends for years. She's a nice, uncomplicated girl who trusts me. I wouldn't dream of dragging her into your perverted world,' said Fiona furiously.

Duncan smiled at the irony of hearing Fiona protect possibly the most uninhibited mistress it had ever been his good fortune to have. However, he knew that despite Fiona's promise, it was important that she was in the right mood to go along with his plans for Alessandro Trimarchi.

'I like your hair loose,' he murmured. 'It reminds me of the first time I saw you, that day I came to see your father.'

'Considering that was probably the unluckiest day of my life, perhaps I should wear it up tonight,' retorted Fiona.

Duncan grasped her round the waist and pulled her up off the stool. He then sat on the edge of the bed turning Fiona, who was still standing, to face him and trapping her between his knees. He watched the rise and fall of her breasts, held tight within the dress, and felt her draw herself as far away from his body as she could.

Slowly, he let his fingers splay out round her waist, running his thumbs down over the tight silk of the dress across the sensitive hip-bones beneath. Fiona felt her flesh jump in response but kept her face impassive.

'Relax,' murmured Duncan. 'You know you like that. Enjoy it.'

'I used to like it,' she said tightly. 'Now I just wish you'd leave me alone.'

'Surely you'd like some pleasure? I taught you well enough. You can't tell me you don't miss it?'

Fiona shrugged. Inside she was burning with impotent fury. Of course she missed the good sex they'd once had. Duncan had indeed taught her body well. Early in their marriage, once he'd penetrated her natural reserve, he had coaxed forth responses that had astonished both of them and she'd come to anticipate their nights with excited pleasure. But then he'd changed; the sex had become more violent, more extreme, and she hadn't been ready to follow him along the paths he wanted. As soon as she failed to respond as he wanted, he'd deliberately withheld the kind of sex she did enjoy, and although she'd tried to discipline her body into forgetting she'd failed. Her body remembered very well, and when he touched her as he was touching her now her memories became even more vivid and she longed for sexual satisfaction again.

'Let me do what you like,' he coaxed her.

'We haven't time,' Fiona said, trying to sound totally disinterested. 'Anyway, I'm dressed now.'

'I don't have to undress you. I can manage like this,' Duncan assured her.

Imprisoned by his knees, she felt one of his hands edge up beneath the hem of her skirt and then his fingers were teasing the soft delicate flesh at the top of her legs, creeping round to the inside of her thighs and stroking rhythmically back and forth until she felt her hips move forward as her starved body moved towards this possible source of pleasure.

Duncan's thumb brushed against the tight crotch of her panties and he heard her suppress a soft moan deep in her throat. Encouraged, he eased his hold on her with his knees and pulled her carefully round so that she was sitting on the bed next to him. Then he lifted her back a little and knelt on the floor in front of her.

Fiona was wearing black silk hold-up stockings and his hands caressed the silk lovingly, easing her legs apart and moving up to the patch of exposed flesh above the elasticated top.

Fiona shut her eyes. If this was a bribe, then she'd accept it. After last night, the aggressive violence and the pain, she'd earnt some pleasure. Through her tight-fitting panties Duncan's tongue skimmed lightly over the material and she felt herself growing damp both from his tongue and, more shamingly, from within.

His hands slid beneath the cheeks of her bottom and he lifted her slightly off the bed so that he could cover a larger area with his mouth. He sucked at her through the material, drawing her bud of pleasure into a hard little peak and all the time he continued to stroke the delicously responsive flesh of her thighs.

Fiona could hear her own breathing now. Knew that it was ragged and urgent, but she didn't care. He was her husband, and she was entitled to this. Her breasts began to feel too large for the dress; they were swelling in anticipation of a pleasure too long denied.

'Look at me, Fiona,' whispered Duncan.

Fiona opened heavy-lidded eyes, and Duncan saw the hoped-for green flecks that told him, as if her other physical responses hadn't, how excited she was. He felt a flow of triumph and pulled her dress back down again.

'What a pity our guests will soon be here,' he said casually.

The ache in the pit of Fiona's stomach was like a pain, and her clitoris was burning as it pressed against her panties. She stared at him in total confusion. 'Duncan, please! It will only take another minute!'

'A minute I don't have, but I'm sure Alessandro will more than make up for my inability to finish what we've begun.'

Even Duncan was startled by the expression of loathing that entered his wife's eyes as she stared at him, absorbing the full extent of the trick he'd played on her. 'I hate you,' she said, her voice trembling with thwarted passion. 'Why I ever let myself believe it was going to come to anything I can't think, but I promise you it's the last time I'll make such a mistake.'

'We'll see about that,' said Duncan easily. 'If Alessandro doesn't manage to satisfy you, your body will want someone to attend to it, and I am your husband.'

'I wish to God you weren't!' replied Fiona, humiliated and enraged.

'There are plenty of women who'd be more than willing to trade places with you if you wish to leave,' said Duncan smugly, thinking of Bethany.

'They wouldn't be if they knew what you were really like,' Fiona answered.

'You look wonderful now!' enthused Duncan. 'Your eyes are shining, your cheeks flushed; Alessandro won't be able to resist you!'

Fiona straightened her dress, then sat shaking with anger and frustration as Duncan fastened the necklace and earrings. Then, realising that he had no intention of leaving her alone in case she gave herself the satisfaction he'd denied her, she had to take some deep, calming breaths and go downstairs to greet the guests while beneath her cool exterior her body throbbed and her breasts burnt even at the touch of her dress against them.

Eventually the desire that Duncan had aroused died down and it was then that Fiona made a vow that she would never again let anyone arouse her into any kind of sexual response. As for this Alessandro, whoever he might be, well she'd let him paw her and fumble around but it wouldn't affect her, she wouldn't even think about what was happening. She'd detach herself completely from this ageing company director's pathetic imitation of lovemaking and tomorrow she'd tell Bethany something of the life she was having to live with Duncan.

11

At least, that was the way she was thinking until she actually set eyes on Alessandro Trimarchi. Once that happened, it all became more complicated.

He and his long-time girlfriend, Georgina, were the last two guests to arrive that night. Duncan had managed to work himself up into a frenzy by the time they had put in an appearance. If Alessandro didn't come, then Duncan wasn't sure that he could delay repaying his debt any longer, and the truth was that he simply didn't have the money. He had expanded his business too fast and the banks were calling in their loans which made repaying the Trimarchis out of the question right now.

'That's Alessandro,' Duncan hissed at Fiona as the couple were let in by the butler he'd hired for the evening. 'After dinner, once I've had a few words with him, I want you to take him off somewhere *and do whatever he wants*. Is that clear?'

Fiona looked at the man standing just inside the door. He was about six feet, two inches tall, very broad-shouldered but slim-hipped, a combination she'd always found attractive. However, it was his face which really caught her attention. His smooth olive-skinned complexion showed signs of dark shadows round the chin, even though he'd clearly shaved that evening, and he had high cheek-bones and a typical Roman nose beneath which the mouth was set in a tight line which emphasised two sharp lines running from the side of his nose past the corners of his mouth. All of that was enough to make him handsome, but his eyes were totally hypnotic and – had Fiona but known it – they were responsible for making him virtually irresistible to women.

They were coal black, so dark that the irises were difficult to distinguish, and he had long thick lashes, while the eyebrows were set high, enlarging the eyes and off-setting the very heavy lids. Fiona stared directly into his eyes, and suddenly her mouth went dry.

Duncan put a hand in the small of her back, and none too gently pushed her towards Alessandro. 'I don't believe you know my wife, Fiona,' he said smoothly. The Italian took Fiona's hand, lifted it to his mouth and kissed the air above it. It was a practised and meaningless gesture that irritated her. She hadn't expected him to be the kind of man who deliberately played on his Italian charm.

When he bent his head over her hand, she just had time to notice that his blue-black hair was streaked with threads of grey and then he'd straightened up and was staring intently into her eyes for a moment. The look he gave her then wasn't in the least conventional. It was an assessment, a summing-up of her looks and appeal and as his eyes widened in appreciation she turned away, her body suddenly remembering the earlier sensations of the evening.

Duncan, who was watching his wife carefully, noticed her nipples pressing prominently against the bodice of her tight-fitting dress and smiled to himself. At least she wouldn't be difficult tonight. The last thing he wanted was for Alessandro to be turned down by Fiona, but by the look of things his calculated arousal of her earlier was paying off.

Georgina watched her lover with some amusement. Whenever he met an attractive woman he would fix her with the same gaze and make his own private assessment; but although he slept with many he always returned to her because she knew how to keep him happy. Fortunately she had never been the jealous type of woman, and as a fashion editor for one of the country's leading women's magazines she had a job that kept her busy while Alessandro was working or playing the field.

A short, slim woman with cropped dark hair that was smoothed sleekly to her head, Georgina was impossible to ignore. She wore dramatic make-up and even more dramatic clothes, usually sensuous, clinging designs

13

which Alessandro liked. This evening her dress was white with wide black lines cutting diagonally across the front while there were cut-out keyholes at each side of the waist. The strapless top hugged her small, neatly rounded breasts tightly and as usual she wore no underwear.

Following Alessandro into the dining room she hoped that the dinner wouldn't go on too long tonight. It was over a week since the pair of them had been together and she was desperate for the feel of his clever, knowing hands and mouth on her body. Their relationship was the most dangerously exciting and erotic she had ever experienced, and she knew that she was lucky to have met him. He was everything she could have hoped for, and Georgina intended to make sure that he kept returning to her. She didn't want marriage any more than he did, but she wanted to keep her place in his bed and would go to almost any lengths to make certain that she did.

The dinner went smoothly. Duncan had Georgina seated on his right. Although she wasn't Alessandro's wife he knew that they were considered a couple by everyone who knew them, and felt that the Italian would expect her to be treated as though they were married. At the opposite end of the table, Fiona had Alessandro sitting on her left. On the other occasions when Duncan had told her that she had to be 'nice' to certain guests, she had managed to give a good imitation of a sparkling, lively hostess all through the dinner, which made what followed later easier; the men in question already convinced that Fiona was enchanted by them.

This time it was different. The sheer physical magnetism of Alessandro had the effect of silencing Fiona. Having just vowed never to let her body become aroused by any man again, she found herself sitting next to one who even without trying was having a physical effect upon her. Her breasts tingled every time he glanced at her, and the ache at the pit of her stomach that Duncan had originally caused had returned with a vengeance.

When Fiona watched Alessandro handling his knife and fork she found herself studying his hands. The long, slender fingers were delicate, precise; she could almost feel them on her body, touching her where Duncan had been touching her earlier, and her cheeks grew hot.

Later, when he peeled a small tangerine and bit into one of the tiny segments with his white, even teeth and then flicked his tongue into the corner of his mouth to catch the juice her stomach lurched as she imagined what it would feel like to have his mouth kissing hers. She didn't allow herself to picture it in more intimate places.

After coffee and liqueurs, they all left the table and went into the other rooms in small groups. As instructed, Fiona let Duncan take Alessandro away for a few words while she waited in the hallway. Later she would take him into the small drawing room where she had always taken the other men she was expected to entertain, but this was the first time that her heart had quickened with excitement at the thought instead of dread.

She tried to control herself. It was all so pointless. Even if by some miracle this Alessandro Trimarchi turned out to be as good a lover as her overheated imagination was picturing, she couldn't allow herself to respond. What was the point when her married life was so sexually frustrating? It would only make things worse. And yet, another part of her was telling her to go with it. To make the most of the experience if it was good.

Torn between desire and shame at her thoughts, Fiona didn't realise at first what a long time she'd been waiting. People had been passing through the hallway, making for the main drawing room or the garden, but Alessandro still hadn't appeared.

Suddenly, Duncan came out of the door she was watching. 'What the hell are you doing here?' he demanded harshly. 'You should be with Alessandro. He was most unco-operative about the money. It's all down to you now.'

'I haven't seen him,' protested Fiona.

'He left by the other door, but he must be around somewhere. Go and find him, and remember, whatever he wants just do it. Forget that damned puritanical streak of yours. He's a sophisticated man and he'll expect you to match him.'

'I don't get much practice at that kind of thing with you,' retorted Fiona, pleased to see the look of fury on Duncan's face before she hurried away.

She checked all the main rooms, but there was no sign of the elusive Italian. Finally she came to the study. This room was usually kept locked. Duncan kept all his business papers in there, in the safe. She paused outside the door.

There were definitely noises coming from inside the room. It struck her that Alessandro was probably more interested in Duncan's work than in his wife, and that he had somehow managed to get the door open and was now going through her husband's business papers.

She didn't care about Duncan or his business, but she did care about what happened to her parents. If Alessandro crippled Duncan financially then they would again be homeless and she wasn't sure they could cope with that. Added to which if she failed tonight, Duncan would be sure to start on about involving Bethany in one of his depraved games and that was something she didn't want either.

Spurred on by these thoughts she turned the handle of the heavy oak door and pushed it slowly open. If Alessandro was in there, trying to find out business secrets, then she would have to take his mind off them.

She only hoped he found her attractive enough to be a distraction. When she opened the door and crept inside, Alessandro wasn't busy with Duncan's papers at all. He was busy with Georgina.

Georgina was lying on her back across Duncan's huge writing desk, with her head towards the door. The top of her dress had been pulled down to her waist and Alessandro, standing on the far side of the desk between her legs, was bent over her, his hands on the desk to support his weight while he bent his head over her breasts.

Neither of them had heard Fiona's entry. Alessandro's tongue was moving in long, slow strokes up the undersides of Georgina's breasts and then circling the nipples lazily without ever actually touching them. Fiona stared at the taut erect nipples standing up from the small breasts and listened to Georgina's frantic moans as she tried to pull her lover's head directly onto them.

Alessandro ignored her movements. He continued to lap at the soft undersides of the breasts, and every time Georgina's hands grabbed at his head to move him directly onto the nipples he deliberately moved further away from them, his tongue teasing the surrounding aureoles with tiny swirls instead while Georgina's nipples continued to grow, changing from pale pink to red as they became suffused with blood.

The blood was coursing through Fiona's veins as well. She found that she was totally hypnotised by the sight in front of her. Her throat was tight, it was impossible for her to swallow, and even worse, every stroke of Alessandro's tongue across Georgina's breasts seemed to sear Fiona's breasts as well and her nipples felt just as swollen and desperate as Georgina's looked.

Now Georgina began to move on the desk, her hips writhing as her moans increased. Slowly, Alessandro lifted his head to move lower down his mistress's body and it was then that he saw Fiona. For a few brief seconds they stared at each other in mutual shock, but then Alessandro's mouth lifted in the briefest of smiles before he returned his attention to Georgina and continued as though Fiona wasn't there.

His hands slipped languourously down Georgina's hips and then up under the skirt of her dress, just as Duncan's had done to Fiona earlier, only this was so different that it was as though the two incidents were entirely unrelated.

Georgina, who still wasn't aware of Fiona's presence, began to gasp. 'Yes! Yes, now! Now!' she cried, her voice thick with passion. Alessandro gripped her more firmly round her hips and pulled her across the desk so that she was nearer to him. Then, to Fiona's excited horror, he reached down to unzip his flies while at the same time staring directly into Fiona's eyes.

He was actually going to enter Georgina while she stood there and watched, she realised. Well, she wasn't going to let him. Georgina's pleas increased, and finally Fiona managed to wrench herself away from the erotic scene that was unfolding before her and almost fell out of the room, pulling the door closed behind her.

As Alessandro slid into Georgina and they fell into their familiar rhythm he found that it wasn't Georgina he was thinking of. Instead it was Fiona, her face and neck flushed, her nipples plain to see beneath the dress and her breathing almost as rapid as Georgina's.

Beneath him, Georgina was close to climaxing. She always came quickly the first time after they'd been apart for a few days, but Alessandro was nowhere near a climax. He was busy trying to work out the complexity of the signals Duncan Sheldon's wife had given out. Through dinner she'd been off-hand, but clumsy as though he unsettled her. Her body language wasn't that of a sensual woman, she held herself too tightly constrained, and her arms were often crossed across her body in an unconscious gesture of protection, yet watching her just now he'd known that his first instinct on meeting her was right. She had the potential to be an incredibly sensual woman.

Georgina, lost in the sensations of her own orgasm, didn't realise at first that Alessandro wasn't sharing her release. It was only when her body finished its final shudders of pleasure that she realised he was still hard and erect. Quickly she slid from the desk top and started to kneel in front of him but he pulled her up and straightened her dress. 'I'll save it for when we get back,' he said casually. 'This was just for you, because I was pleased to see you again!'

Georgina hoped that was true. He looked as though his thoughts were miles away, but he'd been keen enough to take her on Duncan's desk, no doubt encouraged by the risk of interruption because danger always added an edge to his excitement. She smiled brightly. 'I can hardly wait for us to leave.'

Casually he patted her on the bottom, a gesture she loathed but had never summoned up the courage to complain about, and ushered her towards the door. He was now highly excited at the prospect of what lay ahead of him. The plan had been worked out weeks ago, long before this dinner party and his first sight of Duncan's enigmatic wife. It had aroused him then, but now that he'd seen Fiona and knew more about her the idea seemed like a stroke of genius.

Over the next few weeks he'd have a chance to work out Fiona's true potential for sensuality at his leisure, and introduce her to a whole new world. He smiled at the thought.

Chapter Two

As soon as the last guest had left, Fiona went straight to her room. She'd tried to find Bethany but her friend seemed to have gone up already. She hoped this didn't mean Beth had been bored. Fiona valued their friendship, but now that Duncan was so caught up with his obsession about having Bethany join them for a threesome she knew that she'd never be able to have her friend to stay in the house again. It was a pity, but she decided that she'd tell her truthfully why it was, so that Bethany didn't think it was because Fiona no longer wanted to see her.

No sooner had Fiona taken off her dress and slipped into a satin nightgown that Duncan barged into the bedroom. He never knocked on his wife's door, although she always had to knock on his on the rare occasions she needed to go there to speak to him. They'd never shared a bedroom, not even at the start of their marriage.

'Well?' he demanded, pushing her down on the bed while he stood over her. 'How did you get on with Alessandro?'

Fiona tried to remain calm. 'I didn't "get on" with him at all. He was totally wrapped up in his girlfriend. I wouldn't have been of any interest.'

'You mean you didn't even try?' asked Duncan incredulously.

Briefly, Fiona considered describing the scene in his study to Duncan, but she decided against it. He'd probably only say she should have taken off her clothes and joined them. 'He spent all his time with his girlfriend. I couldn't even get him to come outside with me for a stroll round the gardens,' she lied, hoping to appease Duncan a little.

Duncan's face went white with anger, and then a dull flush of fury spread across it. 'You mean I still owe him the money? You stupid bitch! You know why he wasn't interested in you don't you? It's because he could tell you're frigid. Men like that, men of experience, they know these things. The one good thing about you when I met you was that you were beautiful. Not just beautiful, but sexy as well. Men looked at you and they wanted to take you to bed. Now they don't give you a second glance and they're right, because you're a cold, self-centred woman who doesn't know the meaning of passion. Unless you're lying underneath me and I whisper sweet nothings in your ear before doing everything according to your old-fashioned ideas of what's right, you're not interested are you? Well, are you?'

Fiona had heard it all before, but never shouted so loudly and never accompanied by such a look of hatred. 'If you mean I'm not perverted, no I'm not!' she retorted. 'I don't like having to seduce men you need for your business purposes, and I loathe it when you invite other women to join us in bed. That isn't what sex is meant to be about.'

'You've no idea what sex is meant to be about. You're the most puritanical woman I've ever met.'

'If I don't know what sex is about perhaps that's because you haven't been able to show me,' Fiona shouted, goaded into raising her own voice.

'Well I'll show you now,' replied Duncan. 'If you can't please me in my public life then you'll damn well

21

please me in private. Tonight we're joining your little friend Bethany for an interesting *ménage à trois*.'

'No!' shouted Fiona, trying to pull her hand free of his grasp but he was far stronger than she was and buoyed up by fury over what method the Trimarchi family might now use in retaliation against him, he dragged her along the landing and hammered on Bethany's door.

Fiona went to shout a warning, but he put a hand over her mouth and to her dismay Bethany immediately opened the door, wearing only a silk pyjama-jacket and a pair of brief silk panties.

As Duncan pushed Fiona into the room ahead of him, she heard Bethany give a startled scream of fright, but because her back was to the door Fiona failed to see her turn the key in the lock once they were all in the room.

Bethany was tremendously excited. Here was Duncan, the best lover she'd ever had and the only man she'd ever wanted to marry, actually in her bedroom with his wife, who happened to be her best friend. Not only that, but Fiona was so clearly against the incident that her resistance greatly added to the thrill. It was very difficult for Bethany to pretend to be afraid.

Duncan pulled Fiona's robe off and pushed her down onto the double bed. 'Get over here,' he said curtly to Bethany. She hesitated a moment, to make it look to Fiona as though she were only doing what he said because she was afraid for her friend. 'Hurry up!' he snapped, and this time she did as he said, inwardly burning with excitement.

'Hold her legs apart!' he ordered her.

Fiona kicked at him, her legs flailing in all directions. 'Don't do it. Go and get help!' she shouted, but she could see from Bethany's wide, terrified gaze that there was no chance of help. Because Bethany cared for her so much she would do everything that Duncan said, just to keep Fiona safe, in the same way as Fiona had tried to protect her, thought Fiona.

Duncan realised that Fiona wasn't fighting so hard now and quickly seizing her naked thighs in his bare hands he pressed them wide apart. 'Hold her knees,' he repeated to Bethany. Fiona felt her friend's small hands on the insides of her knees, the touch tentative. 'Wider,' ordered Duncan, and Fiona closed her eyes at the shame of exposing herself in front of her friend.

Bethany looked down at Fiona's closed eyes and jolts of pleasure shot through her. This was what she'd wanted all along. To see her friend humiliated like this in front of them both, totally unaware that Duncan and Bethany were already lovers and had been for over a year. It made up for the times she'd had to watch Fiona on Duncan's arm at official functions when it should have been her.

Fiona, her eyes closed, waited to see what would happen next. She didn't have to wait long. Suddenly Duncan's hands were pulling roughly on her outer nether-lips, separating them to expose the shiny pink inner lips to his and Bethany's intense satisfaction. He glanced briefly at Bethany, whose eyes were glowing with the thrill of the long-awaited moment.

Now Duncan lowered his head, and suddenly Fiona's hips jolted off the bed as her husband's tongue slid up and down the channel between her inner and outer lips. His hands pulled her apart more widely so that she could feel her secret opening being revealed to his own and Bethany's gaze and she cried out for him to release her, despite knowing that the appeal was useless.

Now his tongue was pressing harder, jabbing roughly at the place where the small hood of flesh covered her clitoris and again Fiona felt her hips jerk as sparks of sensation shot through her. It wasn't pleasure because his tongue was too rough, but neither was it pain, it was like an electric current running through her.

Suddenly, she felt Bethany's hands release her knees, and now Duncan was ordering Fiona to keep her legs apart herself if she knew what was good for her. She kept her eyes closed and obeyed. All she wanted was to save Bethany too much humiliation. It wasn't the first time she'd had to share her husband with another woman, but she felt sure it was the first time Bethany had ever been in this situation.

'Suck on her nipples,' Duncan ordered Bethany, who obeyed with such speed that Duncan wondered if Fiona would guess she was a willing partner in all this. Fiona bit on her bottom lip as she felt Bethany's small mouth closing round her right nipple, the soft lips barely touching her delicate flesh. 'I'm sorry,' Bethany whispered in Fiona's ear, but she wasn't really. She was delighted, especially when she felt Fiona's nipple begin to harden in the soft velvet of her mouth.

Between Fiona's thighs, Duncan's hands were now busy. He inserted two fingers into her vagina and began to work them in and out, slowly at first but increasing the speed as his tongue continued to lick and jab at her inner lips and clitoris.

Bethany's mouth was softly insistent, and she sucked appreciatively at Fiona's tight nipple before releasing the pressure, while her right hand enclosed the other breast, gently kneading it until the globe began to swell slightly.

Fiona fought frantically against the sensations that her body was experiencing. Bethany's touch was particularly knowing, the delicate sucking of the nipple almost too pleasurable and her hesitant fingers were massaging in such a way that arousal was almost impossible to fight.

Between her thighs, Duncan's tongue was as usual, too heavy and rough for the kind of pleasure Fiona had always wanted, but it was still effective, as was the rhythmic movement of his fingers and as her body began to gather itself together into a tight knot Fiona knew that after the earlier stimulation by Duncan, and then the extraordinary scene in the library, she wasn't

24

going to be able to deny herself the release that was close.

It was utterly shaming, but the pleasure grew and grew, until it seemed like a tight bright white light slowly shrinking into a pin-point that would then explode. Fiona tried to distract herself, to remember the humiliation of her position and Bethany's situation, but just as she thought that she was succeeding, Duncan managed to slide the protective hood of her clitoris back with his fingers and then jabbed at the exposed mass of nerve endings with the end of his tongue.

As the same time, Bethany, carried away by watching the heaving ripples of Fiona's stomach muscles as she tried to bring herself under control, closed her teeth over the tight nipple in her mouth and grazed its peak between them.

The culmination of the two sensations proved too much for Fiona and her hips rose up off the bed as her body convulsed in a spasm of pleasure that shook her from head to toe while Bethany and Duncan watched her and smiled at each other across her shaking body.

The relief after so much frustration was indescribable, but all pleasure for Fiona was ruined by the knowledge of the situation she was in.

'Open your eyes,' Duncan ordered her. She did as she said, and saw that Bethany, now totally naked herself, was lying next to her on the bed, eyes full of apprehension. 'Get your friend on her hands and knees,' said Duncan. 'I'm ready for her now.'

Fiona shook her head. 'No, I won't.'

Bethany could have screamed with frustration. She was desperate to have Duncan enter her while Fiona watched. It was to be the highlight of the evening for them both. 'Do as he says,' she pleaded. 'Let's get all this over with, Fiona, please.'

Fiona nodded. If that was what Bethany wanted, then she'd go along with it. Tomorrow they would both leave the house for good she thought to herself, and this knowledge gave her the courage to go on. Swiftly she positioned Bethany on all fours with her back to Duncan, and then, following Duncan's instructions, she took his already erect penis in her mouth and licked at it until he pushed her away impatiently. 'Some day perhaps you'll learn to do that properly,' he remarked, grasping Bethany round the waist. Bethany immediately lowered her arms so that her forearms were flat on the bed, this gave Duncan a better angle for entry and allowed her more satisfaction, but Fiona thought it was because her friend was so ashamed and she averted her gaze.

'Watch us, Fiona,' Duncan ordered her. 'Watch, or I shall have to do it all again.' Instantly, Fiona turned back to look at him, and felt a peculiar hollow sensation in the pit of her stomach as he eased the swollen head of his penis into Bethany's exposed opening. For a moment he paused, rotating his hips and letting the head of his penis tease Bethany's entrance until she whimpered with passion and nearly gave the game away by thrusting back against him.

Aware of her rising and almost uncontrollable excitement, Duncan quickly thrust himself into her fully, and then continued thrusting while his right hand slid beneath her and manipulated her clitoris.

Bethany loved the feeling of fullness when he was inside her and playing with her clitoris at the same time, and when she heard him order Fiona to slide beneath her stomach and play with her breasts hanging down in their voluptuous fullness she nearly climaxed with the novelty of the situation. It was all so bizarre and stimulating, having her lover and her best friend, who were also husband and wife, making love to her at the same time, that she felt she might faint with the intoxication of it.

Fiona did as she was told, but her touch was hesitant and uncertain. She barely brushed Bethany's nipples at all, and Bethany had difficulty stopping herself shouting at her to pinch them in the way she liked, but in the end the very hesitancy became arousing in itself and when Fiona's reluctant tongue finally grazed Bethany's stomach it was the trigger for her climax.

When it came, it was the most intense Bethany had ever had, and she couldn't stop herself from crying out in delirium while her body twisted and turned, still impaled from behind on Duncan who was just reaching his own climax, which was hastened by the intense spasms of Bethany's inner muscles.

When it was over, Duncan collapsed on Bethany's back while Fiona slid to the edge of the bed and stroked her friend's auburn hair, certain that Bethany was muffling her face in the bed to silence her sobs of humiliation and shame.

After what seemed an eternity, Duncan stood, pulling Fiona up with him. 'None of this would have happened if you'd done as I said with Alessandro tonight,' he told her. Fiona burned with fury to hear him blaming her for what he'd done to the two of them. 'You can explain that to your little friend here in the morning,' he added as he drew her out of the room.

As soon as they'd gone, Bethany sat upright, a wide smile of contentment of her pert little face. It had been just as good as she'd anticipated, possibly even better. Watching Fiona climax in front of them had been something she'd never expected to witness and it had provided the biggest thrill of the whole evening as far as she was concerned. Satiated and content she slid between the sheets and slept.

Finally alone in her own room, Fiona lay wide awake. She was furious with her body for betraying her in the way it had, determined it would never do so again and equally determined that by tomorrow night she and Bethany would be far away from Duncan's Mayfair home. In thinking this she was quite right, but not in the way she imagined.

* * *

The next morning, Fiona stayed in her bedroom until she knew Duncan would have left for work. Then she went downstairs, drank some coffee and waited with trepidation for Bethany to appear. So had no idea how they were going to face each other after the horror of last night.

She was surprised but relieved when Bethany, yawning sleepily, finally joined her and proceeded to chat about the dinner party the previous evening without any sign of awkwardness. It was as though the previous night's humiliation had never happened, and Fiona was grateful for her friend's tact.

'I need to buy some new clothes,' Bethany remarked. 'Why don't we go to Oxford Street and have a good look round? I hate choosing things alone and you've got such wonderful taste.'

Privately, Bethany thought that a lot of Fiona's clothes were boring. They suited her, and she always looked well-groomed, but there was no hint of sexuality about any of them. She'd mentioned this to Duncan, but for once he'd stuck up for his wife, saying that it was all right for a mistress to flaunt her sexuality but not a wife. This typically chauvinistic remark had rankled with Bethany for some time and now she was determined to tempt Fiona into buying something that Duncan would consider more suitable for a mistress.

'I'm not sure,' said Fiona, aware that she still had bruising on her body from her last two sexual encounters with her husband, and anyway the chauffeur wasn't free that day and she hated driving in London.

'Come on!' urged Bethany. 'We need to get away from this house. I want to talk to you about last night.'

Fiona lowered her eyes. She knew that Bethany was right, they had to talk, but even the memory of her own body writhing in pleasure in front of her friend was unbearable. How could she ever speak about it, let alone apologise enough? 'All right,' she agreed faintly.

'I shan't buy anything myself, but we'll talk properly over a long lunch.'

Half an hour later the two young women were setting off down the driveway, towards the garage where Fiona's smart red Celica was kept. Just as they approached the garage doors a large florist's van drove up and parked opposite the garage. Fiona didn't recognise the name on the side.

Bethany glanced across at it. 'Duncan must be feeling guilty,' she said in surprise. 'He's probably sent you a gorgeous peace offering.'

'You too I hope,' remarked Fiona. 'I can't begin to say how awful I feel about . . .'

She never finished her sentence. Suddenly the back doors of the van were thrown open and three masked men jumped out. Before the women even had time to scream they were roughly seized, their arms pulled up behind their backs and then they were bundled into the van which sped off at breakneck speed.

As soon as she felt herself hit the hard floor of the van, Fiona began to scream. The actual attack had taken her by surprise, but now she began to kick and fight, all the time making as much noise as possible. Beside her she could hear Bethany sobbing, and it crossed her mind that her friend had shown far more composure than that last night.

'Shut up,' said one of the masked men curtly. Fiona ignored him and continued to fight and scream while the jolting of the van threw her body around the hard floor. 'If you don't stop we'll shut you up,' the voice continued and all at once two pairs of hands grabbed hold of her, her mouth was forced open and a thick gag pushed inside. At the same time her wrists were handcuffed behind her and then a thick blindfold was tied round her head so that the only useful sense left to her was her hearing.

Now she began to panic even more and kicked out frantically, but she heard the men laughing and then

29

her ankles were quickly fastened together. Fear turned to terror as she realised how helpless she was, and for the first time she wished that she'd told someone where she and Bethany were going.

The van turned sharply left and Fiona was thrown against the legs of one of the men. He put his hands down, at first she thought to steady her, but then she felt them cupping her breasts through the silk of her blouse and she twisted desperately away from the touch, pulling her knees up and kicking out as best she could considering that her ankles were fastened. 'Quite a little fighter,' she heard a voice say. The next moment her blouse was being ripped open and hands were releasing the front fastening of her satin bra.

A scream built up in her throat, but she couldn't release it because of the gag, and, because of the blindfold, she had no idea where the kidnappers hands would go next. She began to shiver with shock and terror, and then she heard another voice say: 'Better not; the boss won't like it. Put the bag over her if she won't keep still. We'll have plenty of time to look at her later.'

Fiona wondered what kind of a bag they could be talking about, but she didn't have long to wonder because immediately a hessian body-bag was pulled over her head right down to her fastened ankles, where it was tied with a draw-string.

She wondered how on earth she would ever get enough air to breathe and her panic increased until some cool air hit her face and she realised that there had to be some air holes in the top of the bag. After that, there was nothing for her to do but lie silent and shaking at the feet of her abductors, and listen to their desultory exchanges and the intermittent whimpering of Bethany.

After a very long journey the van turned off the road they'd been following and Fiona could faintly hear the crunch of gravel beneath the wheels. Then at last her bruised body was given some respite as the van came to a halt. She was rolled to one side as the men opened the doors and then one of them picked her up and pulled her into a crouching position as he unfastened her ankles, before manhandling her out of the van and over the gravel.

Fiona's legs had turned to jelly and she stumbled several times, which merely amused her kidnappers. The sensation of having to walk into a wall of blackness was horrific and she wanted to hold her hands out in front of her, but they were still handcuffed behind her back.

'Steps here,' said one of the men and she drew back, afraid of falling. 'Come on, put your right foot down, surely even ladies of leisure know how to walk down steps!' he laughed. Tentatively she lowered one foot, and then when he prodded her in the back she moved the other, but all the time she was petrified of being pushed and pitching down into some kind of hole. Behind her gag she was whimpering and her eyes beneath the blindfold stung with hot tears.

At last, after several steps, she reached level ground again and the body-bag was pulled off over her head. Cool air surrounded her, and now the sound of Bethany crying was much louder. Somewhere a door was closed and bolted and Fiona waited tensely for whatever was to happen next.

The silence in the room was thick and heavy. No one was moving, nor could she hear the sound of any breathing except her own and Bethany's, but she knew they weren't alone. She realised this was all part of some kind of sadistic game, designed to terrify her and even though it was working, she vowed that she wasn't going to let her fear show.

After a good five minutes, during which time Bethany's crying increased in volume, someone abruptly unfastened Fiona's handcuffs and removed the constricting gag from her mouth. She drew in great gulps of air, grateful for the chance to breathe freely. She realised the Bethany couldn't have been gagged or she wouldn't have heard her crying. Again she decided that this was a calculated move. Bethany's distress was meant to unsettle her further.

She waited for the blindfold to come off, but it was left in place and now men's hands began to strip off her blouse and skirt. Her bra was refastened but her hold-up stockings were peeled off and she obediently lifted each foot in turn so that they could be removed. At that moment she felt that all she could do was go along with their demands if at all possible and wait to hear why she'd been taken.

Bethany had stopped crying now, but once or twice Fiona heard her friend give a sharp intake of breath, and every time that happened their kidnappers laughed with a new edge of excitement in their voices.

Once she was stripped down to her bra and pants, Fiona was left alone. Unable to see anything she was permanently tensed against the next touch, or the removal of one of these garments, but nothing happened. She wished that she could see. Being blind made her feel hideously vulnerable and unprepared, so that she had to bite her bottom lip to stop herself from whimpering like Bethany.

Then there was the sound of another door being opened, one at the opposite end of the room from where they'd entered, and for the first time Fiona heard the sound of a woman's voice.

'What a pathetic pair they look!' the woman exclaimed, and Fiona heard the newcomer's footsteps approaching her. She lifted her chin in defiance. 'I don't think Alessandro will care for the underwear,' the voice went on. 'Marcus, take off Mrs Sheldon's bra and panties for us, please.'

Fiona's hands moved protectively across her chest even as her brain absorbed the name of Alessandro. The thought that he was behind this, and that he would

32

presumably soon be coming to witness her humiliation was such a shock that she could hardly keep standing because of the weakness in her legs.

'Don't try and resist, Mrs Sheldon,' continued the woman's voice. 'Marcus would be only too happy to have to use force. I suggest you let him do as I say. Perhaps you'd be happier with the blindfold off as well?'

Fiona didn't answer, but as Marcus unclipped the front of the bra and peeled the satin cups away from her breasts, the woman stood behind her and untied the blindfold. Because of the pressure that had been against them it took some time for Fiona's eyes to adjust to the light again, and by the time they did, Marcus had already slid his thumbs up the sides of her panties and pulled them down round her ankles.

'Step out of them,' said the woman, still standing behind Fiona. When she ignored the instruction Marcus began to let his hands drift back up her legs, his work-roughened fingers harsh against the tender skin of her inner thighs. Quickly she did as she'd been told and the woman laughed. 'That's better. Now turn round. Let me have a look at you.'

Fiona was now facing the man called Marcus. He was short and dark with a heavy forehead and a sullen expression and beside him stood another taller man with fair hair and appreciative blue eyes that were lingering on her naked body with obvious excitement.

Quickly, she turned to face the woman. She recognised her at once. It was Georgina Prior, the woman she'd last seen spreadeagled over Duncan's desk while Alessandro Trimarchi made passionate love to her. At the memory Fiona's face grew warm.

Georgina's eyes swept up and down Fiona's body. 'You've a nice figure, Alessandro will appreciate that, but you don't hold yourself very well. Put your shoulders back more, it will make your breasts stand out better.'

33

Fiona simply looked at the other woman with loathing. 'Why have we been brought here?' she asked, wishing that her voice didn't sound so nervous.

Georgina smiled. 'Alessandro will tell you all about that. He should be here soon. In the meantime we must make you and your friend secure as well as comfortable. Your friend wasn't part of the plan, she just happened to be in the wrong place at the wrong time. Still, the more of us there are the greater the fun!'

Just then, Fiona heard Bethany give a gasp and she turned quickly to see her friend, naked except for a black G-string, being held from behind by the fair-haired man while another dark-haired man was nuzzling against her naked breasts, his heavy stubble leaving red marks against her fair skin. To Fiona's amazement, Bethany's nipples were standing out fully erect.

'Your friend is less inhibited than you it seems!' laughed Georgina, her eyes also caught by Bethany's visible excitement. 'Still, no doubt Duncan already knows that.'

'Duncan?' asked Fiona in astonishment. 'Bethany's *my* friend. If this is all some plot against Duncan you must let Bethany go. She's innocent.'

'She may be a lot of things, but innocent isn't one of them,' laughed Georgina. Then she signalled to the men to release Bethany. 'Get them both into the cuffs and sit them in the corner. Alessandro will come and see them as soon as he arrives so handle them carefully, you understand?'

The men nodded at Georgina turned and left the room. Although she hadn't offered any kind of comfort, Fiona had still felt safer with another woman in the room. Now she found that she was trembling again, and when the man called Marcus advanced towards her with what looked like a chain in his hands she backed away, horribly aware of her nakedness and inability to fight.

He held his hands out in front of him, wrists together and indicated that was what she was to do. As she obeyed, he fastened leather cuffs round each of her wrists, then pulled on a strap that ran between the two and pulled her wrists tight against each other. The chain he was holding was then threaded through a loop in the strap and Fiona was pushed into a sitting position in the corner of the room where the process was repeated with leather cuffs on her ankles. Now, with her ankles held fastened about an inch apart, the chain was drawn down from her wrists between her knees and into an opening on the ankle cuffs, then pulled tight until the only way she could sit comfortably was with her back upright against the wall, her hands held in front of her breasts, elbows resting on her knees which were drawn up and spread about six inches apart.

All three men studied her carefully. Fiona knew that they could see her most intimate parts quite clearly, while her breasts and nipples shrank beneath their gaze. 'That will do,' said the fair-haired man. 'He should approve. The chain can be altered if the position isn't quite right.'

'Bring the other one over,' murmured Marcus.

Fiona watched as Bethany, fastened in exactly the same way, was lifted over the floor and pushed down next to her. The only difference was that Bethany's breasts were standing out proudly, her nipples still stiff. As they sat her down, one of the men let his hands wander down the side of her body, lingering at the curve of her waist and Bethany's breathing snagged in her throat. Fiona, trying to make herself as invisible as possible, couldn't believe the look of excitement in her friend's eyes.

With one last look, the men finally left the two friends alone.

'I'm cold,' whimpered Bethany. 'Who are they? Why are we here?'

35

Fiona assumed that it must be the cold making Bethany's nipples so erect, and not the manhandling by the men. 'I rather think we're here because Duncan owes the Trimarchi family a lot of money. Obviously they intended to kidnap me, and you were unlucky enough to be with me at the time. I'm sorry, Beth,' she added miserably. 'I seem to bring you nothing but bad luck.'

'Well, Duncan will pay as soon as he hears won't he?' said Bethany.

'Of course. He's a great one for preserving outward appearances. Kidnapping his wife is hardly something he's likely to let these criminals get away with.'

'Will they ask for more money because I'm here too?' asked Bethany miserably.

Fiona would have laughed if she hadn't been so frightened and humiliated. 'Hardly. It isn't as though you mean anything to Duncan.'

This remark silenced Bethany completely. She hoped that it had been a genuine mistake to kidnap her as well, only she had a nasty feeling from what the woman had said that they might be aware of the fact that she was Duncan's mistress, in which case Fiona would soon know too.

Chapter Three

*A*s all their personal possessions had been taken away with their clothes, neither Fiona nor Bethany had any means of telling the time, but it seemed to Fiona that over an hour must have passed and still they were alone. The room, which she thought was a cellar, had no form of heating and she felt cold and uncomfortably cramped. Although anxious for some form of human contact before too long, she dreaded the arrival of Alessandro because of the position in which she had been left, with no part of her body hidden from his eyes when he came to look at her.

'How long will we be left do you think?' whispered Bethany a little later.

'How should I know?'

Bethany looked hurt. 'There's no need to be nasty. If you remember, it's your fault that I'm here.'

Fiona felt a rush of guilt. 'I'm sorry. I'm just so scared and . . .'

At that moment the door opposite them opened, and in walked Alessandro Trimarchi. He was followed by a younger, slightly shorter man, who was so like Alessandro himself that it was obvious he must be his brother, and Georgina Prior. The three of them advanced towards the two young women, and Alessandro's eyes never wavered from Fiona. While his brother, Edmund couldn't take his gaze away from the ample charms of Bethany, who was staring back at him with equal enthusiasm it was Fiona who held Alessandro's attention.

The sight of Fiona naked except for the cuffs and chain was indescribably arousing to Alessandro, and even the way she was shrinking back against the wall trying to hide her breasts as best could within the restrictions of the chain and cuffs, rather than sitting upright as Bethany was doing, didn't displease him. He'd felt certain that Duncan had somehow failed to release her full capacity for passion, and seeing her like this, he knew that she had a great deal to learn and he was going to be the one to teach her. He would quite happily have written off the money for the sheer thrill of the days that lay ahead.

Here, in this remote country house in Norfolk, set in eight acres of ground and secure within the encircling ten foot brick wall, patrolled by guard dogs day and night, he and his family and friends could play out their fantasies in the full. It was a house where everything was possible, and there were no limits except those chosen by the participants – a sensualist's delight.

He glanced briefly at Bethany. There would be no problem with her. He already knew from the reports his men had compiled that she was Duncan's mistress and a woman who enjoyed almost any form of sensual pleasure. The sight of her now as she made intimate eye contact with his brother merely confirmed this.

Fiona was different. She clearly hadn't learnt, or hadn't been given the opportunity to learn, all the things that were possible between men and women in order to give and receive pleasure. By the time Duncan got her back she would be a different woman and Alessandro knew that during her journey of discovery she would give him as much pleasure as she in turn would gain.

Bethany, quickly summing up the situation, realised that it was the taller more intense looking of the two men who was in charge and she decided to turn a pitiful gaze on Alessandro. Tears filled her eyes and she gave a small but heartbreaking sob.

Fiona, still pressed back against the cold wall of the cellar, turned to look at her friend in dismay but Alessandro simply leant over Bethany and tugged sharply on the middle of the hanging length of her chain. This jerked her wrists and ankles painfully tightly and forced her to lean forward so that her hair hung down, partially obscuring her breasts. She hadn't expected his response, and now genuine tears of dismay filled her eyes. It seemed the older of the Trimarchi brothers wasn't as impressed by her as the younger one was.

Fiona saw Alessandro's actions and swallowed hard. She was already trembling from head to foot, and didn't know how to cope with whatever lay ahead of her. Alessandro reached forward, ignoring her instinctive flinching, and pressed a small button on one of her cuffs. Immediately the chain lengthened and she was able to let her arms hang at her sides and straighten her legs. Darts of pain shot through her cramped muscles as she did so.

Alessandro waited a moment, reached out with both hands, took hold of her by the shoulders and pulled her to her feet. Then he walked into the middle of the cellar and Georgina led Fiona by the hand until she was positioned in front of the tall Italian. He murmured something beneath his breath and slowly ran the middle finger of his right hand from under her chin down between her breasts, across her nervously tensed stomach until it came to rest at the top of her pubic hair.

Fiona, her skin burning everywhere his finger had been, waited rigid with tension for what was to come, but to her surprise he simply removed his finger, withdrew his hand and nodded to himself. 'You expect pain, not pleasure?' It was a question, but she didn't think he expected her to answer. 'Is your husband a sadist, or simply careless?' This time he smiled, his white teeth flashing for a moment.

'Perhaps we should ask Bethany,' suggested Georgina, sweetly.

Fiona stared at Georgina in astonishment, and Alessandro frowned angrily at his mistress. 'First, we must explain to our guest why she is here, *cara*. I am afraid, Fiona, that your husband is refusing to repay us a considerable sum of money. It should have been returned three months ago. As a result you are our hostage. As soon as the money is paid, you will be freed. At first I thought it unfortunate that your friend here had to be involved as well. However, since she is your husband's mistress I think that it will speed up his reaction. What man wants to be without either his wife or his mistress?'

Fiona tried to moisten her dry mouth. 'Bethany isn't Duncan's mistress. She's just a friend of mine who happened to be staying with us for a few days.'

Alessandro's black eyes stared into hers. 'You really believe this?'

'I know it. You're the one who's got it wrong, not me. Bethany's been my best friend for over ten years.'

Alessandro signalled for Edmund to bring Bethany across to them. When the two women were side by side her turned to the shorter, red-haired woman. 'Tell your "best friend" the truth, Bethany.'

'He's mad, Fiona,' babbled Bethany. 'I don't know what he's on about. You know what happened last night. I was as shocked as you when Duncan brought you into my room. I had no idea what he was like. I thought he was in love with you, a gentleman, not . . .'

Alessandro reached out and closed his fingers round one of Bethany's nipples. 'So, last night you enjoyed the pleasures of three in a bed? How exciting, and right up your street I imagine. Just the same, you're lying. Tell Fiona the truth.'

'I've told her the truth!' shouted Bethany.

Alessandro's fingers tightened. Fiona tried to go to her friend's assistance, but Edmund held her tightly from behind and she couldn't move. At first, as pain darted through her breast, Bethany's eyes shone with excitement, but the pain increased beyond anything that was enjoyable and she could tell by the look in Alessandro's eyes that he had no intention of stopping until she admitted her affair to Fiona.

'Stop it!' she cried out at last. Alessandro's fingers released the crimson nipple, leaving it throbbing as much with desire as pain. 'It's true,' she muttered, turning towards an astonished Fiona. 'I've been sleeping with him for over a year.'

Fiona just stared at Bethany, her mind a turmoil. Visions of the previous night rushed through her head, and she realised that Bethany must have been a willing conspirator in the whole affair.

'It's your fault,' Bethany rushed on, shaken by Fiona's silence. 'He said you were hopeless in bed, that you wouldn't do anything he wanted. I didn't love him,' she added quickly. 'but I enjoyed the sex. I always enjoy sex with a good lover.'

Alessandro smiled. It was clear to him that Bethany was signalling her willingness to have sex with them as well.

He turned back to Fiona. The shock and humiliation of Bethany's remarks were all too clearly imprinted on her face and he felt a moment's pity for her. Then he remembered the money Duncan owed them, and how much he could teach the young woman in front of him before she left and the pity vanished to be replaced by his earlier excitement.

'Bring them both upstairs,' he told Edmund. 'I'd like to see the difference between them for myself.'

Quickly the two women were pushed through the doorway and up some steps into a modern kitchen. Georgina pulled on Fiona's chain, leading her through an arched doorway into a huge sunny room filled with couches and chairs, with numerous cushions of various sizes scattered all over the floor.

Alessandro gestured to Marcus and Craig, two of the men who had seized Fiona and Bethany earlier that day, and were now standing waiting against the far wall. Quickly they began to collect together cushions and pillows from around the room, and furniture was pushed back so that the cushions could be made to form two high, soft beds set side by side in the centre of the room.

'Edmund and Marcus are excellent masseurs,' Alessandro told Fiona as she stood tense and wide-eyed in front of him. 'I'm sure that both you and your friend will feel more relaxed after their attentions. It must have been a highly alarming day for you.'

Fiona backed away from him. 'They're not touching me,' she said furiously. 'I want to speak to Duncan. Get him on the phone. He'll pay the moment he hears what's happening here.'

'He already knows,' said Alessandro softly. 'Unfortunately he's having a little difficulty raising the money, which is why I want to make you as comfortable as possible. Plus, I wish to see for myself why he has taken your friend here as a mistress when he has such a lovely wife. I shall watch the massage with interest.'

Georgina, standing beside her lover, was aroused by Fiona's flushed humiliation and also intrigued by the contrast with Bethany's obvious eagerness to take part in what lay ahead. The red-head was already lying face down on one of the piles of cushions, her ankles now spread about a foot apart as Marcus had loosened her chain, and her arms stretched out above her head, palms down but still held by the cuffs.

Fiona stared down at Bethany's back. She saw the

softly dimpled buttocks, the creamy white skin of a true red-head and the soft outsides of her breasts where they showed beneath her ribs which were pressed against the cushions.

The knowledge that she too would look just as naked and be equally accessible to any of the men's touch was terrifying, but she knew that the last thing she wanted to do was give the Italian the satisfaction of showing her distress, so finally she lowered herself reluctantly onto the softness beneath her.

Both Edmund and Marcus already had bottles of massage oil in their hands. Carefully they each poured some into the palm of one of their hands and then warmed it by rubbing their hands together.

Fiona closed her eyes. Her mouth was tightly shut, her jaw aching with tension and when Edmund's hands first touched the tightly knotted muscles at each side of her neck she nearly cried out with terror and shock. Alessandro, who saw the way her whole body was taut compared with Bethany's limp and passively receptive muscles, moved to stand by Fiona's head. It was then that he saw the small purple bruises just beginning to turn yellow at the edges, and he silently pointed them out to his brother who nodded, and was careful to avoid them as he began.

His touch was light to begin with, and as his fingers slid smoothly across her flesh Fiona found that her breathing was becoming less constricted. No one had ever given her a massage before, and it was impossible to stay so rigid beneath such skilled hands.

As she slowly relaxed, Edmund allowed his hands to press more firmly on her back, moulding his palms to her soft contours and kneading at the flesh rhythmically while he worked his way down towards the small bones at the base of her spine.

As soon as he began to work on the tightly rounded cheeks of her bottom, Fiona felt herself tense again. Duncan had often started to caress her there before proceeding to humiliate her with painful indignities that gave her no pleasure at all. She guessed that this would be no different.

Edmund felt the change in her body beneath his hands and was surprised. Most of his women enjoyed it when he began working there, and usually their automatic reaction was to open their legs wider, but Fiona was definitely trying to close hers, without success since he was now kneeling between her outspread legs. He glanced across at his brother for guidance.

Alessandro, who had been watching Bethany as she sighed and wriggled beneath Marcus's less skilled but highly enthusiastic manipulations, caught his brother's eye and stood over Fiona again. He sat down on the cushions next to her and slid a hand beneath her naked stomach.

For Fiona, who had briefly imagined that Alessandro had been telling the truth and she might begin to relax a little, his hand was a sure sign that he, like Duncan, had been lying. She drew in her stomach muscles and tried to pull herself up off the bed, but Edmund pushed her firmly back down.

She could feel Edmund's hands continuing to glide over her buttocks, his fingers sliding into the surrounding creases and trailing down the backs of her legs, while at the same time Alessandro's hand was spread open over the middle of her stomach and all of his fingers were rotating very lightly.

Gradually, a warm glow began to spread through Fiona's lower body. Every time Alessandro moved his fingers the flesh lower down between the tops of her inner thighs was pulled slightly, and this gave rise to sparks of pleasure that tingled briefly before dying away.

Fiona knew what was happening. It was the same as it had been with Duncan. Despite herself she was becoming aroused, only this time she was quite determined to shut the sensations off before they grew out

44

of control. She tried to think of other things, of what Duncan might be doing now, of how much food was left in the freezer and whether or not she'd asked the gardener to weed the front borders.

Both Alessandro and Edmund could feel her body's reactions starting to fade. Alessandro frowned. On the pile of cushions next to them, Bethany had already been turned over and Marcus was now working his way carefully round her breasts and across her stomach, but he was careful not to actually touch either her breasts or her genitals until he was told he could.

Alessandro decided that it might be better if Fiona were in the same position. 'Turn over,' he said quietly. Fiona, her eyes still resolutely closed, ignored him. He sighed. 'Turn over, Fiona, or I'll turn you myself.'

Quickly she turned onto her back, but her eyes stayed shut because she couldn't bear to see the men and Georgina watching her. 'Look at us,' he murmured. 'You're escaping through your mind, I think. That's a mistake. Give yourself up to the pleasure. Open your eyes.'

Next to Fiona, Bethany was groaning voluptuously and longing for Marcus to touch her straining breasts. As her sounds increased in volume, Alessandro turned and nodded at Marcus who quickly let his oiled palms enfold the creamy globes that he'd been longing to touch from the beginning. Bethany arched her back, trying to get him to move one of his hands to between her thighs where her body was already damp from excitement.

Fiona could hear Bethany's cries and moans and it didn't help her control her own body's responses. She bit on her lip, and seeing this Alessandro gently licked one of his fingers and pulled her lip free of her teeth before inserting his finger into her mouth, sliding it around the inside of her lips and gums.

Startled, Fiona found herself automatically sucking on his finger and she was so distracted by this that her

45

eyes flew open and she found him staring down at her intently while his brother's hands continued their expert manipulations over the front of her shoulders, round her breasts and down across her flat stomach.

As he worked, Marcus's hands finally moved to Bethany's inner thighs and his strong fingers dug into the creases at the top so that her sex-lips began to move with each manipulation. For Bethany it was like paradise; this man was an expert at what he was doing, and her body loved every moment of what was happening. She began to tense in readiness of the time he actually began to explore her secret parts.

Fiona could hear Bethany's breathing becoming louder, and her friend's muted cries of excitement only heightened her own body's awareness of the sensations the two brother were arousing. Alessandro decided that he wanted to change places with his brother and at his signal, Edmund stopped the massage and went to sit by Fiona's head while Alessandro poured plenty of the scented oil into his own hands and carefully began to work on her lower stomach and thighs.

Fiona's body was almost out of her control now but she still fought to dampen its reactions. Alessandro was surprised to find that when he carefully parted her legs and opened her outer lips she was still quite dry. Their attentions had not caused any self-lubrication at all.

He hesitated, uncertain as to why that could be. It was obvious from her relaxing muscles and slowly engorging breasts that she was enjoying the experience, but it seemed that she was only willing to enjoy it up to a certain point. Quite why any woman should choose to shut off her natural sexuality to that extent he wasn't sure, but certainly if she was to be taught the ways that pleased him most then this simple exercise in arousal couldn't be allowed to fail.

Because of the oil on his finger it was a simple matter for him to slide it down the inside of her outer labia, where he paused to briefly circle the small opening he

46

would one day penetrate, before running his finger back up the inside of the inner lips.

Fiona's breath caught in her throat as his finger skimmed lightly across such a sensitive area, and at the same time she felt her nipples start to rise.

Alessandro saw this too, and leaving a finger still in her mouth he bent his head and licked lightly on each of the rosy buds in turn.

Fiona's increasingly stimulated body jerked, and Alessandro saw her inner sex-lips starting to turn a deeper shade of pink as her arousal grew. Encouraged by this he flattened the palm of his hand against the whole of her vulva and massaged gently, pulling the skin round in slow circles so that Fiona's clitoris was stimulated indirectly beneath the surface and her legs began to tremble.

Next to them, Marcus finally allowed his hands to move deeper between Bethany's thighs and as his finger slid into her already warm and moist opening she gave a cry of pleasure and within seconds her body was in a spasm of blissful release.

Her cry aroused both Alessandro and Edmund, but they tried to keep their rhythm and pace the same as Fiona gradually lost her battle to control herself and refuse them the satisfaction of seeing her reach a climax. They were simply too practised, and guided purely by her body's responses it was impossible for them to fail.

Alessandro continued to rotate the palm of his hand until he saw the flush of sexual excitement begin to appear on Fiona's chest and neck. Then, and only then, did he carefully part her tender inner lips and although she seemed to resist for a moment he let his finger draw a little of her own moisture from her now aroused and more open entrance and drew this up between the inner labia until he finally touched the emerging tip of her clitoris with such delicacy that Fiona wasn't even certain it was a touch.

All she knew was that the sensations that had been

building up inside her, the dreadful aching tightness that had grown despite her attempts to quell it, suddenly exploded into a mass of sensations that flooded her whole body making her groan aloud with relief and she felt her own moisture between her thighs as she finally fell back against the cushions, limp and briefly at peace.

Alessandro gave her a few minutes to recover then rose and stood over her. She stared back up at him, and he was surprised to see that resentment rather than passion clouded her gaze. 'How hard you made us work for that one simple orgasm,' he said lightly. 'Your friend has a much better understanding of sexual satisfaction. But, it is no great matter. At least we now know that your body is willing, it is your mind that resists. I think that before very long your pleasure will come more easily and frequently. Once you have mastered that, then perhaps you can learn how to please me!'

Georgina tucked her arm through Alessandro's. 'I thought you were going to fail,' she laughed.

'She was definitely hard work. This, I assume, explains the mistress.'

'But you prefer the wife all the same don't you?' asked Georgina.

Alessandro nodded. 'Yes, I definitely prefer the wife. I look forward to tomorrow, and a new approach.

Fiona, who was listening to all this, prayed that before tomorrow came, Duncan would have paid off the debt. Then, as Alessandro and his mistress left the room, she and Bethany were once again taken back to the cellar, their chains tightened, blankets thrown round them and there they were left for the night with only a bucket in the corner of the room for company. They didn't exchange a single word all night.

In the morning, after a long and virtually sleepless night, the two young women heard the door open and they looked towards the doorway with totally differing emotions. Fiona was dreading seeing the dark-haired menacing figure of Alessandro, while Bethany was hoping against hope that it would either be him or his younger brother Edmund. From what she'd seen of Edmund the previous day, he would be a wonderful diversion while they waited for Duncan to get them released. She thought Alessandro was probably the more inventive lover, with a dark streak that his brother lacked, but she was a realist and understood that Fiona was his main interest. His aim was to make Duncan suffer, and in an Italian's mind wives were more important to men's honour than mistresses.

In fact, it was a stranger who entered the cold cellar; a tall, slim fair-haired girl wearing cut-off jeans and a white blouse knotted below her bust, exposing a tanned bare midriff. She stared at the chained women in fascination.

'Hey, that's neat! Is it uncomfortable?' Neither Fiona nor Bethany could be bothered to answer her. Their aching muscles fuelled their resentment at the stupidity of the question. 'I'm Tanya,' the blonde girl went on. 'Edmund's girlfriend. I'm a model, so I was on my way back from the Bahamas when you got here last night. But Edmund's told me all about you.'

'A model?' asked Bethany. 'I'd have liked to have been a model if I'd been taller.'

Fiona closed her eyes. How Bethany could even begin to make small talk considering their position was beyond her understanding. She wondered why she'd never realised before how shallow and deceitful her friend could be.

'You both look exhausted,' Tanya chattered on. 'Not to worry, you're in for a treat now. I've come to take you upstairs for a bath. Georgina's gone to London, she works there some days and from home the rest of the time, so I've taken over from her. I'll get Marcus and Craig to help you upstairs. The restraints can't come off until you're safely inside the main part of the house.'

'Do you think we could use the bucket first?' asked Bethany. 'It was left too far away for us to reach it during the night.'

Tanya glanced into the corner and pulled a face. 'Ugh! There's no need, the bathroom you're using will be much nicer. Marcus, you can come in now!'

Marcus went straight to Bethany, pulling the blanket off her. Letting his hands wander over her exposed breasts and buttocks he began to half-carry her from the room. Craig, the tall fair-haired bodyguard, was more careful in the way he handled Fiona, but he still managed to cup one of her breasts in his hand. She tried to flinch away from him, but he only laughed and tightened his grip.

'Come on,' said Tanya impatiently. 'I've got to get her ready for Alessandro in half an hour and you know how he hates to be kept waiting.'

This time Bethany and Fiona were taken up a second flight of stairs and found themselves in the middle of a thickly carpeted landing with numerous doors leading off it. They were lifted bodily into one of the rooms and both stared around them. It was a huge bathroom. There were two shower cubicles, a big old-fashioned enamel bath, a basin, bidet and lavatory, and two small round tubs which Fiona realised were spa baths.

'Sit on the floor,' said Tanya, but they had already fallen down, their cramped legs unable to bear their full weight after their uncomfortable night. Marcus produced a key and both their sets of cuffs were removed and thrown into a corner. To Fiona's dismay, Marcus and Craig showed no sign of leaving, but turned their backs while the women went to relieve themselves.

'Right,' said Tanya brightly, once they'd finished. 'You can have a spa bath each. Marcus and Craig will look after Bethany, while Edmund and I take care of you, Fiona!' She saw the look of apprehension on Fiona's face. 'Just enjoy it,' she told her with a smile. 'This house is where the Trimarchi family all come to enjoy themselves. They work from their London penthouse and play here. Believe me, it's quite an experience knowing any of the Trimarchi men.'

'An experience I could do without,' said Fiona shortly.

'I'd like to stay here, become a Trimarchi woman,' confessed Tanya, 'but I don't think I ever will. Alessandro doesn't approve of me.'

Fiona couldn't have cared less if Alessandro had wanted to marry the stupid girl himself. All she wanted was to be given her clothes back, and return to her home and the comparative safety of life there. After this, even the house in Mayfair seemed inviting.

'There you are!' said Edmund, walking in on the scene. His eyes went first to Fiona, sitting in a shivering heap on the floor, and then to Bethany who was sitting upright and looking towards the spa bath with obvious anticipation. He wished he could be the one to see to her this morning. Bethany was his kind of woman, but Alessandro's orders had been clear and it was never worth disobeying him.

'You're to get in the bath,' he said to Fiona, reaching out and taking hold of her right arm. She pulled back, trying to wrench her arm free. 'There's no point in all this,' he said as patiently as he could. 'With Craig and Marcus here to help me, why make trouble for yourself?'

If he didn't understand why she was resisting then there was no way she could explain thought Fiona. Obviously none of the Trimarchi family had any sense of moral decency at all. Nor, for that matter, did Bethany. She was already stepping into one of the spa baths with Marcus helping her negotiate the two steps, and she looked perfectly happy.

Horribly aware of her nakedness, Fiona reluctantly let Tanya take her hand and help her to the second bath. The water was calm and the first step clearly visible beneath the surface. On shaking legs, Fiona stepped down and the warmth of the water felt blissful. At that moment she was chilled to the bone, at least this might help.

'There's a second step,' warned Edmund, slipping an arm round her and letting his left hand linger on her hip-bone. 'Once you're down on that you sit on the first. Tanya and I will just take our clothes off and then we can join you.'

Her neck and spine aching with nervous tension, Fiona finally sat herself down in the water and waited. Tanya and Edmund deliberately stripped opposite her so that she had to watch, and as soon as Edmund peeled off his jeans she saw that he had an enormous erection. The swollen purple head of his penis had emerged from the surrounding foreskin and as Tanya stepped out of her skimpy briefs she laughed at him and with her right hand carefull manipulated the loose skin up and down his shaft for a few seconds, causing his member to rise even higher towards his stomach. Then, with a giggle, she stepped into the spa bath and slid round along the seat until she was on one side of Fiona while Edmund sat on the other.

Fiona sat stiffly upright, trying to forget what she'd just seen. From the other bath came the sound of Bethany's delighted squeals and the low murmur of Marcus and Craig. 'Relax!' said Edmund, pushing his brown hair back off his forehead. 'This is meant to be fun.'

Fiona ignored him. With a sigh, because Edmund always enjoyed his sex and liked the women to be light-hearted about it too, Alessandro's brother reached over the side and pressed the button so that the jets of water began to erupt beneath them until the surface was covered in bubbles.

'She isn't in the right place,' Tanya pointed out.

Edmund glanced down. 'No, she isn't. I'll move across. Come along, Fiona, you have to sit here.'

Nervously, she edged along the slippery seat. The

water was deliciously warm, the bubbles were relaxing her tight muscles, but she didn't want to move. Her breasts were fully exposed above the water line, and when she moved she knew that both Tanya and Edmund were watching them with interest. Suddenly she felt water playing directly between her legs and with a gasp she tried to pull her feet together.

'That's it!' said Edmund with a grin. 'You sit there. Tanya loves it, don't you, *cara*?'

'Mmmm, it's delicious. But you have to keep your legs apart,' she chided Fiona, and hooking one of her feet round Fiona's left ankle forced her to expose her most sensitive parts to the jet again. The sensation was so acute that the whole area between the tops of her thighs began to grow hot and the blood coursed and pulsated through her veins as violently as the water was pulsating through the jets. She found that she was hardly daring to breathe lest she accidentally increased the pleasure.

On her left, Tanya sat watching her with interest. 'It's good, isn't it? Why don't you just let yourself enjoy it? Your friend certainly is!' Fiona knew that, she had already heard one scream of ecstasy from Bethany and by the sound of the muffled cries and laughter coming from that direction there would soon be another one, but Fiona was determined it wasn't going to happen to her, especially not in front of these two strangers.

Gently Tanya leant across and fingered Fiona's nipples. Fiona immediately went to slap her hand away, but Edmund prevented her. He gripped her wrists in his hands and held them beneath the water while Tanya continued to lightly caress the small aureoles round the stubbornly flat nipples.

'You've got sweet nipples,' she said cheerfully. 'Let's see if I can get them more interested in what's happening shall I?'

'No, you hold her hands and I'll get them interested!' said Edmund. With a pout, Tanya did as he said. Now

Fiona had to sit with the jets of water continually stimulating her entire vulva while Edmund carefully took hold of each of her nipples in turn and tugged on them, extending them as far as possible before releasing them. Slowly, they began to grow, and when he saw this he gripped Fiona's waist and turned her so that she was facing the wall of the spa bath.

At the same time, Tanya released Fiona's ankle, then between them Tanya and Edmund pulled the startled Fiona lower into the bath so that she was kneeling on the floor and only her face was above the water. They spread her knees, so that the water beat more strongly against her open thighs, and pulled the top half of her body slightly to one side until she gave a cry of surprise as sprays of water began to stimulate both her breasts as well.

Now the warm water was arousing two of her most sensitive areas, her breasts and vulva, and when Edmund sank lower in the water himself he managed to reach beneath her and pulled open her outer labia so that all at once it was her inner lips and the clitoris itself which were receiving the full force of the water jets.

The hot, tight sensations began to grow and grow in her. Her breasts ached and throbbed and she felt as though she was on fire between her legs. Her face became flushed, and now Tanya pulled at her legs and lifted them up while Edmund put supporting hands below her shoulders until she was lying diagonally across the spa bath. They raised her, letting the jets of water pepper her spine, buttocks and the backs of her knees and thighs, while on the surface their mouths began to wander across the damp and still pulsating flesh of her stomach and breasts as they were pushed above the water line.

Fiona's breath was coming quicker and quicker now. She had never felt a sensation like this before and she tried to force herself to remember that she was being watched, that her tormentors were no better than

Duncan and were using her only for their own amusement, not for her pleasure.

Even so, her body was coming perilously close to betraying her and a knot behind her stomach button grew tighter and tighter until she felt that if it broke her body would totally unravel, and she was frightened by the force of the feeling, which was new to her.

Fear at what was happening to her made her start to twist her body, and for a moment Tanya's grip on her ankles slipped. To Fiona's relief her legs fell back into the foaming water and Edmund had to lower her down to the seat again so that the painfully pleasurable moment of taut sexual tension dissipated.

Edmund knew that they'd missed a golden opportunity to put Fiona in touch with her own sexuality, but before he could suggest to Tanya that they restart the entire process, the bathroom door opened and Alessandro strode in.

Chapter Four

'*I* thought you'd be cleaned up by now,' he said, looking down at Fiona's flushed, wide-eyed face. 'Your friend's enjoying herself,' he added with a brief smile.

Still coming down to earth after her battle with her body, Fiona was once again aware of the cries coming from Bethany's side of the bathroom. 'She isn't my friend any more,' she said coolly.

He nodded. 'Understandable! Come along then. We have work to do, or rather I have work to do.'

Tanya scrambled out of the spa bath and drew Fiona out after her, wrapping her in a huge, soft warm towel as she emerged. 'The bedroom's next door,' said Tanya in a low voice. 'I'll take you in. You're lucky,' she confided when Fiona looked at her apprehensively. 'He's better at oral sex than any man I've ever known.'

The two words 'oral sex' were enough for Fiona. She remembered Duncan's rough, jabbing tongue. The almost painful spasm her body had endured beneath Bethany's gaze and she turned and bolted from the bathroom, dashing headlong along the landing, running blindly with no idea of how she would actually escape.

Alessandro stood in the doorway of the bedroom

where he was waiting for her and watched her flight. He knew she couldn't get far, one of his men, Grant, was always on duty on the upper floors, but he did wonder what had sent her off in such a panic.

He turned to Tanya. 'What did you say to her?' he asked smoothly.

Tanya was annoyed. She only wanted to please Alessandro, because otherwise no matter how much Edmund liked her she knew he'd never marry her and she liked this way of life, but now it looked as though she'd done something to irritate him.

'I told her how good you were at oral sex. What's wrong with that?'

'Perhaps she doesn't like to think that she's sharing me with you!' he said with a tight smile that wasn't in the least amused.

'I thought she'd be pleased to know you were good at it.'

'I didn't really want her to know what we were going to do. How fortunate for you that modelling doesn't require brains. Now go and get her back from Grant, and don't bother talking to her this time.'

Tanya, still nude but entirely unselfconscious about it, obediently went down the long landing and collected a white-faced Fiona from the arms of Grant, who had taken great pleasure in holding her tightly against himself while waiting for someone to arrive.

'Silly girl!' commented Alessandro when Fiona was brought to him at last. 'Where did you think you were going?' She didn't answer and he stood aside for her to walk into the room ahead of him. 'Tell Marcus to come in,' he instructed Tanya. 'The rest of you won't be needed.'

Fiona stared at the huge bed set to one side of the room. It was covered with assorted bolsters and pillows and there was a high footstool at the end of the bed. Apart from that the only furniture was a small wardrobe and a large dressing table with a vast rectangular mirror running the length of it.

'Why can't you leave me alone?' she asked Alessandro. 'If you just want your money back, what's the point of all this? Do you enjoy degrading women? Can't ordinary sex satisfy you any more?'

He seemed surprised by her questions. 'I'm not trying to degrade you; I'm teaching you how to enjoy yourself. I thought when I first saw you that you were being wasted, and I was right. As for ordinary sex, who's to say what's ordinary and what's exotic? It all depends on what you're used to. If I were to ask you a question, it would be why you deny youself the pleasures that normal women crave?'

'Because sex is power,' said Fiona bitterly. 'Once Duncan learned how to give me pleasure he used the knowledge to try and control me. Do this or you won't have pleasure. Do that and I'll make sure you have pain. I'm not going to let that happen again.'

'Women use sex too,' Alessandro said mildly. 'Once they're married it's often a weapon. Do as I want and I'll let you sleep with me. Annoy me and I'll have a headache for a week.'

'It isn't the same,' protested Fiona. 'I'm not saying it's right, but women don't hurt men with sex.'

'Real men don't hurt women with it. Once I've taught you how to receive pleasure openly and fully, you'll feel different about it.'

Fiona looked boldly at him, hoping he couldn't tell how frightened she really was. 'And once I've learned from your expert ministrations – you were highly recommended by your brother's blonde girlfriend you'll be pleased to hear – I suppose I shall be expected to start learning to *give* pleasure.'

'Of course, unless you're safely back with Duncan by then!'

'Well giving pleasure to men doesn't usually give pleasure to women.'

For the first time he looked annoyed. 'Of course it does. That's the whole point of it. Sometimes it's even better to give the pleasure than to receive it. You've had a poor teacher, that's all.'

'I suppose all Italians are brilliant in bed and all English men hopeless?'

His eyes shone with amusement. 'I've no idea, but I imagine there are good and bad in both countries. What really counts is whether a man likes women. I do.'

'Really, in that case I'm surprised you're able to chain us up like dogs at night, leaving us to freeze in your cellar.'

'After tonight you'll sleep indoors,' he said shortly. 'Now, we aren't here to talk. I'd hoped to bring you in straight from your bath and continue what Edmund and Tanya had started, but it seems we'll be beginning from cold again. Never mind. Lie down on the bed. The room is warm, you should be comfortable. I'll take my clothes off.'

'And if I won't?' asked Fiona.

'You'll go back to the spa bath but this time I shall join you there.'

Remembering the sensations of the spa bath, Fiona decided to do as he asked. Oral sex certainly wouldn't arouse her nearly as much as her experience with Tanya and Edmund. She would just have to wait until Alessandro ran out of patience and gave up his lesson.

She was surprised how comfortable the bed was, but even more surprised when he lay down naked beside her and began to stroke her neck and shoulders. His body was brown and muscular with dark hair on his chest spreading down to his navel. She didn't look any lower. His mouth planted feather kisses on the tendons at the sides of her neck while his hands gently skimmed across her tense stomach.

She wasn't used to this. When Duncan wanted oral sex he began between her thighs, and certainly didn't waste any time elsewhere. Alessandro obviously liked

59

a more leisurely approach. His hands settled on each side of her waist, squeezing and releasing the flesh there, and then he slid one long arm beneath her and as he lifted her off the bed Marcus, who had come into the room silently, deftly inserted a bolster sideways beneath the curve of her back and another soft square pillow beneath her buttocks so that the lower half of her body was now elevated.

Alessandro's tongue drifted down the valley between Fiona's breasts and swirled briefly in her navel. Startled, Fiona jumped, but it was a pleasurable feeling and after his tongue had moved on, the tingles of excitement it had aroused continued. Now he was moving lower and she started to tense.

'Try to relax,' he whispered, his hands carefully easing her thighs apart. 'I won't hurt you, I promise. Let the sensations take over. You can trust me.'

His voice was dark and deep, and his hands so soft and caring that Fiona began to relax. She could feel his tongue licking at her inner thighs lazily and lightly, and it felt good. Without realising it her legs fell slightly outwards giving Alessandro better access to her and he felt a flare of triumph.

Still he didn't hurry.

Very slowly he parted her outer labia with his fingers, continuing to kiss and nuzzle the insides of her thighs and when she remained relaxed he slid off the bed and onto a footstool, carefully drawing Fiona's body a little lower on the bed until she was positioned exactly right.

Now he allowed his tongue to touch her delicate, moist inner sex-lips for the first time. Fiona's hands, which had been relaxed at her sides, clenched into fists. Sensing the movement he immediately went back to kissing and tonguing her thighs until her fingers relaxed again. Now he returned to the delicate lips that were exciting him almost unbearably with their pink, moist invitation.

He began to nibble carefully inside the outer sex-lips

but an almost imperceptible tension in her legs warned him against this, and instead he used his tongue like a feather, letting it touch the inner surfaces so lightly he knew she could hardly have felt it.

For Fiona it was an almost unbelievable experience. There was none of the rough nuzzling and biting that had made her so uncomfortable before with Duncan. Instead there was just the silken feel of Alessandro's tongue sliding along her moist channels. He swirled it around the entire area, using the very tip on her inner lips and the full length on the slightly less sensitive areas.

Once again Fiona began to feel as though she was on fire between her thighs. Now his tongue became bolder, his fingers gently eased her wider open and this time he let his tongue snake into her vagina, just entering and circling for a few seconds. Immediately her toes curled upwards and her hands reached down to grab hold on his thick dark hair.

Alessandro felt her hands on his head and knew that now she was fully relaxed and involved in the sensations. Carefully, he began to change his method of arousal, and his tongue began to assault her nerve endings, flicking sharply at sensitive spots before running smoothly down the channels again. He played on her responses, guided by her movements and occasional muffled groans and all the time his own arousal grew until his erection was throbbing painfully, and he felt the preliminary drop of fluid fall onto his own leg. He ignored it. It was Fiona's pleasure that counted this morning.

Fiona was totally lost in the waves of bliss which were engulfing her. Each time his tongue flicked at some vital spot within her inner folds her whole body seemed to expand and she could feel the heat between her thighs spreading upwards though her abdomen and right up to the breasts where her nipples had become painfully erect.

61

Alessandro drew back for a moment. Fiona's entire vulva was swollen and engorged with blood, moisture was seeping from her vagina and her breathing was rapid while her body was starting to move restlessly on the bolster. With infinite care he approached the still-hooded clitoris, running his tongue carefully beneath it, anxious to wait until the last moment before giving direct stimulation.

A pulse began beating between Fiona's thighs; a steadily increasing pulse that was drawing her into herself, until she didn't know what was happening because her whole body was centred on this strange burning need which had a dull ache behind it; an ache that hurt and yet gave her pleasure.

Alessandro felt her fingers clenching frantically in his hair and decided to wait no longer. Carefully he pushed the skin of her pubic hair upwards and then took the newly revealed clitoris between his lips and sucked as slowly and lightly as he could, drawing it further into his mouth and feeling it begin to tremble on the brink of its final pulsations.

For Fiona it was the biggest shock of her life. Suddenly the dull ache vanished. There was only a tight mass of incredibly sensitive nerve endings sending jagged lines of fizzing pleasure across her body as the steady pulse that she'd begun to experience increased. She felt as though her whole body was being drawn down through her stomach into Alessandro's mouth.

She cried out, terrified at what was happening to her, but she really meant 'yes' and he knew it. He continued to suck steadily at the hard, tight bud and Fiona went totally out of her mind as her whole body was racked by an internal explosion which had her arching herself off the bolster and pillow, twisting frantically away to her left with her arms flung over her head as the pulse that had previously been centred between her thighs consumed her whole body and sweat poured from her breasts, belly and thighs as she climaxed with an intensity she would never had believed possible, crying out as she did so.

Alessandro slid back up onto the bed and lay beside her. When she was at last still he put one arm across her and turned her onto her side so that she lay facing him. Fiona closed her eyes, unwilling to meet his piercing gaze at such a moment. The Italian wasn't bothered. This time the closeness was for her benefit. He knew that it was important she should continue to feel human contact once her climax was over. It seemed to him that Duncan had done little more than work out how best to stimulate her physically but mechanically, ignoring the more sensual sides of lovemaking.

Just the contact of their bodies from shoulder to ankles added to Alessandro's already high state of arousal, but he had no intention of actually allowing himself to penetrate Fiona yet. That would only come much later, when he felt that she would welcome him rather than resent him as an intruder, even if pleasure accompanied his invasion.

These were early days. Later, if, as he suspected, Duncan continued to find himself unable to repay the money he owed, then Alessandro intended to teach Fiona more complex and darker ways to pleasure. She'd obviously felt pain, but not the right degree of it. He had tutored many women over the years and knew the exact point at which the pain became bearable, tumbling over into a red-hot pleasure that couldn't be obtained in any other way. It wasn't for all, but it was for most true sensualists and he now felt certain that Fiona fitted this description.

Today, one intense orgasm from oral stimulation had made her cry out, and his erection grew painful at the thought of how she would be in time, when he had taught her the joys of multiple orgasms, group sex and the so-called perversions that he knew he could teach her to enjoy with him.

Beneath his restraining yet comforting arm, Fiona

drifted off into a light sleep, her body exhausted by passion and the broken night she'd spent in the cellar. Once her breathing was even and slow, Alessandro rose from the bed and padded naked out of the room, along the corridor and into the room where he knew Edmund, Tanya and Bethany would have been watching them through the two-way mirror over the dressing table.

'Fetch Chrissie,' he said shortly to Craig who was standing at the top of the stairs. Chrissie had once been Marcus's girlfriend. He had tired of her, but because everyone else in the house had grown fond of her she'd stayed on. She was always a willing partner in their various games and today, with Georgina in London, she would be useful to Alessandro.

As expected, he found the others in the small room behind the mirror, all aroused from the scenes they'd witnessed. Tanya, still naked from earlier that morning, was running her hands over Bethany, who had been strapped into a body harness. This consisted of two metal hoops which encircled her breasts and were suspended from a leather strap that ran round the back of her neck. At the bottom of each of the rings were two more straps. From each side one ran round behind her to meet the opposite one in the middle of her back, while the other two were drawn in to the middle of her stomach where they joined another oval metal hoop. From this hoop a long leather thong divided her rounded stomach and at the point where it reached her pubic hair this thong slipped on to two thick straps with buckles. These straps went up and over Bethany's hips, joining the straps from her breasts in the middle of her back and then continued down between her buttocks and up tightly round her sex-lips, pressing against the most sensitive parts and separating the outer lips a little so that they showed on each side of the dividing line. Exactly at the entrance of her vagina there was an opening, to allow penatration by fingers or a small vibrator.

Although Bethany's hands were fastened behind her back, which had the effect of thrusting her already protruding breasts even more through the metal loops, she didn't look in the least distressed and her large, dark nipples were fully erect.

'She's fantastic!' breathed Edmund, lowering his head to suck on one of the suffused points. Bethany quivered as his tongue travelled round the inside of the metal rim and then brushed to and fro across the whole of the aureole.

Alessandro had to agree that she looked splendid. Her lush auburn hair was a wonderful contrast to her porcelain coloured skin, and her whole body was quivering with arousal. She was made for sex he thought. Not love. Bethany probably wouldn't be interested in love, but she was certainly interested in sex.

He saw her eyes glance at his own erection and smiled at her. 'I'm afraid that's not for you today. Edmund would never forgive me! However, I admit I'm tempted.'

Bethany pouted at him. 'I'm better than Fiona. Duncan says Fiona has no idea how to please a man.'

'She pleases me.'

'So would I,' retorted Bethany impudently.

Alessandro raised his eyebrows. 'You seem to forget that you're here as a hostage, not a guest. I decide what happens to you. Be grateful I've given you to Edmund.'

'Duncan will be more worried about me than Fiona.' said Bethany, then gasped as Alessandro reached forward, took hold of the metal loop in the middle of her stomach, then pulled it sharply upwards so that the strap between her sex-lips tightened, pressing against her clitoris and splitting her outer lips totally apart.

'Don't ever say that in front of Fiona, do you understand?' he hissed.

'Why not? It's the truth,' gasped Bethany, squirming

from the mixture of pain and arousal the tightened thong was causing her.

'It may be the truth but I don't wish her to hear it yet.'

'What's she to you?' demanded Bethany rudely. 'Only a hostage, the same as me.'

'She's his wife, and far more important than you,' Alessandro replied, slowly pulling the ring up further until Bethany was forced to rise up on her toes. The ache between her legs was increasing now, and it was delicious, exactly the kind of sensation she liked best. She continued to stare into Alessandro's deep dark eyes, enjoying the thrill of goading him into stimulating her passion.

He saw the flush of pleasure beginning to suffuse her body, watched the metal hoops start to dig more deeply into the swelling breasts and decided that if this was the kind of game she liked to play then he'd show her how he played it. With one easy, fluid movement he picked her up and threw her face down on the divan behind her. Bethany's tender breasts felt the brush of the chenille bedspread and they tingled even more. She wriggled. Alessandro unfastened the buckle at the back of the harness and let the strap fall from between her buttocks. Cool air brushed against the cleft between them, and Bethany felt long fingers separating each rounded globe.

While Alessandro's strong hands pressed firmly down on her waist, Edmund separated the cheeks of her bottom even more widely with his fingers and then began to lick slowly down the inside of the cheeks until he reached the tight rim of her rear entrance. Quickly Tanya handed him a tube of lubricating jelly and he squeezed some on a finger before inserting it inside the red-head's rectum.

Bethany gave a token squeal of protest, but in reality she was excited almost beyond endurance. She felt Edmund's finger rotating, pressing against every sensitive surface of her tightness while Tanya managed to ease a hand under Bethany's stomach and her fingers quickly pushed at the three ends of leather now lying there loosely. She drew them aside and inserted two fingers into Bethany's front entrance while Edmund continued to stimulate her manually from the rear.

It was only when he removed his finger and she heard him murmuring to Alessandro that Bethany began to worry about what else they might do to her. Duncan had often penetrated her anally, but only after she was well lubricated. At that moment she didn't feel ready, and in any case she suddenly wasn't certain she wanted it to happen with Alessandro and Tanya looking on.

She was vaguely aware of another woman entering the room, and heard Alessandro say, 'Come in, Chrissie,' just as Tanya turned her on her side and pulled her right leg, which was still on the bed, up towards Bethany's chin.

Behind the prostrate Bethany, Edmund had filled the bulb of an anal vibrator with warm water. He now covered the stocky head with lubricating jelly and began to insert it into Bethany's tight orifice. There was a sudden sharp pain in Bethany's rear entrance, and she made a sound of protest. 'What's the matter?' asked Alessandro silkily. 'I thought you knew how to please a man? Well, this pleases me.' She fell silent again, but the pain increased as her sphinctre muscles were forced to expand more than ever before.

'Bear down,' whispered Tanya, 'press out, it makes it easier.' Bethany tried to obey, and suddenly the thickest part of the vibrator was inside her and every part of her rectum was alive with sensations.

At a signal from Edmund, Tanya went round behind Bethany and took his place. Then Edmund lay on his side next to Bethany and at last allowed his straining erection to ease itself slowly into her well-lubricated front opening. Bethany moaned at the feel of him. He

67

was wonderfully thick and when the head of his penis was just inside her he stopped for a moment, rotating his hips, which made her thrust herself towards him.

Tanya hastily pressed against the anal vibrator, afraid that it might slip out with the movement. She watched as Edmund began thrusting in and out of Bethany, his hands groping blindly at her breasts which caused the metal rings to dig deeply into her so that she almost screamed with the pleasure-pain. She gave herself over to the sensations. Edmund's thrusting, which was making the loose ends of the straps brush against her swollen clitoris with every movement, was arousing her to the very brink of orgasm, and inside her rectum she could feel the glorious fullness of what she thought was a dildo.

Then, as Edmund's lips began to curl back from his teeth and his groans increased in volume, Tanya squeezed the bulb on the vibrator, releasing the warm water into Bethany and at the same time turned on the power so that the vibrator began to move against the walls of the red-head's back passage.

Bethany was taken totally by surprise. The rush of the warm water made her bowels cramp, her stomach muscles went into a reflexive spasm, the leather straps suddenly touched her protruding clitoris one time too many and her orgasm was triggered making her stomach muscles ripple even more intensely while at the same time she felt Edmund ejaculate inside her, thrusting so hard that their pelvic bones were crushed against each other.

There were too many sensations and she couldn't control any of them. The whole of her body seemed to be being torn apart by convulsions and every contraction gripped either Edmund's penis or the pulsating vibrator which only made everything worse, triggering spasm after spasm as the leather straps continued their relentless teasing of her now over-stimulated clitoris.

Alessandro watched her heaving body. He pressed

against her shoulders so that she couldn't escape and he allowed Edmund and Tanya to continue their ministrations until Bethany's groans became pitiful. Only then did he signal for the pair of them to stop, while at the same time flicking the black leather straps up from between her thighs to rest against her stomach.

At last the violence of the spasm, the earth-shattering flashes of red and white heat and pain and the incredible feeling of being totally filled in almost every space began to abate and a shaken and aching Bethany lay quite still, suddenly aware that in this family she had almost certainly more than met her match.

Alessandro had been tremendously aroused by watching it all. Quickly he sat down on the side of the divan while Chrissie, who had also been watching the scene with Bethany and was more than ready for action herself, straddled his lap and sat facing him. She put her arms round his neck, her knees on the bed and moved herself up and down on his erection, making sure that she angled herself so that her clitoris was stimulated as she moved.

Alessandro let Chrissie dictate the pace. After watching first Fiona and then Bethany, it was difficult not to come before Chrissie was ready but he prided himself on his control, and it didn't fail him this time either. Chrissie's breathing became ragged, her movements more rapid and she uttered tiny mewing sounds of excitement as her climax built.

Just as he knew she was about to come, Alessandro lifted her off him and turned her round so that she had her back to him. Tanya stood in front of Chrissie in order that she could lean on her for support and then Alessandro was finally able to penetrate her more deeply, gaining extra satisfaction from every thrust while at the same time reaching round in front of her and massaging the whole of her pubic area.

Within seconds of the change of position he felt her inner muscles contracting around him, heard her orgasmic cry and then he was rushing towards his own climax. The blood pounded in his ears, he felt his testicles draw up tightly beneath him and at last with a final deep lunge he was there. He heard himself utter a small sound of relief as he released himself inside of Chrissie in a series of wrenching pulsations.

When it was over, Chrissie slid from his lap and onto the bed where she lay next to Bethany, whose eyes were closed. Chrissie was pleased that for once it was Alessandro who had satisfied her, because out of all the men she'd known in this house, he was easily the best at making love.

While Fiona slept on in the bedroom, and Edmund, Bethany, Alessandro and Chrissie sat or lay in satiated contentment, Tanya hoped that before the day was out there'd be some pleasure for her. She expected that there would be. No one was expected to suffer frustration in this house and it didn't usually take Edmund too long to recover from a bout of lovemaking.

However, Alessandro already had plans for Tanya, and once Fiona was awake he intended to put them into action.

Chapter Five

When Fiona awoke her whole body felt strangely limp and her muscles ached as thought she'd recently played three strenuous sets of tennis. It took her a few minutes to remember where she was and what had caused the feelings, but once she did her face grew warm and she buried her head in the pillows.

Watching through the two-way mirror, Alessandro immediately despatched Tanya to bring Fiona down to the lower floor where they would all have a light lunch before he proceeded with the next part of his day's pleasure.

'I want some clothes,' Fiona told Tanya when she delivered Alessandro's instructions.

Tanya, who was again wearing her cut-off jeans and skimpy blouse, looked surprised. 'What's the point? Today is for enjoyment. Clothes just get in the way and the house is always kept warm so that nakedness isn't uncomfortable.'

'I'm always uncomfortable without my clothes,' said Fiona shortly. 'It might be normal for you and your friends to go about naked, but not for me. I'm not getting off this bed until I get my clothes back.'

Tanya didn't know what to say. Decisions were never

made by her, and she had no idea whether or not Fiona was allowed clothes. 'I don't know where they are,' she explained. 'You could ask Alessandro when you go down.'

Fiona sighed. 'I've just told you; I'm not coming down at all unless I get my clothes back. Can't you understand?' she added with more emotion. 'What do you think this is like for me? You've chosen to live with this horrible family. I'm a prisoner and it's a nightmare.'

At this Tanya smiled. 'You looked as though you were enjoying yourself earlier.'

Tired of waiting, Alessandro had come into the bedroom to see what was causing the delay. He looked at the stricken expression on Fiona's face and turned warily to Tanya. 'What have you said now?'

'Nothing. Fiona wants her clothes back.'

'She was watching us!' Fiona cried out. 'You told me to trust you, to let you do what you liked and enjoy it, but all the time she was watching us. I hate you, you're utterly disgusting.'

Alessandro glared at the luckless Tanya. 'When's your next modelling job? Soon, I hope. Tact doesn't seem to be your strongest suit.'

Fiona sat up, forgetting her nakedness in her temper. 'There's no point in blaming her. You're the one who encourages all this.'

Now Alessandro turned his glare on her. 'Do keep quiet!' he said in a dangerously soft voice. 'Soon you'll be watching other people and enjoying it, just as you enjoyed our sessions earlier. It's never wise to criticise people before you know exactly what it is you're criticising. Why are you still in bed?' he added.

'I want my clothes. I'm not coming down to eat while I'm stark naked.'

He laughed. 'It's over twenty-four hours since you last ate and you can still worry over a few clothes. No wonder Duncan got bored with you,' he added cruelly.

Fiona went white, and all at once he wished he hadn't

said it. 'Duncan had his first affair on our honeymoon,' Fiona said in a low voice. 'I don't think I'd had time to bore him by then.'

An unusual feeling of guilt swept over Alessandro. He knew that Duncan Sheldon was a totally self-centred sadist with an unquenchable desire for fresh conquests, and hurting his wife, who was already in a terrifying situation, was hardly worthy of a Trimarchi. 'Get her a silk gown, full-length, but sleeveless,' he instructed Tanya. 'There are several in Georgina's wardrobe, and they fit any size.'

Once Tanya had gone Alessandro and Fiona stared at each other. She was the first to look away. Quickly he put his fingers round her chin then turned her back to face him. 'You don't bore me,' he murmured, letting his fingers caress her tenderly. 'In fact, you excite me more than any woman has for a long time.'

'You don't excite me,' Fiona muttered, but she couldn't look at him as she said it and he merely laughed deep in his throat before releasing her.

Tanya then returned with the gown, and she and Alessandro watched Fiona's breasts lifting as she raised her arms and let it fall over her head. Alessandro's penis stirred and Tanya wished she could be allowed to make love to Fiona. She knew that she could teach her body exciting new sensations, the kind that, in her opinion, men never managed to arouse in women, not even the best of them.

Once they were sitting round the dining table and eating, Fiona found that she was desperately hungry, but her appetite diminished when she saw what Bethany was wearing. Her friend was still attired in the body harness she had worn earlier while Fiona slept, but now the straps between her thighs had been refastened and it all fitted tightly again.

Fiona could hardly keep her eyes away from Bethany's rounded breasts which were protruding from the encircling metal rings, while her nipples had peaked

73

into hard little points, deep pink in colour. She seemed utterly unconcerned by her outfit and was eating a salad of baby sweet-corn, mange-tout and tiny pieces of apple with her fingers, licking them alluringly as she slowly cleared her plate.

Edmund couldn't keep his eyes off her either, and his erection was highly uncomfortable, trapped as it was inside his tight jeans. He wasn't helped by the fact that Tanya kept letting her right hand wander to the top of his thigh where her fingers would stray towards his crotch, the fingernails scratching at him through the heavy denim.

Alessandro watched them all from beneath lowered eyelids. He knew that Tanya was desperate for some sexual satisfaction of her own, and that Fiona was once again bewildered by her surroundings and Bethany's behaviour. He wondered how the two women had even become friends when they had so little in common, except he realised with amusement, Duncan. At that moment the telephone rang, and he went to his study to take the call only to find it was from Duncan himself.

Duncan sounded a great deal less urbane and self-assured than when he had first come to the Trimarchi family asking for the large loan that he needed for expansion. 'An absolute certainty,' he'd assured them, describing how he was buying up a bankrupt company at rock-bottom price and then using it to double his own commercial dealings.

Right from the start the plan had been flawed, but Alessandro had still let him have the money. In the City everyone knew that Duncan Sheldon was in line for a knighthood. As such he was a useful man to have in the Trimarchi family's debt, and it was this, not his imagined skill in putting over his plan, that had got him the loan. They had known he would fail, but the fall had been even quicker than Alessandro had anticipated.

'I can't raise all the money!' he was gabbling down the phone.

'Do you have half?' queried Alessandro, aware that he didn't because everywhere he went for help the Trimarchi's had been ahead of him, ensuring that he met with refusals.

'Not quite.'

'A quarter then?' persisted Alessandro silkily.

'Yes, yes I'm close to raising a quarter of it.'

'Your wife's fine,' Alessandro said sarcastically.

There was a pause. 'What about Bethany? You shouldn't have taken her, she was just a visitor,' complained Duncan.

Alessandro snorted. 'She's been your mistress for over a year! Do you honestly think we didn't know about her?'

'I don't want her hurt.'

Alessandro couldn't believe his ears. 'What about your wife?'

'Oh, yes Fiona. How is she? I'm sure she's coping well. She rarely loses her composure.'

'I'd hardly call her composed, but then she's experiencing a rather abrupt change of lifestyle here,' Alessandro told Duncan.

'That's all right. Fiona's used to adversity. Her parents lost all their money once and she was a tower of strength to them, but Bethany's different. She's more . . .'

'Highly-sexed?' suggested Alessandro helpfully, sickened by the man's attitude to his wife.

'You bastard!' For the first time Duncan sounded furious. 'Don't you dare lay a finger on her. She's mine, and as soon as I can raise half the money I want her back. That's fair isn't it?'

Alessandro's mind went into overdrive. It wasn't fair to Fiona, but it certainly suited him. He wanted to keep Duncan's wife for as long as possible. He had many plans for her, and it was quite possible that Duncan would raise half the money within the next week. Bethany was of little interest to him. She was already so abandoned that she offered no challenge or intrigue whatsoever.

'Very well,' Alessandro agreed slowly. 'But in the meantime, until we receive the first half, both the women will pay the interest on the outstanding amount for you. Their bodies in lieu of bank notes, yes?'

'I'll get half the money to you by the end of the week,' Duncan promised. 'Look, you're a man of the world, you know how it is with women. Bethany suits me. She's always willing to . . .'

Alessandro slammed the phone down. He wasn't in the least interested in what Bethany was willing to do, and neither was he pleased to think that Duncan imagined he would be interested. Not that the conversation had entirely displeased him. Quite the opposite, it had given him an even keener sense of excitement over the ways in which Fiona could be brought to life while under his roof.

When he returned to the dining table it was Fiona who stared at him anxiously. 'Was that Duncan?' she asked, and he could hear her voice trembling. He was glad she didn't know what her husband had said.

'It was,' he replied briskly.

'Has he got the money?'

'I never talk business over meals.'

'Please!' Fiona exclaimed. 'Don't play with me like this, I have to know. Will we be set free soon?'

'I'm afraid your husband hasn't yet managed to raise even half the amount he owes us,' Alessandro said gently. 'I explained to him that your fate rested entirely in his hands. I'm sure he'll do his best to get you back as quickly as the money men of London will allow him.'

'What about the interest on the loan?' asked Edmund, who always liked to think about money.

'The interest will be repaid by Fiona and Bethany,' said Alessandro. 'It's clear Duncan can't raise more than the original sum and so I think that it's only fair to use our hostages instead. Perhaps they might like to be tutored in the ways of lovemaking that suit us best, so that we too can gain full satisfaction from their stay here. What do you think?'

'Sounds perfect to me,' said Edmund, who didn't think that Bethany would need a great deal of tuition in order to please him, but knew that Fiona was a long way from being the kind of woman his brother liked to share his bed with.

Fiona's appetite had totally gone and she pushed her plate away. 'If my husband raises half the money, can't one of us go?' she asked hesitantly.

'Possibly,' agreed Alessandro. 'Now, I'd like to finish eating.'

'But I suppose you'd keep me,' she rushed on, almost in tears at the thought of being left alone in the house. 'You've no sense of honour, no decency at all. You'd let Bethany go because she's just his mistress, and keep me because I'm his wife and so more important in your eyes. Important to Duncan, but not to you or you wouldn't treat another man's wife the way you're treating me!'

'Don't talk to me about honour!' snarled Alessandro, infuriated by her words. 'Yes, it will be Bethany who is released once half the money is received, but that's because it's Bethany your wonderful husband has asked to have returned first. Now perhaps you won't be quite so quick to question my honour.'

Fiona shook her head violently. 'You're lying. You're just a liar and a crook.'

Everyone at the table fell totally silent and Alessandro pushed back his chair and stood up. 'I do not lie,' he said softly. 'Neither do I take kindly to being told that I do. You may as well resign yourself to a long stay here, Fiona. A stay where you will continue to learn to receive sexual pleasure and be tutored by Georgina to give me the same degree of satisfaction. Personally, I doubt if it will take even Duncan so long to raise the money that

77

my satisfaction will be guaranteed, but I'm willing to take a chance on it.'

Fiona slumped in her chair. She had been hit by one shock after another over the past twenty-four hours and now she felt as though she couldn't take any more. She knew that Bethany was looking at her, but couldn't meet her eye. The very sight of her almost total nakedness conjured up images of Bethany and Duncan that sickened her, as did the recollection of her own abandonment to the physical bliss of Alessandro's expert ministrations earlier that day. Now her few remaining shreds of self-confidence had vanished and she felt little better than a child deserted by its parents.

Neither her husband nor her supposed best friend had ever cared for her in the way she'd imagined, and she knew that marrying Duncan for her parents' sake had been a total waste of her life. They could have managed as they were, but she'd imagined she could make life wonderful for them. Now she'd probably ruined all their lives and been left without even her own self-respect.

Craig touched her lightly on the shoulder. 'Come along. We're all going upstairs again.'

Fiona didn't attempt to argue or resist. There was no point. She was stuck here, at the mercy of Alessandro and his friends, until Duncan finally paid for her release. Even after that she would always know that Bethany had come first, so what did it matter what happened to her.

Alessandro watched her enter the small room behind the two-way mirror and felt a surge of pity for her. He moved to her side and took hold of one of her cold hands. 'Look at the mirror, he said quietly. She let her hand rest limply in his and stared into it. She was amazed when she realised that it was actually a window and on the other side she could see Tanya, dressed in only a tight leather mini-skirt with attached suspenders, black stockings and high-heeled shoes, standing by the side of the same bed where she had earlier given herself over to Alessandro's lips and tongue.

She drew back slightly, and pressed again Alessandro who had positioned himself behind her. 'This time *you* can watch someone taking their pleasure,' he whispered in her ear. 'Tanya took a long time to learn how to be the dominant woman. At first she rejected the idea, just as you reject all your sexuality, but now she loves the role.'

Fiona could feel Alessandro's hands resting gently at each side of her waist. He wasn't forcing her to stand in front of the mirror, but she guessed that if she tried to turn away his grip would tighten. When she continued to stare at the scene that was unfolding he moved closer until she could feel the rhythm of his breathing and the back of her head was pressed against his chest.

Fiona watched Tanya walk around the empty bedroom, arranging items on the footstool where Alessandro had sat, and checking the way the bed was angled. When she was satisfied she went over to the door and now Marcus led a man into the room. He was in his mid-thirites, with brown curly hair and grey eyes that held a look of anxiety. His hands were fastened behind him and he was completely naked except for circles of leather round his ankles.

'He works for me,' Alessandro whispered. 'He made the mistake of trying to practice a little "creative" accounting while doing the books, and he's here to pay the penalty. Men like him are useful for satisfying Georgina and Tanya from time to time, and after this he won't be so quick to cheat again. The photos we'll take will keep him more honest from now on.'

Fiona watched as the man walked hesitantly towards Tanya. Marcus handed her the key to the man's handcuffs and then withdrew, leaving the two of them alone. Tanya reached out and ran her hands down the man's chest and stomach, letting them linger over his totally flaccid penis and limp testicles. Then she turned away

79

and bent over the footstool searching for something. Her miniscule leather skirt rose up, clearly revealing her naked sex and the smooth pale flesh at the top of her stockings. Fiona glanced back at the man and saw that his penis was already stirring, slowly beginning to fill with blood as his arousal began.

Casually, Tanya turned back to him. In her hand she held a light whip which she let hang loosely at her side. The man's nervousness increased, he licked his lips and swallowed hard but his erection continued to grow.

'This kind of thing excites him,' explained Alessandro. 'It's a private weakness that his wife doesn't know about.'

'But he's terrified. How can he . . .?' Fiona's voice stopped.

'He likes to be dominated. It isn't unusual. Men get tired of always having to be in charge. The fear itself is an aphrodisiac to him.'

Fiona could see that was true. His circumcised penis was now almost fully erect and his testicles had swollen to an impressive size. Tanya studied him for a moment, then reached towards him, turning him in order to give the hidden watchers a better view of what she was doing.

Slowly she slipped something onto the man's straining penis. Fiona looked closely and saw that the object consisted of three metal rings, fastened to the base of the penis and round the scrotum by leather straps. As the rings slid onto him and the straps were tightened the man's erection swelled even more and she heard him groan.

'We have microphones in there as well,' explained Alessandro. 'It adds to the pleasure of viewing! Now that the rings are on him, his erection will be sustained. The blood is trapped there and there's no fear of it becoming limp and useless to Tanya!'

'But doesn't it hurt him?' asked Fiona, her palms damp.

'It's uncomfortable after a while, but he shouldn't have tried to cheat me!'

Once the erection was secured to Tanya's satisfaction, she pushed him to his knees and extended one of her feet. He quickly bent his head and licked at the top of the arch of her foot where it rose from her shoe. After a moment she lifted her foot and pushed at his chest with the high heel of the shoe until he tumbled back awkwardly onto the carpet. Then she stood over him and let the heel rotate around the base of his stomach, occasionally allowing it to press into the flesh. Each time she did this he winced with discomfort.

Alessandro smiled. 'She's very good at the slow beginning. Georgina did her tutoring well.'

Fiona shivered, hoping she'd never be expected to behave like Tanya was behaving now. The blonde model suddenly lifted her right hand and let the light whip fall onto the man's unprotected stomach. Immediately his erection strained upwards and Fiona could see the metal rings digging into his flesh.

'Get on the bed,' said Tanya coldly. He hurried to obey. 'Lie face down,' she added, then spread his legs and fastened the ankle cuffs to the corners of the bed. Once she'd done that she unfastened his handcuffs, pulled his arms above his head and fastened them to the opposite corners, spreadeagling him in an X-shape.

Now Tanya climbed onto the bed and shook her head, letting her long blonde hair fly loose about her face. After that she bent her head and began to shake it from side to side, so that the strands of hair brushed against the man's back, teasing back and forth across his shoulder-blades and running down his spine until they came to rest in the cleft at its base.

Fiona watched the way the man's buttocks tightened and trembled as he waited to see what Tanya would do next. She hung her head down and her hair fell right over her face so that it was all over his buttocks, stroking his skin like strands of silk, igniting all his nerve endings. Then she continued on down the backs of his legs and the sheer lightness of the hair-brushing, the very lack of firm pressure, began to drive her victim mad and he strained against his bonds as he attempted to find some firmer pressure to offset the teasing sensations, but Tanya knew what she was doing and refused him.

After what seemed an eternity to the man, Tanya finally threw her head back and the gentle torment stopped. She got off the bed and wriggled out of her leather skirt and stockings while her victim turned his head to watch her.

'Face down,' she said harshly. He obeyed without question. Alessandro felt Fiona shiver, but whether with fear or excitement he couldn't tell. His hands drew her closer to him and crossed her stomach so that he was encircling her from behind and could feel the vibrations of her body beneath the silk robe. He kept silent, letting the scene speak for itself.

Tanya now picked up a small vial and poured a few drops of liquid into the palm of one hand, then she dipped her middle finger of the other hand into the liquid and climbed back into the bed to kneel between the man's legs. Very slowly she eased the cheeks of his bottom apart, and began to circle the rim of his anus with her oiled finger.

The man on the bed groaned and pressed himself down onto the softness of the bed. His erection had never felt so hard or ached so urgently before. He longed for sexual satisfaction, his tight testicles caused the encircling straps to give him pain, and one of them was pressing against the nerve ending of his urethra which only increased all the sensations. However, he had been given his instructions before he ever entered the room and knew that he wouldn't be allowed to climax until the woman had finished with him. It was the most bitter-sweet agony of his life.

Her finger skimmed round the rim of his rear

entrance. The oil was cool and he longed for the finger to enter him there, but she simply continued to tease him. Suddenly he couldn't bear it any longer and with an abrupt movement he thrust his hips up off the bed and Tanya's finger slid inside him. He gasped at the resulting pressure on the walls of his rectum, and the nerve endings blazed with the sensations so that his penis throbbed and he felt the clear pre-ejaculatory fluid dripping from the tips of his glans.

'Stupid girl!' muttered Alessandro to himself.

Tanya was livid. She'd been doing so well, and now the man had dictated the pace himself, which was never allowed. She knew that Alessandro was watching and would consider the mistake hers.

Immediately Tanya withdrew her finger, making sure it didn't stimulate his prostate gland. 'After that you'll have to wait even longer,' she told the trembling man beneath her. Then she pressed a small bell beside the bed and sat back as Marcus and Craig came into the room to turn the man onto his back.

He struggled violently against them, desperate to get at the woman who was tormenting him and hoping for some kind of body contact to precipitate his aching climax, but the men easily re-fastened his bonds and then with a laugh at his straining and tightly imprisoned erection, they left him alone with Tanya once more.

Fiona could now see the man's arousal for herself. The tip of his penis was dark purple in colour with a bead of liquid at the top while his testicles were so swollen and tight that the straps were visibly digging in to the flesh.

Tanya's face was flushed, partly from excitement and partly from annoyance at how he'd nearly defeated her. She was determined to make him suffer to the maximum before letting him have his release.

She sat astride him, brushing his stomach with her pubic hair and then began to wriggle up and down, gradually extending her legs behind her and sliding down his body to press her pubic bone against his rigid thighs to stimulate herself in that way while she nibbled at the tightly stretched skin of his upper chest.

She let her teeth close round his nipples and then bit at each of them in turn. The man cried out in surprise and felt his nipples hardening at the pain and excitement of what she was doing. He felt sure that he would soon explode if she didn't stop rubbing herself against his thigh but the rings not only stimulated but also seemed to impede actual ejaculation. He felt hard, tight and helpless and the ache in his testicles was increasing all the time.

Now Tanya's own sexual excitement was mounting. He looked so desperate and she knew that she was the one who was controlling him. She could decide when or indeed if he was allowed relief and this power aroused her almost as much as the pressure on her pubic bone, the gentle rubbing of flesh against her clitoris as she rubbed up and down him and the feel of his nipples between her teeth.

She let her breasts hang above his face. 'Lick me,' she instructed. Greedily he tried to reach her with his mouth, but she was just out of reach. For a moment she savoured the despair in his eyes, but then her own need outweighed that pleasure and she lowered herself more until at last he could encircle her tiny breasts with his lips.

He sucked skilfully on them, drawing the entire areola into his mouth and exerting firm pressure before releasing it again. Tanya felt the darts of tension in her stomach and moisture began to seep between her thighs.

She let him suck on first one breast and then the other for several minutes until finally she twisted herself round and then the man began to suffer the worst torture yet as he felt Tanya's tongue between his thighs.

'No!' he gasped. 'Please, stop! I can't bear it! I can't!' But Tanya ignored him. She knew that he'd have to bear it. The rings were well designed and he would find that he couldn't climax while they were on even if he allowed himself to try.

In the other room, Fiona's breathing had risen rapidly, and when Alessandro slid his hands inside two openings set beneath her waist on each side of the gown she didn't even seem to notice. He felt her warm flesh, and his hands moved up until his long fingers touched the lower edge of the curve of her breasts. They were tight and already swollen with the excitement of the scene she was watching.

He pressed his hips closer to her, his own erection hard against her buttocks despite his clothing. Still Fiona didn't react. He let his fingers go higher and wasn't surprised to find the nipples hard against them. Placing two fingers each side of the nipples he gently squeezed against the base of the erect flesh. This time Fiona gasped and he felt her body jerk. For a moment he let his fingers tighten and the nipples felt the pressure more intensely, then he released them, letting his fingers simply skim the tight little tips while her breasts thrust up against the palm of his hands. Carefully he continued to massage her breasts and maintained the pressure against her buttocks as Tanya continued to work on her victim.

Tanya was totally lost in the game now. She let her tongue float round the edges of the rings that were imprisoning the man's throbbing shaft, and then moved her mouth over the glans, sucking for just a couple of seconds until she felt his stomach muscles begin to contract beneath her lower body. At that she stopped, and the man shouted his frustration aloud, wondering how much longer he could bear this torment.

Tanya wriggled down until her thighs were each side of the man's head, and this time she didn't have to issue any instructions because his tongue was immediately working greedily at her, licking the moisture where it had seeped out of her and then pressing itself

85

between her outer lips into the more intimate inner parts.

Fiona stared at Tanya's face which was gazing directly into the mirror. The girl's expression was one of pure lust. Her eyes were huge, her colour high and her mouth slightly open as her body began to ripple with the sensations from her victim's mouth.

'She's going to come now,' Alessandro murmured in Fiona's ear. Hypnotised, Fiona continued to watch, and all at once Tanya's head went back, the tendons of her neck stretched taut and her body shook, her breasts thrusting up as she arched her back and her eyes closed in the first moment of release.

The man tied to the bed felt her climax and hoped that this meant his would soon be allowed. The pressure from his imprisoned penis and testicles had now spread to his entire abdomen and his thighs were aching with the tension but Tanya hadn't finished with him yet. Now she drew herself away from his mouth and turned round so that she was facing him. Carefully she raised herself up, then taking her weight on her hands she let her body drift up and down in such a way that the tip of the man's penis brushed up the cleft between her inner labia. He could feel her moist flesh and he tried to buck upwards, only Tanya was ahead of him and lifted herself higher when he did so.

'Please!' he begged her again. 'I can't stand it any longer.'

Tanya didn't even look at him. She closed her eyes and felt the wonderful velvet flesh at the top of his rigid hardness touching her like a lover's and at last the glorious bunching sensation began to build up beneath her pelvic bone. She rotated her hips, letting the man's rod skim her clitoris making her jump with the sudden pleasure and although he was now groaning continually beneath her she continued to torment him and satisfy herself until she was once more gripped by a climax that sent shock waves rippling through her body.

'See how much more intense that climax was,' whispered Alessandro. 'They get better for women, Fiona, as you'll discover.'

Fiona couldn't speak. She couldn't do anything except continue watching and let Alessandro's hands wander across her overheated flesh. She felt him reach lower, sliding down behind her so that he could press against the area above her pubic hair. At once she felt a pulse of pleasure begin between her thighs and she gave a moan that was half despair and half ecstasy.

After her second climax, Tanya finally reached for the last object on the footstool. The man on the bed tensed, wondering what else could lie ahead of him before he was given his release. Tanya's curved back hid the object from his view, and it wasn't until he heard the soft buzzing sound that he knew with sinking certainty that she had a vibrator in her hand.

Tanya heard his cry of disbelief and her own excitement mounted again as she very slowly lowered the tip of the tiny machine onto the man's paper-thin and totally exposed perinium, the small area of flesh running from the base of his penis to his anus, which could give such diabolical pleasure when stimulated.

The victim knew this too, and when the vibrator first touched him there he shut his eyes as flashes of white light exploded in his head and his penis grew so hard that he wondered if the metal rings might break with the pressure. His hips moved of their own volition, he cried out for relief and still the vibrator darted from spot to spot raising his arousal point higher and higher.

At last Tanya realised that he couldn't wait any longer. Swiftly she turned, unfastened the straps at the base of his penis, slid the rings off and then lowered herself onto him. She moved diabolically slowly, only allowing him into the very tip of her opening until she had gained enough stimulation to be at the point of climaxing herself. Then, when the man felt that he was about to lose consciousness with the sensations, she moved faster and faster, up and down on his finally freed erection. Everything spun out of his control as he felt his testicles, drawn hard against his body, finally start to release the fluid that had been so wickedly constrained in them for the past hour.

Tanya angled herself towards him, allowing more friction near her clitoris, and that, combined with watching the man's face contorting into the blissful agony of release, tipped her over into her third orgasm as the man's over-excited body was at last allowed its natural release and he began to ejaculate into her.

As the waves of Tanya's own climax started to die she could feel her victim's penis still within her, and she deliberately tightened her internal muscles one final time. This had the effect of sending ripples of delight through her own abdomen while milking him of every last drop of semen and still she tightened and released despite knowing that he was totally drained, and at this final touch of cruelty the man cried out, but whether in bliss or agony he never really knew.

Chapter Six

*F*iona watched the man's body in its final spasms of long-awaited fulfilment and swallowed hard. She had seen Tanya come to one climax after another, watched the blonde girl's body moving swiftly and athletically to bring about her own maximum satisfaction with no regard for the imprisoned man's pleasure, and her body swelled with burgeoning arousal caused by the scene. Alessandro's hands and fingers had played their part, but most of her growing excitement was due to what she had seen through the mirror, and she was shaken by the realisation that watching had stimulated and not disgusted her.

As the man was released and led from the room, Alessandro picked Fiona up and carried her quickly through into a small bedroom next door. She was silent and unresisting, as though unaware of what he was doing. Without a word, he laid her on the soft, deep carpet and then pulled on each side of her robe, so that the velcro fastening down the middle parted with a tearing sound.

Equally swiftly he pulled off his own clothes and then lay naked on top of her, his body weight supported on his elbows as he stared into her eyes. For the first time he became aware of the flecks of green in them, but unlike Duncan he didn't understand their significance.

'I want you to lie on top of me,' he murmured. She stared up at him, lips parted but still not speaking. Rolling onto his back he pulled her over until she was on his chest and his arms went round her upper back holding her firmly in place. He parted his legs slightly and felt her legs slip between them.

'No, put your legs on top of mine,' he whispered.

Fiona shook her head, remembering the way Tanya had pleasured herself on the bound man's body and suddenly knowing that she couldn't let herself do the same.

'You have no choice,' Alessandro said gently. 'You're paying off Duncan's interest on the loan, remember? If that isn't paid, you'll never be freed.'

'I don't want to,' she said plaintively.

'This is to please me. I want you to.'

He was relieved when she obeyed, but guessed that her aroused body was actually as anxious as he was for this to happen, it was only Fiona's mind that still resisted total surrender to pleasure.

'Now move yourself like Tanya did,' he said, his voice ragged with excitement. 'I want to feel you all over me.'

Fiona stared down into his eyes that were as dark as night and her stomach turned over. There was nothing her body wanted more than to feel the whole length of him, and between her legs there was a throbbing pulse that she was frantic to ease; it was only the thought of the power this ability to please her would give him that held her back.

Roughly, Alessandro moved his hands to her buttocks and he began to move her himself, pushing her up and down so that she felt the pressure building over her entire vulva. When he released her, her body continued moving without any conscious effort on her part.

Now her sharply pointed nipples were rubbing against his firmly muscled chest, and when their nipples met the sensation was so unexpected that Fiona gasped. Alessandro continued to look up at her, his eyes unfathomable.

Fiona's movements grew more urgent. The quicker she moved, the greater the friction between their bodies, the more the aching need increased in her. Her breasts felt huge now, as though they'd swollen to twice their normal size and they were so sensitive that she found herself longing for the cool touch of Alessandro's tongue on them.

Without thinking what she was doing she moved higher up his body, just as she'd seen Tanya do, until her breasts were within reach of his mouth. Alessandro raised his head and flicked his tongue up the underside of each of her breasts in turn, just as she'd seen him do with Georgina in Duncan's study.

It felt every bit as good as she'd imagined then, and she found that she was trying to press more of her breast into his mouth, so that he could suck on her throbbing nipples and ease their heat as well.

Alessandro curled his tongue round the outer edge of the nipples instead, never quite touching the most sensitive tip until he actually heard Fiona moan with desire. Then he took the tip into his mouth, his teeth grazing it for a second before he began a swift sucking rhythm that pulled her down onto him and sent long curling tendrils of pleasure shooting along her body, all focusing between her thighs where she felt warm and sticky with desire.

As though he could read her thoughts, Alessandro raised one leg, making sure his left thigh was in such a position that she could press her entire pubic area against his thigh bone and she did exactly that, and at the increase in sensation she became almost frenzied with desire and moved frantically, afraid he'd remove his leg and the source of such gratification.

Alessandro left her alone to do as she wished, taking his pleasure from her increasingly flushed face, the brightness of her eyes and the growing wonder that he could see in them as she learnt to arouse herself to new heights, just as Tanya had done.

After a few minutes he felt her stomach muscles tense, and then Fiona began to slow, aware that she was rushing into a climax before she wanted it all to end. However, Alessandro's hands took over and kept her moving. He wanted her to come, in order to take her on to a second and third climax and show her that she was no different from Tanya in her sexual ability.

Fiona gave herself over to him. She let him move her against his leg and chest, and allowed the throbbing to grow and grow until all at once there was the headlong rush into release that was signalled by her stomach muscles contracting sharply as she climaxed more swiftly than ever before.

When the climax had died away, Fiona began to move away from Alessandro, but he held her fast. 'Where are you going?'

She stared at him. 'I don't know. I suppose you . . .?' She blushed, aware that there had been no peak of pleasure for him and ashamed that she'd forgotten all about him in her own personal world of ecstasy.

'Turn round, I want to taste you,' he whispered.

Fiona felt she couldn't bear to have him see her the way she felt at that moment. 'No, please don't. I'm not . . .'

'This is just the beginning. There's nothing to be ashamed of. This is what real sex is all about. Besides, you can hardly say I've done well out of this yet!'

Despairingly, Fiona twisted round on top of him, so that she was crouched over his body and looking down directly at his erection. His hands gripped her thighs and he manoeuvred her back further so that he could lower her legs until her entire vulva was over his mouth and face.

Fiona wanted to die of shame. To her disbelief, he put his hands up and parted her very tenderly, drawing the outer sex-lips apart and licking at the sticky seepage that had leaked from her during her first climax. As his tongue caressed her there her body began to grow hot again, and she felt the blood coursing in her ears while her breasts slowly started to tingle with re-arousal.

He burrowed more deeply into her secret parts, his nose nudging at the place where her inner lips joined to form the small hood of flesh that covered the clitoris. At this touch Fiona gasped aloud, and Alessandro felt the tip of her bud emerge as it became filled with blood and once again her labia swelled with excitement.

Now she was growing steadily more and more moist and Alessandro lapped at her secretions, swirling his tongue around her channels so that he covered her with her own juices. Fiona's arms could hardly support her, so intense were the sensations he was causing, and the muscles of her abdomen grew hard while her aureoles darkened and the nipples stood out proudly with desire.

Alessandro moved his head for a moment. 'Lick me,' he said quietly but firmly. 'Let me feel your tongue, just as you can feel mine.'

If she hadn't been so utterly distracted by the feelings she was experiencing, Fiona would have refused. She hated giving oral sex to Duncan, hated the way he thrust himself into her so that she nearly choked, and it was the last thing she wanted to do now, but because she didn't want Alessandro to stop what he was doing to her she bent her head and licked apprehensively at the purple head of his erection.

He had never had a woman lick him so uncertainly. Her lack of expertise, the obvious ignorance of what was needed to please him most, gave the act an unexpected piquancy and although he knew that in time she'd learn to be far more expert and skilful, this almost

93

virginal approach to pleasing him with her mouth gave him a new kind of pleasure. He found that he was filled with tenderness towards her, and when she finally mustered the courage to actually take him in her mouth and move her lips lightly over his shaft he nearly came with the novelty of the sensations.

'That's enough!' he gasped, terrified that he'd come in her mouth when that was the last thing he wanted to do at this time, and Fiona stopped gratefully. Then he curled the sides of his tongue up and using the tip like a tiny brush flicked rapidly three times at her protruding clitoris.

Fiona screamed, her body shot off his as though she'd received an electric shock and then her head was thrown back as her climax engulfed her again and she ground herself against his face while the waves continued to pulsate through her.

When he knew that it was over, Alessandro lifted her off, laid her on the carpet next to him and leant over her, his right hand reaching across to squeeze one of her breasts. 'One more,' he urged her. 'Let's see if you can manage one more.'

Fiona had no idea if she could or not, she only knew that the dull ache between her thighs was still there, less insistent but definitely present. When she didn't protest, Alessandro gave a small smile. The corners of his mouth lifted and his top teeth showed briefly for a moment while his eyes glittered. 'I think I'm beginning to know you better than I'd dared to hope,' he murmured. The hand that was holding her breasts tightened, then eased, and he kept doing this while his other hand travelled down her body with the fingers bent allowing his nails to scratch lightly across her skin.

It was an entirely new sensation to Fiona, and when he drew his nails across the stretch of stomach between her hip-bones, her legs jerked and she felt herself thrusting her pubic mound into the air seeking some kind of relief from the ache that still wouldn't go away.

Releasing her breast for a moment, Alessandro reached for the small object that he'd put in his trouser pocket earlier that day. He put that into the hand that had been delicately scratching her responsive flesh and returned again to the steady squeezing pressure on her breast.

Then with the other hand he quickly switched on the battery that worked the round ball nestling in the palm of his hand and waited as it grew pleasantly warm, vibrating against his skin. When it was fully activated he parted her loose thighs and began to massage her with steady circular movements that tugged and pulled at all her nerve endings until the distant ache grew into a painful need that had Fiona crying out restlessly.

She was heavily lubricated now, and it was easy for Alessandro to insert the vibrating ball into her vagina while continuing to stimulate the surrounding area. Fiona was suddenly aware of something filling her, something warm and throbbing that stretched her in a different way from a penis and filled her so that the ache eased briefly before the vibrations made it flare up again and she found herself pressing down against the heel of Alessandro's hand.

He moved his fingers down until they were near the entrance to her bladder, and there he played with exquisite lightness upon the delicate membranes while at the same time the vibrating ball continued its warm stimulation of her internal muscles.

Fiona had never imagined it would be possible to have three orgasms in a row, let alone three of increasing intensity, but now her body was being racked by glorious sensations that banished all her inhibitions, leaving her nothing but a mass of yearning, pulsating nerve endings that were filling her body with a pressure that threatened to split her wide open if it wasn't released.

Alessandro watched her closely from beneath his heavy lids. His own excitement was controlled now.

Georgina would be home that evening and it would simply increase the pleasure he enjoyed with her. All that mattered to him was getting the timing right for Fiona's third orgasm.

Beneath the fingers of one hand he felt her breast tissue pressing against the stretched skin and between her thighs her clitoris retracted beneath the protection of its hood of skin. He knew that this meant her climax was imminent, but judged that to manually expose the clitoris to his touch would probably cause too intense a sensation after so much titillation, instead he concentrated on the area just below it, moving his fingers faster in firm circles, tugging at the base of the clitoris without actually touching the bud itself.

Deep inside Fiona the ball continued to vibrate while Alessandro's skill brought her excitement to such a pitch that she felt like screaming aloud at the piercing darts of hot pleasure that were multiplying inside her. Her abdominal muscles seemed to contract inwards, drawn by the tightening knot of desire until, with one final featherlight caress of her slippery, swollen inner lips Alessandro precipitated her headlong rush into fulfilment.

Fiona lost all sense of everything, time, place and appearance as her body exploded in an orgasmic rush that drew her legs up to her body in a reflexive movement while the middle of her back lifted upwards and her head thrashed from side to side. She found that she was sobbing with the incredible, overwhelming wash of sensations that made her whole body throb and glow.

She thrashed and twisted for endless seconds, and at the very peak of her release she nearly lost consciousness, so overpowering was the sensation. Alessandro watched her, and wondered how it would ever be possible for her to return to Duncan now that he had shown her what her body could safely enjoy. It wasn't a problem he intended to let spoil this moment for him, nor the days that lay ahead. It could wait. He had discovered that many things in life resolved themselves with time.

At last Fiona's body was still. Damp with sweat she opened her eyes and stared at him, her gaze unfocused as she slowly came down to earth again. Alessandro quickly inserted two fingers into her and removed the vibrator, then pulled her towards him and held her close. 'You see, it's safe to give yourself up to sensuality. Safe and exciting, don't you think?'

Fiona, who wasn't able to think clearly about anything other than the hardness of his body and the clever way he'd aroused her to such heights of bliss, only murmured something unintelligible.

'Tomorrow, Georgina will show you how best to please me with your mouth,' he added quietly. 'You have a lot to learn, but Georgina is probably the best teacher possible. Once you have seen her with me, you'll understand what is wanted. Then we'll give and receive equal pleasure from each other in that way.'

'I don't want to watch you and Georgina,' protested Fiona, amazed at how much she resented the thought of his mistress with him.

'But I want you to watch us, and that's what counts. Now you'd better go and take a bath and get changed. There are plenty of clothes in a wardrobe in the dressing room next to the bathroom. Choose something sexy, I like my women in sexy clothes.'

'I'm not your woman,' she muttered.

'You are until Duncan's paid for your release!'

Fiona sighed as she felt his arms releasing her. Slowly she pulled on her robe and made her way to the bathroom, her body replete and the dull ache finally banished, at least for the moment.

They all ate dinner together at eight o'clock, by which time Georgina had arrived, flown in by Alessandro's helicopter for which he had a landing pad in the grounds. Fiona was pleased that she'd taken Alessandro's advice when choosing her clothes. Her black and cream clinging Lycra dress, with a scoop neckline but dramatically plunging back was both comfortable and highly flattering. Georgina, her short dark hair in tousled curls tonight instead of sleek to her head, was dressed in a bright red silk blouse and a tight red and blue skirt that ended at the top of her knee. Although striking it emphasised her lack of height, while the skirt looked far from comfortable, riding up whenever she sat down. Bethany, in a sheer black, patterned bodystocking that concealed nothing, was the only one of the women who seemed out of place, because Tanya had changed too, into a long button-through cotton dress that suited her tall, slim figure.

Throughout the meal, Alessandro, Edmund and Marcus discussed what they knew of Duncan's continued efforts to raise money to repay them. Once or twice they burst into laughter, and Fiona had to bite hard on the inside of her cheek to control herself. Tanya glanced at her sympathetically now and again, but the men seemed to forget that she was in any way concerned with the outcome of her husband's efforts.

Georgina, bored by the talk, turned to Fiona. 'How did you enjoy your day?' she asked with a smile.

Fiona shrugged. 'It was all right. At least we left the cellar. I thought we'd freeze to death there last night.'

'I heard you had a *very* good time,' Georgina continued, her eyes probing Fiona's more deeply. 'Was Alessandro telling me fibs?'

Fiona flushed, and wondered how many more times she was going to be humiliated before she got away from the Trimarchi family. What had happened between Alessandro and her had been private, or so she'd imagined. The thought of him talking about her to Georgina was utterly mortifying. 'I'm sure Alessandro doesn't tell "fibs",' she said curtly. 'He seems to go in for grand gestures. I imagine it would be lies or nothing.'

Georgina stared at her, no longer smiling. 'You're saying Alessandro's been lying to me then?'

Her voice was deliberately loud, and Alessandro turned his head to look at the two women. Fiona felt his eyes on her and experienced a moment of fear. She knew how Duncan would react to being called a liar, and it seemed likely that the Italian would take the slur on his honour far more badly. 'I've no idea,' she said as calmly as possible. 'How can I judge when you haven't told me what he actually said?'

Alessandro's brow darkened and he scowled at his mistress. 'Be careful, *cara*, I thought you understood the need for discretion in all things.'

At this unexpected and public rebuke, Georgina felt a flare of anger, but it was directed at Fiona and not her long-time lover. The other woman had outwitted her verbally, and she wouldn't forget that in a hurry. Alessandro rarely lost his temper with Georgina, and she prided herself on knowing how to keep him happy. She didn't intend to let Fiona alter that, but knew that she must be more careful in future dealings with this important hostage.

'I only heard that you'd watched a show through our mirror,' she said lightly.

Fiona relaxed a fraction. She'd thought that it was their own lovemaking Alessandro had discussed with Georgina. 'Yes, we did,' she admitted. 'Tanya enjoyed herself.'

Now Georgina permitted herself another smile, but less pleasant than the earlier one. 'Of course. I taught her how to enjoy being dominant, because when she first came here she was basically subservient which bored us all after a time. I'm a good teacher – as you'll learn tomorrow,' she added.

Fiona turned her head away. She wasn't going to think about tomorrow. There was tonight to get through first, and once they were alone together she knew that she had to talk to Bethany. As soon as the meal had ended, she and Bethany were taken from the room by Chrissie. This time they were left in a bedroom on the top floor of the house. It was quite large, with two single beds, and a tiny toilet with handbasin off it. There were mirrors on all the walls and the ceiling.

'Once you've used the bathroom you have to be tied up for the night,' said Chrissie apologetically. 'Alessandro doesn't want to risk either of you escaping. I can do it, or I can get the men to help me.'

Bethany came out of the bathroom and stripped off her body-stocking leaving herself naked before the other two women. 'I shan't resist. I'm exhausted; all I want to do is sleep.'

Fiona would have liked to resist, but she didn't want Marcus and Craig to have another excuse to put their hands on her, so she decided to go along with Bethany's attitude.

'You have to take all your clothes off,' said Chrissie when Fiona went to lie on one of the beds in the brief and bra set that she's put on under the Lycra dress.

'Why?'

'Alessandro said. There's a special cover on the beds to make sure you're . . . well, comfortable,' and she smiled at Bethany knowingly.

Bethany's eyes went to the bed and she saw the fitted sheepskin covers stretched over the mattresses. At the thought of lying naked on the soft fibres for the night she shivered with delight. 'At least we'll be warm,' she told Fiona and promptly lay down on her side.

'You both lie on your stomachs. It's easier to fasten you that way,' explained Chrissie.

Fiona sighed. 'I'm surprised we didn't have to come up half an hour earlier with this performance to get through.' Then she stripped off her underclothes and lay face down as instructed. Chrissie, who had been told that the only trouble was likely to come from Fiona, immediately spread the young woman's feet apart and fastened them securely with cuffs and straps, then did

100

the same with her arms. Fiona realised that she was now in the same position as the man she'd watched through the mirror earlier that day. After Chrissie had secured Bethany in the same way she put a tiny pillow at the base of each woman's spine, drew a strap tightly round the bed and across the top of them, then pulled a cotton sheet over their bodies and left the room, turning out the main light but leaving a small night light glowing in the corner.

Fiona lay quite still. The sheepskin was tickling her whole body, and the pressure of the pillow against her lower spine meant that her lower half was pressed more firmly against the material than the top. With her legs parted as they were this ensured gentle but continued titillation of the area between her legs. Because her flesh was already learning the joys of sexual pleasure, her nerve endings began to respond to the sensations, and to her shame it wasn't long before she felt the increasingly familiar dull ache returning at the base of her stomach.

To distract herself she turned her head towards Bethany. 'I must say you've been a great friend to me,' she said furiously. 'I invited you into my home as someone I could confide in. I thought we were close, that you liked me and would understand what I was going through, but all the time you frowned and pretended to feel sorry for me you were actually sleeping with my husband, weren't you?'

Bethany, who had spent an incredible hour with Craig and Edmund before dinner and whose body was still highly sensitive, snuggled against the sheepskin and sighed voluptuously. 'So what?' she asked casually. 'You didn't enjoy sex with him. I wasn't taking anything away from you.'

'He treated me abominably. How could I enjoy the sort of sex he allowed me?'

'Duncan's a terrific lover,' protested Bethany. 'You just didn't know how to have fun. It's probably not

101

your fault. Your parents were pretty old weren't they? Duncan thought you'd had a repressed childhood.'

'I did not!' protested Fiona violently. 'He was always hurting me.'

'I never mind that!' laughed Bethany. 'Anyway, he told me you were frigid, whatever he did.'

'There's nothing wrong with me. I know that now. Alessandro . . .' Fiona suddenly fell silent.

Bethany laughed. 'Quick, tell me, what did Alessandro do? Something good? I wish he'd do it to me as well. He's fabulous. So fierce and handsome. God, I shall go mad tied up like this all night. I'm so close to coming already I could scream.'

'Shut up!' hissed Fiona. 'Can't you think of anything but sex? You seem to love it here. You let them put you in the most disgusting clothes, giggle and laugh when the men manhandle you, and yet claim that Duncan's the best lover in the world. Well, where's your loyalty to him then?'

'We're stuck here until Duncan pays for our release,' said Bethany practically. 'If I can enjoy myself while I wait, so much the better. Duncan won't ever know.'

Fiona fidgeted restlessly, and strands of the sheepskin brushed against her vulva, making her catch her breath. Bethany heard the sound and laughed. 'I told you, it's incredible isn't it? The pillow's a great help. It gives enough pressure to open us up but we've still got sufficient freedom to move around a bit. It doesn't look as though I'll sleep much after all!'

'I'm not listening to this,' Fiona exclaimed. 'You're totally without any moral principles, and I think you and Duncan deserve each other.'

'Good,' said Bethany, stung into retaliation by Fiona's words. 'In that case you won't mind if he dumps you and marries me after this is all over, will you?'

The ache in Fiona's body was increasing, and now she was starting to feel hot and uncomfortable between her thighs. 'He'll never marry you. He just likes your type as a mistress. You're not the first, and you won't be the last. Duncan marries for other qualities than sex, and you don't possess them.'

'I'll still be out of here before you,' Bethany muttered, knowing a climax was approaching and losing interest in the conversation. She felt her outer lips opening, flattening themselves back and exposing the innner lips to the sheepskin's caress as the excitement rose. This made it easier for her to ensure that her emerging clitoris was able to experience the same gentle stimulation and at once her excitement rose to a higher level and her nipples hardened until they too were rubbing against the bed covering.

Fiona could hear Bethany's straining attempts at bringing about her own satisfaction. She listened as her friend's breathing grew more rapid and small groans issued from her mouth.

'Stop it!' Fiona cried. 'Don't you see, this is what they want. We're just bodies to them. They're trying to make us as depraved as they are.'

A thin film of sweat was covering Bethany's back as she tried to wriggle her hips from side to side. 'They're not depraved,' she managed to mutter. 'They simply know how to make full use of their sexuality. There's nothing wrong with that.'

'There is! We're their prisoners, we shouldn't be . . .'

But Bethany's cries were louder now and Fiona gave up the attempt to talk to her. She had to listen to the small rubbing sounds of Bethany's body as it strained against its bonds but quite quickly the sheepskin and the pressure from the pillow above her did the trick and with a gasp Bethany felt her body's internal muscles start contracting, sending ripples of pleasure through her. She wished there was a man there who could enter her, in order for her vaginal muscles to have something to contract around, giving her the feeling of fullness that she adored.

For Fiona, listening to the uninhibited sounds of

103

Bethany was an added source of arousal and she tried to calm her body by thinking of her home, her life before her marriage and the day when she would finally be freed. To her annoyance, it was more difficult than she'd expected. Instead, images of Alessandro's hands and mouth on her body earlier that day kept darting uninvited into her brain.

In the end, exhaustion triumphed over stimulation, and Fiona slept, but during the early hours of the morning she awoke after a vivid dream in which all the men in the house were playing with her body, touching and entering her until it seemed that there was no part of her body that wasn't alive with excitement.

When her eyes flew open she realised that it was her inadvertent movements against the cunning sheepskin cover that had caused the dream, because all the front of her body was alive and tingling with pleasure and the pressure against her stomach and pubic bone was adding to her accidental arousal.

She felt burning hot, as though she was running a fever, and longed for a cool drink or some air in the room, but there was only the warmth of the central heating and the windows were closed against the cool night air.

Now Fiona knew why they had been fastened on their stomachs. If she could have turned over, eased the pressure against her breasts, nipples and engorged vulva then the sensations would have died away, but she couldn't. Instead she lay wide awake, determined for her own pride not to allow herself any kind of sexual release from their cruel game. For the rest of the night she kept totally still, forcing her eyes to remain open in case by sleeping she accidentally triggered the spasms of release her flesh was craving.

It was daylight before anyone came to see them, and then it was Edmund and Tanya who arrived. They had to wake Bethany, who had spent the greater part of the night bringing herself to orgasms, but Fiona was awake and looked heavy-eyed. Edmund guessed why she'd stayed awake.

Tanya released the bonds and both young women were allowed into the bathroom, although the door between the two rooms was left open which Fiona hated. After that they were hurried down to the first floor and pushed beneath the shower one after the other, then Bethany was led away by Edmund while Tanya took Fiona into a different bedroom. 'Georgina and Alessandro intend to give you your first proper lesson now,' she explained, pushing her through the door.

Chapter Seven

*F*iona walked slowly into the room, her heart beating loudly in her ears. Georgina was sitting on the king-size bed at the far end of the room. It was covered with a cream and black duvet and the head of the bed was piled high with pillows. Above these rose a headboard at least four feet in height, while silk curtains were suspended from a rail in the ceiling, and drawn back on each side of the headboard leaving an area of gold and white wallpaper exposed behind it.

Georgina was wearing white patterned stockings fastened to suspenders that hung from a blue and white satin teddy. This had been unfastened beneath her crotch and pushed up round her hips although it was still covering her breasts. Round her neck were three heavy gold chains which gave off a soft glow against her skin.

Alessandro was standing naked at the foot of the bed. He signalled for Fiona to come nearer to him as his eyes swept over her. 'You look tired. Didn't you sleep well?'

'No, I had bad dreams,' she retorted.

His mouth curved upwards in a smile. 'What a pity. I'd hoped your dreams would be pleasant ones.'

'You were wrong. Bethany seemed to have a good night though.'

He nodded. 'Of course; Bethany doesn't fight against her nature like you do. Sit down on the chair there. Georgina is going to teach you how to make love to me properly with your mouth. Yesterday was pleasant, but only as a novelty. You have a lot to learn, so watch her closely. Later today we'll see how well you've absorbed the lesson.'

Fiona swallowed hard. She wanted to close her eyes, but knew better than to try and defy him, and anyway there was something compellingly sexual about the sight of him standing before her, his erection already making itself evident.

He stood sideways on to her and signalled for Georgina to join them. Carefully Georgina dropped to her knees in front of her lover. Fiona watched as the other woman nuzzled at Alessandro's lower stomach, sucking lightly on the skin while her hands went round his buttocks and her fingers caressed them.

Then, as Alessandro's hands went to her head, Georgina began to lick very softly at his testicles. Immediately they started to swell and tighten, pulling up towards his body. Georgina increased the pressure of her tongue a fraction and the testicles expanded further while Alessandro's head went back and his eyes closed.

Fiona watched, her mouth dry with a feverish excitement she'd never experienced before. Georgina was so obviously enjoying herself, while Alessandro's rigid thighs and taut belly indicated clearly how stimulating it was for him. Once his testicles had drawn up, Georgina allowed her tongue to travel slowly along the skin beneath, licking back and forth but using only the tip of the tongue to give the sensitive perineum maximum pleasure.

His penis was fully erect now, the glans a dark purple, the shaft thick and rigid. Georgina raised her head a little and licked the underside of the shaft, making sure that she spread plenty of her own saliva along it as she went because the lubrication was essential for his enjoyment.

Once he was thoroughly moist, she stopped licking and instead used her parted lips, pressing them against the bottom of the stem and then rubbing them up towards the head of his erection. Alessandro sighed with enjoyment, and all at once he turned his head towards Fiona, taking in her high colour and noticing the way that her previously flat nipples had risen from the surrounding aureoles. These too had darkened in colour, and he knew that she was finding the whole experience arousing despite her initial objection to watching.

Feeling her lover's hands gripping her hair more tightly, Georgina proceeded to take the head of his penis into her mouth. She opened her lips wide, making sure that her teeth didn't graze him, and then once he was inside her mouth, she began to suck lightly, feeling the clear seepage of liquid from the slit escaping into her.

She knew that she wasn't allowed to have him climax in her mouth today, and reluctantly she slid her lips over the tip of the glans again and then she began to do what he liked best, to lick and kiss the almost unbearably sensitive skin where the glans joined the rigid and straining shaft.

Alessandro's whole body jerked as Georgina's skilled mouth and tongue played on him there, and she increased the amount of saliva covering him until all he could feel was the slippery movement of lips and tongue as searing bursts of blissful sensations filled his sexual organs.

He was no longer looking at Fiona, but allowing himself to be swallowed up by his mistress, taking his pleasure to the full. It was only when she put her mouth over his glans again and began to move her head up and down the shaft with rapid movements that he came back to his senses and pulled her away from him, knowing that if he didn't stop her he would lose control.

Georgina tried to take him back into her mouth. Aware that Fiona was watching them in hypnotised fascination, she suddenly wanted to demonstrate her power over the Italian. She wanted to show Fiona just how well she knew Alessandro, and if she could make him come in her mouth against his will then she felt that she would have scored a point over a woman she was begining to fear might be of more than passing interest to Alessandro.

She closed her lips about him and sucked hard. Startled, Alessandro grabbed hold of her hair and jerked her away from him again, only this time his hands hurt her and her neck was jarred by the force with which he thrust her away.

'What are you doing?' he whispered and she pretended to look apologetic.

Alessandro's chest was rising and falling rapidly and his legs trembled with sexual tension, but he wanted the end of Fiona's lesson to be as erotic as possible and quickly he picked Georgina up, lifting her onto the bed and positioning her so that she was standing with her arms resting behind her on the large headboard, her body thrust towards him.

Her teddy was still up round her waist, and now he pulled the straps down Georgina's extended arms until her breasts were revealed. Standing in front of her, balancing carefully on the thick mattress, he pushed at the undersides of her breasts with his hands and then tongued the exposed surfaces vigorously before letting his hands slide down the sides of her body to cup her small, firm buttocks. His fingers felt the top of her silk stockings and he touched the flesh beneath, at the same time pulling her hips closer towards him until he could finally thrust his engorged and throbbing erection into her.

Georgina, moist and warm from the thrill of demonstrating her sexual expertise to the naïve Fiona, welcomed him with a low cry. Her hands gripped the head of the bed tightly as Alessandro moved her lower body roughly to and fro, and every time he penetrated her the area around her clitoris was pulled tight, increasing her excitement.

Fiona watched them in utter silence. Between her thighs she could feel moisture seeping out onto the cushion of the chair, and her breasts were tight and aching, while in the pit of her stomach there was a strange rippling sensation as though her muscles were coiling up in readiness for action. She was totally aroused, and utterly unable to take her eyes off the couple on the bed.

Alessandro knew that he was about to come. He had delayed his climax as long as possible while Georgina went through her entire repertoire of oral tricks, and now that he was encased in her moist warmth he was losing control, but he knew that Georgina wasn't quite ready to climax.

He slid a hand further round her back and while he increased the depth of his penetration from the front he inserted a finger inside her rear entrance and rotated it, pressing against the highly sensitive skin just inside the opening.

This, combined with the feeling of Alessandro's own climax, was enough to trigger Georgina's climax. As her vaginal walls contracted around her lover's penis the muscles of her rectum contracted too and red hot shafts of pleasure lanced through her from front to back so that she flung her head back with a cry of release while Alessandro shuddered in the final spasms of ejaculation.

Fiona knew that it was over, but was unable to move. She didn't know what was expected of her, or what was going to happen next. What she did know was that it had been incredibly arousing, and that she had briefly hated Georgina for being so experienced and able to give Alessandro such pleasure. She was ashamed of her own pathetic efforts the previous day.

Georgina sank down onto the bed, turned on her side and closed her eyes. Normally Alessandro would lie down with her, his arm across her back while they talked of small unimportant things, but this morning he left her and went over to where Fiona sat waiting.

'Do you think you can remember all that?' he asked, his eyes still soft from lovemaking.

'No, and you disgust me,' said Fiona, determined not to let him see how aroused she was.

Alessandro drew her to her feet and slid a hand between her naked thighs. 'You seem to have enjoyed yourself, despite your protestations!'

She squirmed, terrified that his touch might precipitate further visible signs of her stimulation. He let his hands run softly over her breats, and felt the nipple peak again beneath his touch. Fiona gave a tiny groan. 'Please, don't,' she whispered.

'Why not?' His voice was just as low.

'Because it feels too good,' she admitted, dropping her eyes.

Alessandro nodded and released her. 'For once you're honest with me! See how I reward you? I do as you ask! But later, you shall have an opportunity to show me how well you studied Georgina, and after that I will give you the release you need now.'

'The only kind of release I want is my freedom,' protested Fiona.

He flicked at her rosy, erect nipple and laughed. 'These tell a different story! I shall get Craig to take you back to your room now. You can rest on your bed again until I'm ready for you.'

She stared at him. The sheepskin had been bad enough last night. After what she'd watched here it would be unbearably arousing, and she could have cried at the thought of what would undoubtedly happen to her body once she was fastened against it.

Alessandro watched the play of emotions across her face and was well pleased. Soon the lessons would move on to more erotic things. Group sex, the pleasures that could be found from playing with all her sensitive openings, but this morning's lesson was sufficient for one day. He was anxious not to rush her.

Fiona was led away, and Alessandro began to think about the afternoon, surprised to find his penis stirring again so soon after sex with Georgina. He assumed it must be because Fiona was so different from all the other women he was uséd to having.

On the way back to the small bedroom, Craig handed Fiona a set of skimpy underwear. She took it from him without a word. Already she was beginning to get used to being naked for much of the time. She guessed that quite apart from being useful for their erotic games, it helped allay Alessandro's fears of her attempting to escape. Without clothes she would find it difficult to go anywhere.

Craig opened the bedroom door and Fiona steeled herself to lie down on the bed again, but to her shock Bethany was still in the room, and she wasn't alone, Tanya and Edmund were with her.

Craig quickly retreated, shutting and locking the door behind him. An equally startled Bethany lifted her head and gazed into Fiona's astonished eyes. The red-head was spread sideways over her single bed, her arms stretched out to rest on a padded chair that had been placed between the two beds. Her breasts were hanging down towards the floor and Tanya was sitting beneath her, sucking at the dangling nipples with obvious relish.

Edmund was kneeling on the bed between Bethany's outspread thighs, and the pillow that had been on her back during the night was now beneath her abdomen so that her buttocks were elevated, allowing him easy access to all her intimate parts.

Fiona tried to escape from the room, but the handle didn't turn. Trapped, she turned again to look at

Bethany, and knew from her friend's sparkling eyes and glowing skin that whatever was happening here it was giving Bethany great pleasure.

Edmund frowned. 'Why are you here?' For the first time his voice held a touch of Alessandro's arrogance.

'I'm meant to rest until after lunch,' she explained, wishing that the room wasn't so full of the scent and sounds of sexual arousal.

'Then lie down,' he said abruptly. 'Tanya, you'd better fasten her. I expect Alessandro wants her on the sheepskin while she waits.'

Tanya reluctantly left Bethany's breasts and did as Edmund commanded. Fiona could turn her head away from the other three people, but there was no way in which she could ignore the sounds and movements going on around her. Eventually, in order to try and distract her own throbbing flesh, she decided to try and see exactly what was happening.

Bethany's head was lifted up and she was arching her shoulders back as Tanya attended to her breasts with hands that were encased in silk gloves. The feel of the smooth, cool material on such an erogenous zone was wonderful and Bethany wished that the manipulation could go on for ever.

While Tanya worked on her breasts, Edmund was exploring between Bethany's thighs. He had already used a vibrator around her vulva, one shaped like an electric toothbrush with bristles that stimulated the soft flesh of the inner lips so greatly that it had almost been too intense an experience. Then he had threaded small beads joined together on a string into her anus, twisting each one around as she took it inside her, and continuing to insert them until she felt so full that internal cramps racked her and made her cry out.

To her surprise this hadn't deterred Edmund and now that Fiona was in the room with them he seemed intent on making Bethany accept yet another bead while

113

her body told her that it wasn't possible. She gave another small cry, and this time he stopped.

'What is it?'

'I feel full,' Bethany moaned. 'It's uncomfortable.'

'But Tanya can take three more than this. You'll have to wear an anal plug for a day. That will stretch you more.'

'It's nice too,' Tanya assured Bethany. 'When you clench the muscles of your back passage with a plug inside you, you get an orgasm almost immediately.'

Fiona wished her hands were free so that she could cover her ears. She had a terrible feeling that this kind of thing lay ahead of her too, and while it wasn't troubling Bethany it was something that she couldn't bear to contemplate.

'I don't want to be stretched any more,' said Bethany sulkily. 'Why won't you enter me?'

'Hostages don't make demands of their captors!' laughed Edmund, smacking her lightly across her upper thighs.

Tanya stopped the stroking of Bethany's breasts and peeled off her silk gloves. Then, to Fiona's amazement, the blonde model picked up what looked like a pair of long-handled scissors and reached up towards Bethany's nipples with them. Fear closed Fiona's throat and she couldn't even cry out a warning to Bethany.

She needn't have worried. They weren't scissors but nipple clamps. The circular ends fastened round the already extended tips of Bethany's breasts and then Tanya tugged, pulling them down yet further so that Bethany's pleasure began to turn to the kind of pain that she enjoyed, a sharp darting pain that made the surrounding breast tissue feel warm and swollen.

Bethany was so busy savouring what Tanya was doing she didn't pay full attention to Edmund. Fiona however, trying vainly to lift her tense and tingling body from the insidiously caressing sheepskin, did. She watched as he took something from the table next to the bed and when she couldn't see what it was she glanced in the mirror on the wall opposite him.

The sight she saw there was so arousing that deep inside her the coiled springs of sexual tension gathered yet more tightly and the pupils of her eyes dilated. She could see the whole of Bethany's naked back, the cleft between her buttocks and Edmund's massive erection which was jutting out at a sharp angle from the base of his stomach.

It was what he held in his hands that startled her the most though. She realised that it must be a two pronged dildo, but both of the prongs were amazingly realistic replicas of a penis, one longer than the other and complete with veins and holes from which she guessed that real fluid could seep.

Swiftly, Edmunds smeared the tips of both dildos with lubricating jelly and then he tugged on the cord protruding from Bethany's rear entrance and Fiona watched as the round beads he had inserted popped out from between the tightly puckered opening, one after the other.

Bethany gasped at the sudden sensation, and automatically clenched her sphincter muscles, which trapped the last bead tightly within her. 'Push down,' said Edmund in annoyance. Bethany had never been treated like this even by Duncan and she was beginning to feel the first stirring of real fear. But, as Edmund and Tanya had guessed, this fear was only a greater aphrodisiac to Bethany's body, and her level of arousal grew.

Once the last bead was out, Fiona saw in the mirror that Edmund was liftening Bethany's abdomen off the bed and inserting the first dildo into her vaginal opening. With her head away from him and facing down, Bethany had no idea that this was about to happen, but when she felt the thick hardness of the imitation penis gliding into her she gave a sigh of relief, still unaware of what was to follow.

As the front dildo slid home, Edmund angled the

115

adjoining one correctly, then quickly pushed it into Bethany's second opening, which was still recovering from the beads.

At this second intrusion Bethany shouted out in protest, but she couldn't move because Tanya still held the nipple clamps tightly to her breasts and so she was forced to lie motionless as Edmund began to move the double dildo in and out of both her orifices.

He moved very slowly at first, building up speed gradually, and Fiona could see how Bethany's round creamy buttocks were tensed against the invasion, but she was throwing her head back further and her cries of discomfort were tinged with an increasing amount of excitement as Edmund found the rhythm that suited her best.

Deep within Bethany's vagina, small nodules set beneath the protective covering of the dildo started to move, rubbing against her vaginal walls and one of them touched her G-spot causing her to utter a cry of surprised delight.

Fiona's own body seemed to feel the fullness of the dildos and she found that her hips were moving as much as her bonds allowed in time to the rhythm she was witnessing in the mirror. She was burning hot again, and no longer cared about pride. She needed to climax just as badly as Bethany did, but because of her own inhibitions and the lack of direct stimulation she was afraid that it wasn't going to be possible.

Bethany, in the meantime, was steadily climbing towards a massive orgasm. She could feel herself reaching the very edge of that final shattering moment, and although the muscles of her anus were protesting, the messages from the over-stimulated nerve endings were blissful and Bethany only wished that Tanya would release the nipple extenders so that she could let her upper torso twist and turn as she neared the final explosion.

Tanya knew better than that. Bethany had experienced too much pleasure from her captivity, and she had to learn that not everything she wanted could be hers, so Tanya kept the clamps firmly in place and watched Bethany struggling to keep her breasts still despite the contractions sweeping up her body.

Edmund's hand slowed for a moment, making Bethany hold her breath, terrified that he was going to stop before she'd finished, but then when he re-started, her body grasped its chance and exploded into orgasm. It was too much for the red-head to cope with and without thinking she twisted her chest around and immediately her nipples felt as though they were being pulled from her body. The pain was great, and it ruined Bethany's moment of release, shutting out the peaks of pleasure and bringing her crashing back to earth with such abruptness that she began to sob with frustration.

Tanya released the clamps and tenderly stroked the inflamed nipples. 'You were silly. Why did you move?'

'I couldn't help it!' sobbed Bethany 'That wasn't fair.' 'I thought you liked pain,' said Edmund, carefully withdrawing the double-pronged dildo from her slumped body.

'Only when I choose it!'

'Never mind,' laughed Edmund. 'I think you'll remember the experience!'

Bethany knew that he was right. Already she was replaying the whole morning in her brain, and she found that if it were to happen again she wouldn't mind her nipples being constrained because the sharpness of the pain was such a delightful contrast to the sweetness of the flooding climax.

Fiona kept her head turned away from them. She didn't want them to know that she'd been watching in the mirror, nor did she want them to guess at the desperate longing that was consuming her for her own sexual release.

Edmund got off Bethany's bed and signalled for Tanya to tie her on it again, as Fiona had been. Then he sauntered over to the other bed and looked at Duncan's wife. He knew full well that she'd been watching in the mirror, and guessed too that Alessandro and Georgina had thoroughly aroused her with their morning's tuition. It seemed a shame to leave her there unsatisfied when everyone else was having a good time.

He sat on the edge of the bed and let his right hand slide beneath her until his fingertips could feel between her outer sex-lips. As he'd guessed, she was soaking wet and when he moved the tip of his middle finger in tiny circles Fiona gave a low cry and buried her mouth in her pillow.

'Let me help you,' he whispered, and Tanya smiled at him across the room. She knew that in a few minutes she and Edmund would be in bed together and that all this foreplay with the two young women would simply mean they would have an even better time than usual together.

Fiona felt his finger gliding over her shamingly damp and tender flesh and for the first time ever she actually felt her clitoris begin to swell with the excitement of his touch. Edmund felt it too, and was surprised at its size when it emerged from the surrounding folds of flesh.

He wasn't sure what she liked best. Some of his women liked the clitoris to be touched, some preferred him to stimulate around it, but somehow he thought that it wouldn't matter too much what he did because Fiona was simply bursting with pent-up desire that needed to be assuaged.

Turning the palm of his hand uppermost he slid his finger up her until it reached the point where her inner lips joined together. Once there, he flicked very quickly and lightly, then drew his finger down the length of her inner channel and back up to the top where he repeated the flicking motion.

Fiona felt as though all her sensations were centred on the part of her body that he was touching. Her breasts no longer ached, her nipples were almost quiescent, it was just there, where his hand was moving, that her straining body had decided to focus its need and when he reached upwards and flicked at her again something seemed to explode behind his hand and her stomach muscles bunched tightly inwards while her feet drummed helplessly in their bonds and her head turned from side to side on the pillow.

The waves of ecstasy flooded over her, threatening to drown her in their liquid heat. Then, to her horror, she realised that his fingers were still there and just as her body began to quieten he played them lightly against the tight, moist skin again so that further shock waves were triggered and this time the contractions were so fierce that even the pillow couldn't mask her cries of gratitude.

Edmund at last felt Fiona's outer lips begin to close against him, and then he knew that for the moment she was satisfied. He withdrew his hand and ran a finger, still moist from her own juices, down the length of her spine. 'Alessandro's a lucky man! I can't wait until I'm allowed to join you,' he whispered.

Fiona lay limply against the sheepskin. It no longer aroused her because she was incapable of being re-aroused. Her whole body was sated, her muscles slack and heavy. She felt her eyelids beginning to close and knew that now she would sleep.

'I should think Duncan would have been surprised to see that,' she heard Bethany say, but she was unable to reply because she was already too far into sleep.

This time it was Bethany, irritable and shaken by Fiona's obvious ability to be sexually aroused, who stayed awake. She was beginning to wonder why it was the Duncan hadn't got any response from Fiona when both the Trimarchi brothers seemed to be able to do so with increasing ease. She also wondered why it was that she, who had always prided herself on being a sexual animal, was of less interest to them than the more aloof Fiona.

Her only comfort was the knowledge that at least Duncan preferred her, and she would be the first to be set free. If she told Duncan what the men had done to Fiona during her imprisonment and how she'd responded it was always possible he wouldn't bother to get her back at all, and on that pleasant thought she was at least able to sleep.

In fact, both women spent the rest of the day in their room. Alessandro had to fly unexpectedly to London to talk to colleagues about Duncan's companies, which he intended to take over once the man had been forced into bankruptcy, and in his absence no one was allowed to touch either of them.

Georgina brought them food and released their bonds in the middle of the afternoon. Although she looked searchingly at Fiona, she didn't speak to her, but she left a pile of fashion magazines for them to leaf through.

'You might find some of the tips useful,' she said to Bethany with a smile. 'I don't suppose you've ever tried the sophisticated look, but it might help you if you want to get on in life.'

'God, she's a bitch!' Bethany remarked when she and Fiona were alone. 'I can't think what Alessandro sees in her, can you?'

Since Fiona had been given precise visible evidence of exactly what Alessandro saw in Georgina, she couldn't really agree with Bethany, but she made a non-committal sound and hoped she'd let the matter drop. Bethany however wanted to talk.

'You know, I honestly thought you didn't like sex. I mean, I wouldn't have gone with Duncan if I'd thought the pair of you were happy, but you weren't. You told me so yourself. It wasn't just his word.'

Fiona felt sickened by Bethany's attempts at self-justification, 'No, we weren't happy because he very quickly lost interest in making me happy, but since you knew what a wretched time I was having, did you think sleeping with him would help? Of course you didn't!

All you thought about was yourself, and the kind of sex the pair of you enjoyed.'

'What's wrong with that?' Bethany muttered.

'Nothing, only don't try and make it sound as though you did me a favour, because you didn't. And I would like to know another thing, Bethany. Was that three-in-a-bed nightmare as much of a surprise to you as you pretended, or was it something the two of you had planned together?'

Bethany couldn't look at Fiona. 'We talked about it,' she admitted.

'So you and my husband enjoyed humiliating me. No doubt you were going to have a good laugh about it when you next met up. How unlucky for you that the Trimarchi brothers kidnapped us before that could happen.'

'He said you'd had threesomes before,' Bethany protested.

'Against my will, because I was too weak to stop him.'

'Then you should have walked out,' said Bethany. 'I'd never do anything I didn't want to do.'

'Firstly, I can't imagine anything you wouldn't want to do,' Fiona retorted, 'and secondly I didn't walk out because I had the stupid idea that I was keeping my parents safe by going along with what Duncan wanted. I realise now that was ridiculous. They'd never have wanted me to be treated badly, but all I could think about was how hard poverty had been for them, and how much better off they were once Duncan started providing for them.'

'You're enjoying the sex here though, aren't you?' asked Bethany slyly.

Fiona felt her face go hot. 'The men are very skilled at arousing women. I never realised sex could feel like it does with them, but that doesn't mean I like them, it just means that my body likes what they do.'

'So it isn't your fault!' laughed Bethany. 'I hope Duncan understands that piece of logic.'

Fiona looked sharply at the other woman. 'Duncan won't ever know.'

'He will if I tell him.'

Suddenly Fiona felt bewildered. 'Why would you do that? Do you want him to know how you've been behaving too? You can't think it will please him to learn that you've thrown yourself into the pleasures of the flesh from the moment we arrived. At least I tried to resist.'

Bethany smirked. 'You forget, I shall see Duncan first. Whatever you tell him later, I'll deny. He'll think you're just saying it to cover up for yourself. No, I really think that once we're both free you'll probably find yourself an ex-wife, Fiona, and I shall become the new Mrs Sheldon.'

'Don't worry,' exploded Fiona, enraged by this further betrayal. 'There's no way I intend to stay Mrs Sheldon once I'm freed, and it really doesn't concern me who takes my place. All I want is to get out of here and start living my own life.'

'I shouldn't hold your breath,' cautioned Bethany. 'It seems to me that Alessandro wants to keep you here for as long as possible.'

After that they didn't speak to each other again, but the hours passed slowly and the next morning seemed to be a long time coming for them both.

Chapter Eight

Craig woke the two young women, unbound them and then Amy, his wife of six months and a fresh face to Fiona and Bethany, brought them their breakfasts on trays. Amy was young, no more than nineteen with the clean-scrubbed face of a much younger girl. Her fine fair hair hung loose to her shoulders, held off her face with an Alice band. However, her body was anything but innocent. She was wearing a short navy-blue skirt with a tiny white apron over it, while her ample breasts were bursting out of a low-cut frilly white blouse. Fiona looked at Amy's legs, encased in black stockings, saw her stiletto heels and the black satin bows on the front of her shoes and realised that Craig was into the 'French Maid' line of fantasies.

When Amy leant over Fiona to place the tray across her naked lap it was also clear that Amy's eyes were at odds with her seemingly girlish innocence. They were deep blue in colour, and looked as thought they had already seen everything there was to see, and taken full pleasure in it.

'I hope you slept well,' she murmured, her voice husky. 'I've been away for a few days, visiting my family in Sweden. Craig's told me all about you though.'

'Did you lose your clothes on the journey?' asked Fiona.

Amy smiled. 'Craig likes me to dress like this, and I like to please him. In this house, we do as we wish.'

'As Alessandro wishes you mean,' replied Fiona. At the sound of their employer's name Craig and Amy glanced at each other. 'Of course we'd never do anything to offend Señor Trimarchi,' said Amy quickly. 'He particularly wanted you to have your breakfast in comfort before seeing you this morning.'

'We're very grateful,' Bethany assured her. 'I'm starving.'

'We'll come back for you later,' said Craig, as he and his wife took their leave.

'Alessandro certainly knows how to keep his employees happy,' Bethany remarked cheerfully. 'Imagine being able to do just what you like all the time.'

Fiona felt like screaming. 'They can't do just what they like! They work for him twenty-four hours a day, and in return they can dress up in stupid clothes and play out their pathetic little fantasies whenever they've got a spare moment. He's hardly being generous, merely shrewd. I always knew men used sex to manipulate women, now it looks as though the Trimarchis use it to manipulate men as well.'

Bethany shrugged. 'You can call it manipulation if you like I think it's a great atmosphere here. They all look happy and . . .'

'They're thugs!' Fiona shouted at a startled Bethany. 'Alessandro and his brother are nothing but financial crooks, and they surround themselves with a gang of heavies to make sure of a safe retreat from the business world when things get too hot in London. Are you totally mad, defending them like this? We're their prisoners, and I didn't notice any of the men were too careful in the way they handled us during the kidnapping. I hope they all end up in prison. They certainly will if I have anything to do with it.'

Bethany finished eating and put her tray on the floor. 'There you go again, playing Miss Prim for all it's worth. I don't know why Alessandro's so keen on you. I think Duncan was right, you're a waste of time. No matter how much pleasure you get from the sex here you're never going to admit it, are you? All you do is keep banging on about it not being "right".'

'Kidnapping is against the law,' Fiona said, enunciating each word with exaggerated care. 'If Duncan has any sense he'll already have alerted the police.'

This time it was Bethany's turn to stare at her one-time friend in astonishment. 'You really do live in another world, Fiona! Duncan can't call the police. He's the one who's up to his neck in law-breaking. None of his financial transactions are ethical, and some are positively illegal. There's no way he'll ever let the police start nosing around his affairs. The Trimarchis knew this before they ever took us. If you truly think they're crooks, think again. Your loyalty to Duncan was even more misplaced than you thought, wasn't it?' With a gurgle of laughter she went back to leafing through the magazines Georgina had left the previous day.

While Fiona was still absorbing what Bethany had said, the door opened as Craig and Amy returned. When Amy fussed around with the trays and picked them up of the floor they could see clearly that she wasn't wearing anything beneath her skirt. Craig took hold of Fiona's arm. 'Time to come and see the boss.'

She shook his hand off. 'Let go of me! I'm hardly likely to run away without any clothes on am I?'

Craig released her but watched her closely. If she ever did manage to get out of the house there would be hell to pay for someone, and he was determined it wasn't going to be him.

'Is it on the first floor?' Fiona asked. When he nodded she walked ahead of him down the small flight of stairs from their attic bedroom. As she'd guessed, Alessandro was waiting for her in the bedroom where she had watched him and Georgina the morning before, but this time he was alone.

Fiona moved slowly into the room. One of the windows was open and the heavy brocade curtains, pulled back to allow in some of the early morning sun, moved gently in the breeze. Fiona inhaled. It was the first chance she'd had to breathe in fresh air since her capture.

For a moment Alessandro watched her as, with her eyes closed, she lifted her head and breathed deeply, her breasts rising and falling with the action. At that moment he wished she was here with him by choice, and not held against her will. The wish took him by surprise.

'Fiona!' Because of his surprise he sounded curt and her eyes flew open as she turned her head anxiously towards him. He softened his voice. 'It's time to see how well you learnt yesterday's lesson.'

Fiona's mouth went dry and her heart began to thud in her chest. She looked at his naked body, the smooth perfection of his olive skin and the well-developed muscles across his shoulders and chest but she refused to look lower to where his manhood was waiting for her attention.

Alessandro led her to the large bed. Sitting down on the side he pulled her between his knees, running his hands down the sides of her hips and along the outsides of her long legs. He felt her tremble beneath his hands. Carefully he edged further back on the bed until his legs were extended on the mattress. He patted the space between his thighs and Fiona reluctantly knelt where he indicated, her legs beneath her buttocks.

'Let's see what you remember,' he said softly.

Now Fiona had no choice but to look at Alessandro's penis. It was curled into a semi-circle, apparently totally unaffected by her nakedness and physical closeness, while his testicles were loose, nestling against the duvet.

126

She swallowed hard and then put out a hand to lift his shaft so that she could begin to lick it. Alessandro stopped her. 'No! First you begin with the stomach, remember?'

She couldn't remember anything. All she knew was that she was faced with a flaccid penis and was expected to use her mouth, lips and tongue to bring it to full erection when she knew that with Duncan she was quite hopeless unless he was already aroused.

She heard Alessandro sigh, and quickly tried to conjure up images of Georgina. This proved easier than she'd expected. Sharp vivid pictures like slides on a screen began to fill her brain, and at last she was able to begin softly kissing the skin of his lower abdomen.

Alessandro felt her lips sucking delicately on him and immediately his penis stirred. To his agreeable surprise, Fiona didn't hurry to attend to it but instead lingered on his abdomen, even kissing the delicate edge of his navel. When she swirled her tongue deep in the depression he caught his breath in surprise.

Excited and emboldened by his reaction, Fiona bent her head lower, at the same time letting her hair brush between his thighs. He put his hands in her hair, loving the feel of the long, thick tendrils between his fingers. He had grown used to Georgina's short hair style, but this was how he really liked a woman's hair to be.

Because he was reacting so positively to her, Fiona's task was much easier than she'd expected. His rapidly hardening penis no longer seemed threatening, but instead was something to be teased and excited as he had previously teased and excited her flesh. She let her tongue encircle each of the testicles in turn, then moved lower and allowed it to dance along his perineum, gratified to see his testicles swelling and tightening as she went.

Alessandro closed his eyes and when the sensations grew too intense he pulled gently on her hair to bring her up to his rigid penis. Once she was there, Fiona grew more tentative, and her tongue moved with less assurance along the skin of the bottom of his shaft.

'You can press harder than that,' he whispered.

Fiona did as he said, and then remembered how Georgina had used her lips to kiss and suck at the skin as well. Alessandro felt her mouth on him and his stomach muscles clenched with the thrill of knowing she was finally doing what he'd been imagining for the past twenty-four hours.

After a time, Fiona knew that she had to move still higher and take the dark purple glans into her mouth, but now her own enjoyment began to diminish. She was terrified he would come in her mouth, thrusting himself down her throat in the way that had made her feel so sick with Duncan.

Alessandro sensed her fear. He lifted his head from the bed and looked down at her. 'It's all right. I shan't let myself come. You can do what you like quite safely. One day you'll want to taste me fully, and then it will be different. Today I'm saving myself for other things.'

To her surprise, Fiona believed him. Now she really let herself go, and her tongue and lips were all over him, sucking and kissing while her tongue even slid into the tiny slit at the top of the glans to lick away the clear fluid that had gathered there.

He grew harder than he could ever remember, and still Fiona worked on him until she gathered up enough courage to let her mouth fully enclose the width of him and began to move her head up and down his rigid hardness, while at the same time one of her hands gripped the base of his penis firmly between its fingers.

The suction of her mouth combined with the pressure of her grip, and the sight of her chestnut hair spread out over his stomach and thighs tested Alessandro's control to the limit. For a few minutes he allowed himself to savour the sensations she was giving him but then, remembering his promise to her, he had to catch hold of the back of her neck and stop her movements.

'That's enough!' His voice was hoarse with longing for a pulsating climax in her astonishingly clever mouth, but Fiona thought that she'd done something wrong and froze.

'You've done well,' he assured here, letting his hand caress her scalp. 'Even Georgina doesn't do any better than that. You learn very quickly!'

Slowly, and to her own surprised reluctance, Fiona let him slide out of her mouth, her teeth just grazing the skin beneath the glans as he withdrew, which nearly precipitated his already painfully denied climax.

His legs tensed and he breathed deeply through his mouth to calm himself while at the same time drawing Fiona's head up along his body until she was lying on top of him. Then he turned her until they were looking into each other's eyes. He noticed the green flecks of arousal in hers.

'You see, that wasn't so bad was it! I told you that to give pleasure was as exciting as to receive it.'

She nodded, unable to speak because she was still amazed at how right he'd been and was trying to understand why doing what she'd just done for him should have left her own body tingling with excitement and caused lubrication between her thighs.

'Now for your reward,' said Alessandro softly. He turned Fiona on to her back, kissing her deeply on the mouth for a moment, his tongue searching for hers. It was a deep, passionate kiss and Fiona's whole body responded as she pressed up towards him.

Now Alessandro slid down her. He parted her thighs and saw that her outer sex-lips were already open, pressed back to reveal the inner lips and glistening flesh beneath.

He licked his middle finger and then moved it straight to the tiny area around the opening to Fiona's urethra. He heard her gasp, and saw that her vaginal opening was closing while the rest of the area between her thighs opened up to him even more and her lubrication increased so that he knew she was close to an orgasm.

Quickly he rotated his finger on this small area that so few women realised could give them pleasure. Fiona didn't know what he was doing, all she knew was that suddenly the excitement that had been beginning to surface, the slow arousal that working on Alessandro had wrought on her, was gathering together with incredible speed and she felt the area between her thighs growing warm and throbbing with delicious pulsating beats that made her hips writhe.

Alessandro was delighted with her reaction. As she began to arch herself off the bed with the approaching climax he continued to stimulate around her urethra while simultaneously sliding another finger into the mouth of her vagina and moving it quickly from side to side.

The combination triggered an incredible explosion in Fiona and she hurtled into the most intense climax she'd had yet. It was as though every possible nerve ending in her vulva had been aroused to fever pitch and then exploded at the same time. Without realising it she screamed, 'Yes! Yes!' as her body threatened to shatter into a thousand pieces.

Quickly, Alessandro stopped. After such an intense orgasm he knew that she wouldn't want further intimate caresses, but he was intensely pleased with the way she'd responded. It was all highly encouraging considering the plans he still had for her.

For a time he left her lying on the bed, eyes closed and body spent while he made telephone calls from the far end of the room. They were all business matters, several of them concerning Duncan, but Fiona didn't hear a word. She was lost in this new world of heightened sexual responses that Alessandro was opening up to her.

Nearly an hour later she sat up, stretched lazily and then realised that Alessandro was still in the room. The memory of her experience was so vivid in her mind that she nearly smiled at him before realising that whatever he was able to do with her sexually, he had no right to keep her here and forced the smile away.

Alessandro's eyes were amused as he took in her sated look, but he kept his voice dispassionate because now he was about to move her on to more extreme joys and he knew that this would involve more intense resisitance from her, until she realised that these new experiences too could give her great sexual satisfaction.

'I hope you're rested?' he enquired politely.

Fiona nodded, and went to swing her legs off the bed.

'Stay there,' he instructed her. 'Georgina is going to join us now. We now move on to your next lesson. Such an able pupil shouldn't have any difficulty taking it in,' he added.

Fiona didn't want any more lessons. Her body felt as though it had taken quite enough stimulation for one day, and in any case she hated watching Alessandro with Georgina. When he had kissed her she had felt closer to him both physically and mentally than she had ever felt to Duncan, and although she knew that was wrong she couldn't help it. Knowing that her feelings were inappropriate and one-sided only made her resent Georgina more.

Before she could voice a protest, Georgina came through from the dressing room. She glanced at Fiona, noticed the tousled hair, bruised mouth and dreamy-eyed look of sexual satisfaction and felt a moment's hatred for the woman Alessandro called his prisoner. She was looking forward to the next half hour. This lesson was one she felt certain Fiona wouldn't enjoy.

Turning her head back to her lover she smiled at him, and he smiled back. He was well aware of Georgina's increasing antagonism towards Duncan's wife, and guessed that Fiona's emotions were becoming more mixed where he was concerned, but that was all part of the novelty of the situation and as such they simply increased his satisfaction.

'Shall I bring in Bethany?' asked Georgina. 'She and Edmund are outside.'

He nodded, and Fiona drew her knees up to her chin in a gesture of protection. She didn't want Bethany seeing her as she was at this moment, so satiated and satisfied by the man who was using her as a weapon against her own husband.

She needn't have worried. Bethany had no glance to spare for Fiona. She was looking thoroughly miserable, and for once her breasts weren't thrusting so perkily through the body harness that had been put on her that morning.

'Bethany didn't feel she needed this kind of tuition,' Edmund told his older brother. 'She's been sulking ever since we insisted.'

Alessandro gazed at the red-head and his eyes were cold. 'It seems to me that you've been very spoilt Bethany,' he commented, flicking at her nipples with his long, hard fingers. 'Duncan obviously indulged you far more than he indulged his wife.'

'Duncan and I like the same things,' Bethany muttered.

'Unfortunately Fiona and Duncan didn't,' replied Alessandro.

'She wouldn't ever experiment,' said Bethany.

'But we're getting you to experiment, and it seems that you don't care for that yourself. I fail to see how Fiona was any different from you in her reluctance to go along with her husband's desires.'

'I just don't need to do what Edmund wants. I'm . . .'

'Your needs are immaterial to me, just as Fiona's were immaterial to Duncan. Maybe, Bethany, by the time you leave here you'll have a little more understanding of the predicament in which Fiona found herself. I doubt it though, because deep down there's nothing you won't do. I'm sure you'd be willing to cross the lines that limit the rest of us in this household.'

Bethany looked at him and for a moment he saw deep into her soul. What he saw told him that he was right. 'How should I know?' she asked, but she did, and so did he. He had no compunction about using her as the model for what they were about to teach Fiona. There was nothing this red-head would ever reject, all that she resented was not being in control.

'Sit at the bottom of the bed,' he told Fiona. 'Watch closely, and listen to what we say, but don't speak. You can ask questions once we've finished with your friend.'

Fiona did as he said, her eyes fixed on Bethany. Now Georgina began to release the leather straps that enclosed Bethany's sex-lips and buttocks, then that part of the body harness was pushed up to her waist and she was turned so that her back was towards Fiona.

'Bend down and touch your toes,' said Alessandro. As Bethany bent over, Edmund spread her buttocks carefully apart and Fiona saw a round white piece of plastic nestling between them. It was like the rim of a baby's dummy.

Georgina grasped the ring and began to rotate it, moving it round in slow circles while Bethany started to groan. 'Inside her rectum is a short, thick plug which is attached to the ring,' explained Alessandro in a detached voice. 'This has been left inside her all the morning. She was told to clench and unclench her muscles against it, to strengthen them so that when Edmund penetrates her there she will be able to tighten herself round him. If she does it right she will also get considerable pleasure because the nerve endings in that area are very near the surface and can quickly trigger orgasms.'

Fiona's eyes grew large and she began to tremble. This was something she knew that she didn't want to learn about. The few times that Duncan had talked her into anal sex it had been painful and given her no

133

satisfaction at all. She didn't believe a word Alessandro was saying.

Now Georgina began to move the plug in and out of Bethany, never entirely removing it but bringing it very close to total withdrawal. Bethany started to groan again and after a few minutes Georgina pressed the plug back in. Then Edmund moved a chair into the middle of the room and spread Bethany across the two arms so that her feet were just touching the floor on one side and her head hung down on the other while her stomach was stretched unsupported between the two arms.

Alessandro put a velvet glove on his right hand, reached beneath Bethany, then slowly slid it along her stomach and up between her breasts. As her muscles leapt at the sensual touch her buttocks clenched and Bethany felt the intruding plug touching the unbearably aroused walls of her rectum.

'Don't do that!' she gasped.

Alessandro ignored her, continuing to sweep his hands across her stomach, paying particular attention to her hips and the area above her pelvic bone. He continued the massage for a long time, and all the while Fiona could see the cheeks of Bethany's bottom contracting in rippling spasms with the result that a sheen of perspiration began to cover her buttocks and lower back.

Georgina and Edmund watched too, gauging the red-head's reactions carefully. Finally Georgina whispered in Alessandro's ear and he stopped his ministrations and pulled Bethany off the chair, pressing her down onto the carpet at his feet.

'Crouch on your hands and knees,' he said softly. Bethany remained flat to the ground. Georgina immediately parted the red-head's buttocks again and began to turn the plug in the circles that so inflamed the other woman's over-aroused back passage. Quickly, Bethany rose up onto her hands and knees, deciding that it was better to do as she was told than run the risk of losing control of her bowels and disgracing herself in front of everyone.

She'd always enjoyed anal sex with Duncan, but then she'd been in control, telling him when and how to do it. This time it was different, and she wasn't enjoying it nearly as much, despite the fact that the actual sensations were the same, or possibly even better.

Edmund took hold of the rim of the plug and tugged sharply on it. Bethany felt it rush out of her body so abruptly that it seemed as though the insides of her stomach were going with it, so strong was the drawing tug on her inner muscles.

Fiona continued to watch in silence as Edmund thoroughly moistened the end of his huge erection with lubricating jelly, and then he stood over Bethany while Georgina parted the red-head's creamy globes for him. Edmund pressed the tip of his glans against the entrance and Bethany tensed, waiting for the swift thrust that she was used to from Duncan, but Edmund continued to nudge against the entrance, then slid the glans inside her, rotated his hips and removed it again.

Flashes of pleasure shot through Bethany, darting towards her abdomen and causing moisture to start seeping from her vagina. Now that the plug was out she realised how well it had done its work because her muscles wanted something to fasten round, she longed for Edmund to penetrate her in order that she could tighten herself on him and milk his ejaculation with her contractions.

She pressed back against him, making his glans slide in deeper than he'd intended. At once he withdrew. At the same time he pulled her legs down so that she felt the lower half of her body collapsing against the carpet, although she didn't dare lower herself from her elbows.

Alessandro watched her lower body fall and walked round to the front of her, tugging her head up to make her look at him. 'Now I'm going to lie down between your arms, Bethany, and you're not to lower yourself onto me until I say, is that clear?'

Bethany nodded. She was frantic for some kind of stimulation again. The plug had been withdrawn, Edmund was no longer nudging at her rear entrance and yet her whole body was on fire with need. As Alessandro lay on his back and slid under her, her arms were aching so much she didn't know how to keep supporting herself, but aware of the delight that lay ahead if she obeyed, she gritted her teeth and waited for him to let her rest on his body.

Finally, Alessandro found the right position. Then Georgina lifted Bethany's hips and pressed on her thighs until Alessandro was able to slide his erection into Bethany's front opening. Once he was safely encased in her, he allowed her to relax her arms until she was lying on her forearms with her breasts dangling over Alessandro's mouth.

Idly Alessandro began to suck on one of the large nipples but otherwise he stayed totally still, content simply to fill Bethany while Edmund at last pulled her buttocks as far apart as he could and then plunged into her second opening. He was thick and long, and it seemed to Bethany that she had never been so completely filled.

Edmund started to thrust vigorously, and his movements caused Bethany to jerk up and down on Alessandro. She was crying out with excitement now, and Georgina glanced across at her friend. Small beads of moisture stood out on Fiona's upper lips, and she was clearly unable to tear her gaze away from the scene in front of her, but there was fear as well as excitement in her eyes and Georgina smiled to herself.

'Use your muscles,' she instructed the red-head. 'Hold Edmund as you've been holding the plug. Show us how well you've learnt your lesson.'

Bethany was only too pleased to do as the other woman told her. She gripped Edmund as hard as she could, and heard his intake of breath as she held him tightly for a few seconds before releasing him briefly and then tightening again.

The muscles of her rectum triggered similar movements in the walls of her vagina, and Alessandro felt her tightening around him. His lips gripped her nipple more firmly and when his teeth fastened around it, Bethany gave a protesting noise because now there were too many sensations and she was losing all control.

Alessandro ignored her protests. She wasn't meant to be controlling them, and so as he felt Edmund continuing to ravage her from behind and sensed her growing nearness to release he inserted a finger between her inner sex-lips and pushed up against the hood that was protecting her clitoris.

Bethany squirmed. She was so aroused she didn't want her clitoris touched, the sensations would be too much for her at this level of arousal, but Alessandro didn't care what Bethany did or didn't want. She was already soaking wet with excitement, high on stimulation and certain of the kind of over-intense pleasure tinged with pain that she thrived on. Now he would be the one to topple her into the abyss of dark satisfaction that was her natural habitat.

Bethany felt him push the hood aside and knew what was coming but she was powerless to do anything about it, and Edmund was thrusting so fiercely into her that the red hot sparks of pleasure were almost melting her flesh and her head went back as she opened her mouth to gasp for air.

As her head lifted, Alessandro's finger flicked mercilessly on the unwillingly exposed clitoris and every muscle within Bethany tightened in a huge contraction that gripped both the brothers' erections, causing them to pump their sperm into both her passages as all three of them shuddered and shook with the force of their internal explosions and all the time Alessandro continued to bite on Bethany's engorged nipple and flick at the mass of nerve endings contained in her tiny unprotected sex-button.

Fiona watched the three of them listened to their cries and groans of satisfaction and knew that soon they would expect her to take Bethany's place. She had never in all her life witnessed such a scene, and its erotic power amazed her just as much as the thought of participating herself shocked her.

Finally, it was over. The men withdrew. Bethany collapsed face down on the carpet and the two brothers slumped on the bed, one on each side of Fiona. She shrank away from them, but Alessandro's hand grasped her left wrist.

'Wait there. In a moment Georgina will put a plug in you. It will stay there until this evening, then we'll see what you've learnt from it.'

'No, I don't want to. I don't like it,' she cried.

'How do you know? You've never tried it!' said Alessandro softly, his breathing still laboured from his exertions with Bethany. 'If you don't like it after you've tried it, that will be different. But it's something I like, and so you must at least try it for me.'

'When's Duncan going to pay the ransom money?' Fiona whispered.

The brothers ignored the question while Georgina shrugged. 'Who knows? Next week, next month, it could be any time. He's getting some of the money together, we know that much. You'd better make the most of your remaining time here. Not many people can teach you as much as we can!'

Fiona ignored her. Held fast in Alessandro's grip she had to wait until he had recovered. Then Bethany was carried from the room by Edmund, her eyes closed as she remembered the ecstasy of the past half hour, and finally only Georgina and Alessandro were with Fiona.

Alessandro put his feet to the floor. 'Lie across my knees,' he said softly.

Fiona took a deep breath and obeyed. She felt his thighs press against her tender breasts and then she was pushed further over so that it was her waist that was against him while her head hung down towards the floor.

'Relax your sphincter muscles,' he said gently. 'Breathe through your mouth and bear down, that will open you fully and the plug will go in with the minimum of discomfort. Georgina will use plenty of lubricating jelly.'

He could feel Fiona's body shaking against his legs, but was determined to push her on to new experiences, confident that she'd soon enjoy them as much as he and his other women did. He spread the cheeks of her bottom himself, and when Georgina had lubricated a new plastic plug he got her to hold the round globes while he tenderly eased the tip into Fiona's tightly puckered opening.

'You must bear down,' he said patiently. 'It will expand you more.'

Fiona felt hot tears of humiliation behind her eyelids but finally managed to do as he said, and to her surprise there was just a feeling of coolness and then a sensation of being full that was different but in no way painful. She stopped bearing down, and immediately her rectum felt more full. Involuntarily she clenched her muscles against this intruder, and to her astonishment electric shocks sparked through her.

Alessandro helped her off his knees. 'There, that's in. Now, remember to keep working your muscles on it and from time to time we'll check on your progress. Georgina will put you in a body harness because that's the most effective way of keeping pressure on the plug.'

Georgina then led her from the room into the changing room beyond. There she stood docilely while a body harness was put on her, only protesting when Georgina stroked her breasts to make them large in order for the rings to be fastened. Georgina smiled. 'Don't be silly.

Women are better than men at this kind of thing. They know what feels good.'

Her hands stroked and squeezed, manipulating Fiona's tender breast tissue until it was straining within the confines of the metal hoops. Then she licked twice across each aureole leaving her saliva to cool in the air and watching Fiona's nipples leap erect.

'You see! I was right. Your breasts look glorious. Now I'll tighten the straps and you can go back to your room. Lunch will be sent to you there.'

The straps were fastened, the pressure on the plug increasing the jolts of near-pleasure that Fiona was experiencing, and then she was taken back to her room and left to sit as best she could considering the plug buried deep within her.

She stayed totally silent until Georgina had gone and remained that way even when Bethany finally returned. Her mind was now focused on one thing only, escape. She had to get away, before she became as dependent on the pleasures of the flesh as eveyone else in this household.

Chapter Nine

*F*iona's chance came late that afternoon, when she and Bethany were dressed in calf-length kaftans, given sandals to put on their feet and told that they were to be allowed fifteen minutes in the gardens. Craig and Marcus were to accompany them.

Bethany, who had entirely recovered from the morning and was secretly hoping that she might be allowed another session with the Trimarchi brothers before she obtained her freedom, was in high spirits. She flirted shamelessly with both their guards, talking about what had occurred earlier and hinting that she'd have liked it even better if she'd been with them.

Fiona, who would normally have been appalled by Bethany's behaviour, was extremely grateful. Marcus tried once or twice to engage her in conversation, but her replies were so terse and grudging that in the end he gave up his efforts and enjoyed Bethany's uninhibited reminiscences instead.

Because of the size of the grounds it was impossible for the men who patrolled them to cover the entire area. Instead, Alessandro relied on dogs and before the two women left the house he gave orders for the Japanese Tosas to be released. As long as none of the four left the area he'd designated for their walk, the dogs would be no threat. If one of them strayed, it would be a different story.

The sun was still warm, and because of the danger Fiona felt herself breaking out in a sweat beneath the cool silk of the kaftan. She'd noticed that they were walking in a large circle, along a path that surrounded a glorious rose garden, but there were other paths off this and one of them led straight into a densely wooded area. This seemed to offer her the best chance of staying hidden until she reached the perimeter wall. Once there, she hoped that fear would help her find the necessary agility to scale it and fall to safety on the other side.

Craig now had an arm round Bethany, and his hand was cupping one of her large breasts. He could feel the nipple hardening beneath his touch and his own penis began to stir. Bethany was very much his kind of woman.

Marcus, aware of Craig's interest in Bethany, kept a careful eye on Fiona but she was staring at the ground most of the time. Knowing that she'd been with Alessandro for much of the morning he guessed that she probably didn't have a great deal of energy left over for anything.

Although confident of her good behaviour, he would never have allowed her the opportunity she needed if the lace on one of his trainers hadn't come undone. Realising that if he should have to run it could trip him up, he bent down to secure it. Fiona glanced at Bethany and Craig who were walking ahead of her and then, realising that the path she'd chosen as her escape route was directly to her left, she made her dash for freedom.

After a few yards the branches of the trees began to close over her head and without the sun's warming rays the air turned cool. Behind her, Fiona heard a shout, but this only served as a spur to her already flying legs.

Adrenalin flooded through her and she ran faster than she'd ever run before, expecting at any minute to hear footsteps closing behind her, but there were none. Just the same she continued to run at full stretch.

Bethany watched Fiona disappear down the path and heard Craig shout 'The dogs!' She saw Marcus, who had started off in pursuit, stop in his tracks and glance back at the other man.

'They'll tear her to pieces!' he cried. Craig had gone so pale he looked as though he might be sick.

'What dogs?' asked Bethany, her flirtatiousness disappearing.

'The Trimarchi family keep Japanese Tosas, although they've recently been banned. They're huge, attack without warning, and are trained to kill,' he explained. Bethany began to shake and called out Fiona's name but the sound hung in the air and died away uselessly.

Fiona now had the high brick wall in her line of vision. To her relief there was a tree growing close by and she thought that she could probably use that to assist her in getting over the top. As she ran the final few yards, out of the corner of her eye she spotted a white shape that looked something like a large Pyrenean mountain dog, but she didn't spare it a second thought. In her mind it was Rotweilers and Dobermans that were used for secuirty, not large fluffy white dogs like the one she could see.

The Japanese Tosa showed none of the usual warning signs of aggression. It didn't flatten its ears back, nor did it growl a preliminary caution. All it did was stand watching the running figure for a few seconds before taking off like a bullet from a gun.

Alessandro had fully expected Fiona to try and escape, but even he hadn't expected her to choose this path. Although he had taken a short cut from the house as soon as his outside security cameras revealed what was happening, he still wasn't sure that he was going to be in time to stop the dog attacking her and his heart was pounding as he pushed through the dense bushes.

The dog was within ten yards of her when Alessandro came out into the open. He whistled twice, short piercing sound that the dog knew, and at once it stopped stock still, crouching down in the waiting position while its master approached.

Fiona heard the whistles and stopped for a second, glancing back over her shoulder. At the sight of the massive animal bunched on the ground so close to her she gave a scream and the sound brought the dog to its feet.

'Down!' Alessandro commanded. Slowly the dog obeyed, but it kept its unblinking gaze on Fiona. 'Don't move,' Allesandro added when he realised that she might still try and reach the wall. 'I won't be able to stop him if you touch the bricks. He's trained to stop anyone leaving that way.'

She knew that the Italian wasn't lying. It was there in the dog's eyes for anyone to see, and now the realisation of what had nearly happened hit her and she began to whimper with a mixture of frustration and sheer terror.

Within a few minutes one of the dog handlers arrived on the scene. His face impassive, he clipped a heavy lead onto the dog's collar and led it away, without a single glance at the woman who was standing in front of him.

'That was really foolish,' Alessandro said at last. 'Did you honestly believe that I'd allow you to escape?

Fiona glared at him. 'I had to try. I couldn't stay here any longer, letting you do what you liked with me. After this morning I was too frightened to put up with it any more.'

His coal-black eyes held hers, and he walked up to her until their bodies were touching. 'Frightened of what?'

144

'Of you, of course. You and everyone else in this house.'

'We haven't hurt you. I've seen you squirming with passion and heard you cry out in ecstasy, but not in pain. How can you say we frighten you? The truth of the matter is, you're afraid of what I might teach you about yourself.'

Fiona lifted her head. 'Is that so wrong? Aren't I entitled to choose who teaches me these things?'

'No one would ever have taught you if you hadn't been taken hostage. Your husband certainly wouldn't have bothered, and I don't believe you'd ever have left him, due to your admirably strong sense of duty. Are you saying that you'd rather never have learned about your own sexuality? Was your life with Duncan preferable to your life here?'

'Of course it was!'

'When I saw you at your dinner party you didn't look particularly happy. In addition to which, I understand that you were forced into joining your husband and Bethany later that night after your failure to seduce me! What was so marvellous about that sort of life?'

Fiona hesitated. 'I'm not saying my life with Duncan was marvellous, I'm saying you haven't got the right to use me the way you are. Isn't it enough that I'm your prisoner?'

Alessandro shook his head. 'No, it isn't enough. I like sensual women. I knew you were my kind of woman the moment I saw you. Now I have the chance to prove to myself that I was right.'

'I hate you!' shouted Fiona.

He put his arms round her and pulled her against him. 'No you don't. You hate Duncan and possibly Bethany, but you don't hate me. If you did, your body wouldn't respond the way it does no matter how cleverly I played on it. You like me, Fiona, and one day you'll admit it.'

'I can't wait to get away from here and forget you,'

she retorted, aware that all he was saying was probably true and wishing that she didn't like the feel of his hands against her so much. She wanted to rest her head on his shoulder, give herself up to a comforting embrace of the kind she hadn't known for many years, but instead she tried to pull away.

'Even when you leave, you won't forget me,' he whispered. Then his tongue swirled softly inside her ear and as she jerked involuntarily against him he laughed softly before putting her gently away from him.

'You see! Now, because of what you've done I'm afraid that things will have to change a little. No one is allowed to make me look foolish, and you came very close to that today. How could I have got my money back from Duncan if his wife had been killed by one of my own guard dogs? My sense of honesty would have compelled me to let him off, and that would have meant a loss of face.'

'What are you going to do to me?' she asked with rising fear.

'Nothing too dreadful, but it will be enough to demonstrate that I am not to be disobeyed. For the next few days you will become the personal slave of every member of my household in turn. They all have varied tastes and desires and your sexual experience will probably be expanded far more quickly than would otherwise have been the case!'

She stared. 'What do you mean, slave?'

'You will have to obey their commands without question from six in the morning until six at night. After that the rest of the day will be your own again, although our mutual pleasuring may well continue during the remaining hours!'

'But . . .'

Alessandro held up his hand. 'There's no more to be said. Now I'll take you back to the house and set the arrangements in hand. Tomorrow the punishment will

146

begin. You can think about that while lying on your bed during the long hours of the night!'

Bethany was sitting up on her bed in their top-floor bedroom, her back propped against a mound of pillows, her wrists and ankles once again fastened in the leather cuffs and chain that had been used on them during their first night of captivity. She stared at Fiona in awe. 'I never thought you'd have the courage to try and get away!' she exclaimed. 'Craig and Marcus were out of their minds with fright. I was hustled back here double-quick, I can tell you. What happened? Did one of the guards catch you?'

Fiona slumped on her bed, all resistance drained from her after her ill-fated dash for freedom. 'One of the guard dogs caught me and then Alessandro appeared. If he hadn't I'd probably have been the dog's evening meal.'

Bethany was genuinely puzzled. 'Whatever possessed you, Fiona? Duncan's going to get us both freed in the end, and any fool would have known escape was impossible. Besides, what's the point? It isn't as though we're being badly treated.'

Fiona remembered the sight of the Trimarchi brothers both entering Bethany at the same time and recalled the anal plug she'd seen protruding from between her buttocks and the feel of the plug in her own opening. 'You don't think you've been treated badly?' she asked ironically. 'This morning didn't upset you?'

Bethany shivered. 'This morning was out of this world; totally off-the-wall! I kept hoping Duncan wouldn't get me freed before they had another session with me.'

'Then there's no point in me explaining why I tried to escape. We're totally different people, Bethany, with totally different ideas about sex.'

'I know. I enjoy it and admit it; you enjoy it but try to pretend you don't! We won't argue though, it isn't

147

worth the energy! Just tell me what did Alessandro say when he caught you?'

'Not a lot,' replied Fiona, deciding to keep their conversation private because some of Alessandro's remarks were too similar to Bethany's. 'He was far from pleased, to put it mildly.'   •

'What's going to happen to us now?' Bethany wanted to know.

'I don't suppose anything different will happen to you. I'm to become the personal property of everyone in this house in turn. If I understood the great man correctly it's for daylight hours only, but that's no comfort in this house, where sex goes on all the time.'

Bethany's eyes were huge in her face and her voice trembled with barely concealed excitement. 'You mean, they can do what they like with you? Edmund, Georgina, all of them?'

'Yes. Now if you don't mind I'd prefer not to talk about it any more. I'm well aware that this would be a reward for you, but right now the prospect is more than I can bear to consider.'

Bethany pressed her thighs closely together and felt a tremor of excitement run through her at the thought of Fiona, so aloof and self-contained when she'd been Duncan's wife, having to endure whole days under the control of others. She wished that she'd had the foresight to try and escape.

Fiona was awakened at six the next morning, while Bethany was left alone to sleep. Having been kept awake until dawn by her thoughts, it was as much as Fiona could do to open her eyes.

Tanya was standing over her. 'Come on, you're mine for the day. I want to get you washed and dressed myself. This is the most exciting thing Alessandro's ever let me do,' she added confidingly. 'I've been longing to be allowed to have more time with you!'

Fiona realised that her first day could have been

148

worse. She might have found herself in the hands of Marcus, Edmund or Georgina, but Tanya's feverish excitement was hardly encouraging and she tried to cover her breasts and vulva as she climbed off the bed.

Tanya slapped her hands away. 'Don't be silly! Surely you're used to walking around naked in front of us by now. Anyway, I don't wish you to cover yourself, is that understood?'

The reality of the days ahead seemed to be summed up in that final phrase and Fiona nodded silently as she let her arms fall to her sides.

'That's better!' Tanya's voice was cheerful again. 'Let's go upstairs. We'll start in the bathroom.'

For the second time since being taken hostage, Fiona found herself in the large main bathroom of the house. She fully expected to be taken into the spa bath again, but Tanya was leading the way to the shower cubicle and at the sliding glass door she quickly stripped off her shorts and blouse, then pushed Fiona in ahead of her.

The two of them were now crowded into the confined space, and Fiona jumped as the blonde model turned on the spray and jets of cold water cascaded down onto them. 'It takes a few minutes to warm up,' Tanya explained. 'Mind you, it's very invigorating, especially if you've got a hangover!'

Fiona didn't find it invigorating, but the cold needles made her nipples erect in no time, and immediately Tanya's hands were brushing against them. 'I adore your breasts, they're just the right size. Mine are much too small, but that's lucky for the work I do, and Bethany's are too large for my taste. I shall spend a lot of time on your breasts I think.'

Fiona tried to draw away from Tanya's hands. 'I thought you were in love with Edmund,' she said nervously.

Tanya beamed. 'I am. He's the most gorgeous man in the world, but that doesn't mean I can't appreciate women too. It's just for fun of course, but women do understand each other's bodies better, don't you think?'

Fiona had no idea, she simply swallowed hard and waited for whatever was to happen next. Slowly, the water became warmer, and now Tanya was lathering both their bodies with jasmine-scented shower gel. 'Come on then, Fiona. You're the slave. Start washing me!' Her eyes were alight with amusement.

Fiona hesitantly reached out and began to swirl some of the suds over Tanya's neck and shoulders but Tanya thrust her tiny breasts upwards. 'Do these,' she instructed her. 'Use nice slow circular movements and work from the undersides upwards.'

Fiona obeyed. Her fingers slid across the damp, slippery flesh of the blonde girl and beneath her hands she felt Tanya's nipples growing and heard her sigh with contentment. 'That's very good. Now do my stomach and then my thighs.'

Fiona found that her hands were shaking with a mixture of humiliation and a strangely insidious excitement as she felt the smooth flesh of the other woman responding to her touch. Carefully she worked the suds around the lean abdomen, then on down to the slender thighs. Here she soaped assiduously at the outsides before an impatient sound from Tanya forced her to move inwards and Tanya's legs parted to allow her access to the inner thighs.

Fiona resolutely ignored the fair pubic hairs and pouting outer vaginal lips until she suddenly felt her soaking hair tugged painfully hard. 'Wash me properly!' Tanya instructed her, beginning to grow into the role she'd been allocated for the day. 'I have to be clean everywhere.'

Her eyes watering from Tanya's grip on her hair, Fiona tentatively began to soap Tanya's vulva, and when her fingers slid into the creases on either side of the inner lips she felt the blonde girl's hips twitch with excitement. Now she began to spread the suds inside the lips and down the thin membrane of skin that led to Tanya's rectum. Tanya wriggled and exclaimed with pleasure and then when Fiona's hands caressed her almost boyishly slim buttocks and began to soap around the creases there, the blonde model's eyes closed with happiness.

At last Fiona had soaped her everywhere. Tanya told her to stop, then turned her body towards the spray again, letting it wash off every last vestige of the gel. 'Now I'll clean you,' she said briskly. 'Lift your arms above your head.'

The cubicle was cramped and it was difficult for Fiona to obey, but she managed to lift them high by keeping her elbows bent. Tanya smiled. 'Good. Now, I must make sure you're really squeaky clean for me. I want you good enough to eat off!'

Fiona felt the other girl's hands massaging the foaming gel into her armpits, her fingers teasing the highly sensitive flesh around the edge of her breasts and at the top of her rib cage. Fiona's nipples, already erect, hardened yet more and when Tanya began to clean carefully around the aureoles the nipples felt ready to explode.

'I thought you'd be sensitive there!' said Tanya triumphantly. 'Today's going to be great fun. For now though I'll move on.' Her hands glided down Fiona's body, then plunged straight between her thighs and spread her outer lips apart. 'Hold these open yourself,' said Tanya, her voice becoming husky. 'I want to make sure there's no soap left.'

Fiona gripped her outer sex-lips, hating exposing herself but grateful that it wasn't one of the bodyguards inflicting this torture on her. She watched as Tanya reached up and removed the shower head from its plastic grip on the pole. Slowly, lovingly, Tanya brought it down until it was level with Fiona's stomach. Then she looked deep into the other woman's eyes. 'I'm going to spray you between your legs now. You're to keep your back pressed against the shower wall, your knees bent just a fraction and you're not to move until you've had an orgasm. Is that clear?'

Fiona stared back at Tanya and felt her legs trembling with shock at the explicit way the blonde girl was speaking. It was a shock, but it also created a new kind of excitement in her. 'What's more,' continued Tanya gently, 'you can't come until I say. If you do, I'll have Craig and Amy join us and they'll keep you in the spa bath until you've had so many orgasms you won't have the strength to climb out.'

The words were calculated to add to Fiona's feeling of helpless arousal and add the extra fillip of fear that Tanya knew could heighten all sensations. Unable to speak, Fiona simply nodded. At this, her mistress for the day smiled approvingly and began to let the spray from the shower-head play between her slave's thighs.

As the spray first hit her, Fiona gasped with shock. Tanya was moving the head very slightly, just enough to ensure that the feelings it engendered didn't have a chance to become too familiar, but maintain Fiona's arousal at a constant level.

It was incredibly pleasurable, and very quickly Fiona could feel the delicious warmth spreading through her pelvic area and her clitoris swelled with the relentless play of spray upon it. With her free hand, Tanya pressed against the area just above Fiona's pelvic bone, causing pressure on the nerve endings of the bladder and so increasing her rising sexual excitement.

Fiona gasped and the first slow coils of her climax began to unfold deep within her. Tanya saw that Fiona's abdomen was tightening and moved the spray a little to one side allowing her a view of her slave's swollen sex-lips. She knew very well that Fiona was on the brink of coming.

'Not yet, Fiona,' she said sweetly. 'Remember what I said. I don't want you to come yet.'

Frantically, Fiona struggled against the demands of

152

her burgeoning flesh. She wanted to come, needed the sweet release from the tension that was making her inner muscles contract and causing such a heavy ache behind her clitoris, but she knew that she didn't want to be put in the spa bath with Craig and his wife, and chewed frantically on her lower lip to distract herself from the mounting pleasure.

Tanya moved the shower-head from side to side for a moment, so that the spray wasn't shooting directly onto the swollen clitoris. It gave Fiona a moment's respite from the glorious but unwanted pulsations that heralded her climax and she breathed quickly in relief.

Tanya watched the quick rise and fall of Fiona's breasts and knew exactly what she was going through. Edmund often played this game with her, bringing her right to the edge and then keeping her there by changing tactics and delaying her release for as long as possible. She loved it because the climax, when it was allowed to come, was always breathtaking.

Fiona wasn't loving it. After the short break, she felt the water play on her clitoris again, and her vaginal walls began to contract helplessly with slow movements that brought her closer to her orgasm. 'No!' said Tanya firmly, and knowing that she couldn't control herself if the water continued to play on her, Fiona let her outer sex-lips close.

Tanya slapped at Fiona's breasts, turning the control to cold and moving the spray up and down her body. 'That was naughty! You deserve to be punished for releasing yourself, but because you're trying hard I'll let you off,' she added more gently. The cold water was a shock, and Fiona's arousal level dipped.

'Turn round,' Tanya ordered her. 'Face the shower wall.'

Fiona turned, and now the ice-cold spray was moving up and down her spine, until her body began to tingle all over. 'Pull your buttocks apart,' Tanya continued. As they were reluctantly opened by Fiona she directed the cold spray carefully between them, and laughed as Fiona's hips thrust forward against the cubicle walls with the shock.

Fiona's body was a mass of conflicting sensations as the hot and cold water were used alternately to arouse her. Finally she was put back in her original position and made to spread her outer sex-lips apart so that the warm spray could again be applied to her most sensitive areas.

This time her climax seemed to gather speed even more quickly, causing her legs to tremble with pent-up desire within a few seconds. Tanya watched Fiona's eyes widening with the effort of controlling herself, and she reached forward and pushed the heel of her hand down on the tightly rounded abdomen that seemed to be stretching towards her in a silent entreaty.

She felt Fiona's skin ripple at the contact, and watched as her vaginal entrance closed a fraction. She could hear the other girl's laboured breathing, and cautioned her once more. 'Wait a moment, Fiona. Very soon you'll be allowed to come, just a few more seconds.'

Fiona felt like screaming aloud with frustration. She was burning for release, and the touch of Tanya's hand on her stomach had only made things worse. Frantically she fought against the pulsations of her own flesh but when Tanya saw Fiona's clitoris retract behind its hood of flesh she knew that it was time to let her slave reach fulfilment. Gently she pushed the flesh away from the shrinking button, and Fiona groaned as she realised that now the water would continue to play upon it and she already felt as though she would split open with the pressure of her desire.

'This time you can come,' whispered Tanya, and then the spray was playing on the exposed clitoris and all the sensations drew together and exploded sending Fiona up onto her toes as every muscle in her body went rigid and the delights of the long-delayed climax were finally allowed to engulf her. She heard herself scream with pleasure.

When the spasms at last drew to a close, Tanya replaced the shower-head and stepped out of the cubicle. 'Right, I think you're clean now,' she said casually. 'I'll give you your clothes for the day, and then you can serve me my breakfast.'

On trembling legs, Fiona followed Tanya out of the shower. From a cupboard her mistress of the day was taking out a two-piece costume which she handed over to her slave. 'I want you to wear this, and nothing else. The top fastens down the middle with buttons and loops, while the briefs fasten underneath your crotch. It's pretty don't you think?'

Fiona pulled on the ivory-coloured satin top. It had tiny straps and the bodice was tight, but what made it unusual wasn't the semi-transparent leaf design or the inverted v-shapes above the waist but the separate fastenings each side of the breastbone, level with her nipples. She realised that this meant her breasts could be explosed individually whenever Tanya wished. The briefs were like the bottom half of a modern swimsuit, cut high on the hip, and the narrow band between her thighs pressed tightly against her flesh-lips, keeping them under constant pressure.

Tanya surveyed her with delight. 'You look just how I imagined you would. Innocently seductive! Right, let's go down to the kitchen.'

Fiona realised that everyone else in the house must have been warned about where she and Tanya would be during the day because they had the kitchen to themselves, and there were no sounds of anyone else near. Tanya made a pretence of looking through the cupboards and fridge as she tried to decide what to have for her breakfast. 'I know!' she exclaimed at last. 'I'll have frozen yoghurt. It's in the freezer there. Get the strawberry flavour for me.'

Fiona fetched the round pink-topped carton and

placed it in the middle of the pine table. Tanya looked at her. 'Slide your shoulder straps down and lie on your back on the table. I don't think I'll eat off a plate.'

Awkwardly, Fiona edged herself across the surface of the table and pulled the straps of her bodice down. Tanya moved her over to the edge of the table and peeled the tops of the bodice back off Fiona's breasts. 'I'm going to eat off these!' she said happily. 'I'll lick you nice and clean when I've finished.'

Fiona's body shook against the heavy table as she watched Tanya bringing a metal scoop of the frozen yoghurt close to her left breast. 'I know,' Tanya said suddenly. 'I'll put a mask over your eyes first. That way you can concentrate on the sensations rather than watching what's happening.'

Fiona didn't want a mask over her eyes, but once again she had to submit to the blonde girl's desires, and a thick velvet mask was pulled down over the top of her head. It only covered her eyes, leaving the rest of her face free, but she still felt vulnerable and alone in the dark.

Now Tanya could take her time and enjoy watching Fiona's quivering breasts as they waited for the ice-cold yoghurt to drop on them. Tanya kept her waiting a long time, chattering about her work and how she had to fly off to Greece the next day to do a shoot for winter coats. 'It's always the wrong season's clothes for us. We boil in coats during the summer and freeze in swimsuits in the winter. It's a ridiculous life really!'

Fiona heard the words but all she was waiting for was the cold dessert on her exposed and tender flesh. Tanya was still talking when she let the first spoonful fall on her slave's left breast, and Fiona cried out with shock. 'I think you should keep silent,' Tanya remonstrated. 'No more noise, all right?'

Fiona could feel the yoghurt beginning to melt, spreading slowly down the sides of her breasts, and then Tanya's warm mouth was enclosing the top of her left breast as she licked at the strawberry flavoured drips. The combination of the cold yoghurt and Tanya's warm tongue was exhilarating, Fiona's breast expanded and both her nipples peaked once more into hardness. Tanya bit gently on the left nipple, and it was such a pleasurable pain that Fiona had to struggle not to cry out again. She knew that the other woman sensed her enjoyment because a few seconds later she repeated the movement and Fiona felt the small of her back arch off the table.

Now Tanya let another spoonful fall onto Fiona's right breast, and this time she allowed it to melt before licking it from the sensitive undersides of Fiona's breasts, sucking at the delicious creamy mixture and taking some of Fiona's flesh into her mouth at the same time.

Fiona, whose whole world was focused on the sensations in her breasts, at last gave herself over to Tanya's skilled and titillating ministrations. She let the sensations wash over her without fighting them, and every time Tanya's teeth grazed one of the painfully hard nipple peaks, she had to swallow her groan of delight. To her shame she found that she was wishing Tanya would go on for hours, but Tanya had other ideas.

Once she had eaten the frozen yoghurt off each of Fiona's breasts she took two tiny metal rings from one of the kitchen drawers and then, knowing that the unseeing Fiona had no idea what was coming, slowly approached her from behind her head, reaching down over her bare shoulders.

Fiona felt Tanya's fingers sliding towards her nipples again, and without realising it she thrust them towards the model, but to her surprise she felt cold metal sliding around her rigid flesh and then there was a pinching sensation around them and when Tanya's hands withdrew the metal stayed in place, imprisoning her aroused nipples and making them stand out even more sharply

157

from the aureoles. Tanya promptly took off Fiona's mask. 'Look, nipple rings! Don't you think they look fantastic?'

Fiona struggled upright and stared down at her red, swollen nipples now protruding through tight little circles of gold that had been adjusted to fit her and then clipped shut. 'They pinch,' she protested.

'Only at first; you'll come to like the feeling. Actually, it means that I have to keep your nipples that size or larger from now on, otherwise the rings could fall off. Still, that shouldn't prove a problem. You can have some breakfast now, but not until I've got you dressed again.'

Once Fiona's shoulder straps had been pulled back up, her bodice pressed against the tiny gold rings, and every time she moved they were stimulated by tiny tugging sensations as the material snagged against them.

'See! That's a good way to keep you erect!' laughed Tanya. 'After you've eaten, I'll show you how to give a good massage.'

The rest of the day passed in a haze of sensual sensations. Tanya taught Fiona to massage her, and then massaged Fiona in return. During all that time she never released the tightly pressing briefs and so Fiona was perpetually excited and her nipple rings stayed in place without any difficulty.

Later, she was laid on Tanya's bed while the blonde model used her tongue between Fiona's thighs, at one point letting the tip flick against the entrance to Fiona's bladder. This resulted in an almost painfully intense climax for Fiona, unexpected and forbidden, so later that day Tanya did the same thing again but made certain that Fiona understood she'd be punished if she allowed herself to come. It was the most difficult piece of control Fiona had yet exerted on her overexcited flesh, but she succeeded, only to be flooded with the warm sensation of orgasm a few minutes later when

Tanya's knowing tongue penetrated her vagina and flicked rapidly against her G-spot.

Later, both women used the spa bath, and this time Tanya tried to bring Fiona to orgasm three times in half an hour. She only managed two, but as Tanya had hoped the nipple rings were never in danger of falling off as the relentless stimulation meant that her breast tissue was permanently engorged.

At five o'clock Tanya ate an early tea off Fiona's naked body. She poured wine over her slave's breasts and lapped it off them, then inserted a tiny, firm peeled banana into Fiona's vagina and nibbled away at it, licking at the surrounding flesh as she went and gaining intense enjoyment from the trembling of her slave's thighs and her ever expanding vulva as Tanya got nearer to the centre of Fiona's pleasure.

Finally, when she reached the entrance to her vagina, Tanya told Fiona that she could have her last orgasm as she carefully nibbled and teased the pink and swollen flesh until she felt Fiona's body shattering into waves of orgasmic delight while her thighs closed tightly around Tanya's ears.

At one minute to six, Tanya withdrew the last piece of the banana, unfastened the nipple rings and took Fiona back to her room. 'Enjoy tomorrow!' she laughed as Fiona fell in an exhausted heap onto her bed.

Chapter Ten

*F*iona was left alone in the room for several hours, and she wondered what had happened to Bethany. At nine in the evening Alessandro returned from a visit to his chief financial adviser and, after talking to Tanya, went straight to see Fiona, taking her dinner tray with him.

She was lying on her side with her eyes closed, and he had an urge to cradle her in his arms and make love to her slowly and tenderly until she responded with the kind of fervour that he knew she was capable of, but he didn't. That would come much later, when he was quite sure of her. For now he intended that her sexual horizons should continue to be expanded by others in his household, until she reached her full sexual capacity. After that he would decide where she fitted into his long-term plans.

'I've brought you some food,' he said quietly.

Fiona opened her eyes and stared at him. 'I'm not hungry.'

He smiled encouragingly. 'I'm sure you'll be able to eat something. Tanya tells me she's been eating well today!'

Fiona felt her face turning red and sat up on the bed,

wishing that she was allowed a covering sheet during the day. 'I suppose she told you every detail!' she exclaimed.

'She had no choice. I made her. It seems you both had an enjoyable day.'

Fiona laughed bitterly. 'Is that what she said? Well, she was lying.'

Alessandro continued to smile. 'I think not. Once again you are the one who is lying, to yourself. However, if belonging to a woman for a day wasn't to your liking, tomorrow might prove more interesting. Edmund will be your owner then. The women say he's a very inventive lover, but quite what kind of a slave owner he'll be I can't say!'

'Have you heard *anything* from Duncan?' asked Fiona helplessly.

Alessandro's smile vanished. 'I spoke to him over the phone today. It seems that he nearly has half the money ready. When that is handed over to me, your friend will be released.'

'But she'd rather stay!' cried Fiona. 'It isn't fair that I'm kept here while she goes free.'

'It's your husband's choice,' Alessandro reminded her, and watched as once again Duncan's betrayal bit into Fiona's heart. Alessandro put her tray down on the floor then sat next to her on the bed. 'He isn't worth getting upset over,' he whispered, trailing one lean hand down her right arm and along the inside of the palm of her hand until her fingers closed reflexively around it. 'Soon, you'll be mine for a day, and then you'll know that I'm right. Duncan could never please you as I'll please you.'

'If you're so sure that's true, give me the choice!' exploded Fiona. 'Grant me my freedom and see if I choose to stay.'

Alessandro shook his head. 'I can't do that. Bethany is the one Duncan's chosen. In any case, I'm not sure you'd stay yet, but by the time your visit here is over you'll be as anxious to remain as you currently are to leave.'

Realising that she was still clutching hold of his hand, Fiona relaxed her fingers, drawing away from Alessandro's magnetic figure. 'Perhaps I can eat something,' she said quickly, trying to hide the agitation caused by his physical closeness.

Picking the tray up, he placed it on the bed beside her and left the room. He could see the difference in her every day. Her whole body looked different; more sexual, increasingly aware of itself and more confident of its ability to give her pleasure. He knew that his brother would hasten her progress even more, and felt a knot of excited anticipation at the prospect of the day when it would be his turn.

After she'd cleared everything on the plate and drunk the delicious fruit cup that was also on the tray, Fiona suddenly found that her eyelids wouldn't stay open and before Bethany was returned from a day that both she and Georgina had found mutually satisfying, Duncan's wife was in a deep sleep, induced by the drugged drink. Alessandro had known that she would need to be rested before receiving his brother's attentions.

Once again, Fiona was roused at six and Edmund, wearing tight-fitting jeans but with his tanned torso bare, bundled her out of the room before the effects of the sleeping draught had fully worn off. He hurried her up to the bedroom that he usually shared with Tanya, only today his girlfriend was off to Greece and he couldn't wait to start enjoying Fiona's forced compliance with his wishes.

She stared at the heavy red velvet curtains at the windows and the large four-poster bed with matching curtains round it, which could be closed to shut out the world. 'We'll use that later,' he promised her, but pushed her on through the connecting door to his private bathroom. There he quickly pulled her into the Jacuzzi and pressed the button on the side, so that the

162

pulsations of water commenced, startling Fiona's sleepy flesh into wakefulness.

Edmund pulled her round so that she was sitting across his knees and facing him. 'Pleasure me with your hand,' he instructed her, keeping his hazel eyes fixed on her face. 'Not too much, just enough to make sure I can do what I want to do.'

'What's that?' asked Fiona hesitantly.

Edmund smiled boyishly. 'You'll find out. Hurry up now.'

She reached beneath the bubbling surface and her fingers closed round his already hardening penis. Carefully she let herself grip him and then moved her hand up and down, at the same time squeezing and releasing. His lips parted and he let his head fall back as his arousal mounted.

'That's enough,' he said when the tingling began to grow too intense in the tip of his glans. 'Turn round now.' Fiona slid around on his knees, becoming more aware of the warm bubbles striking her gently between her thighs. 'Press your breasts lower, so that the nipples are in the water,' Edmund continued. Once she'd done this, Fiona's rear entrance was more easily available to him and he let the head of his erection nudge against the tightly puckered rim, enjoying her instinctive tightening and resistance to his movements.

'You can't stop me, whatever I want to do,' he reminded her as his hands reached round her to pull none too gently on her hanging breasts. Her nipples and aureoles still ached from Tanya's attentions the previous day and she nearly cried out at the sharp sensations he was causing to shoot through them again, but then his hands released her, his glans left the crease between her buttocks and she was pushed off his lap.

'Out you get, and fetch me a towel from the heated rail. Then you can dry me.' Obediently she fetched the large white towel and wrapped it around him, patting at the soft fibres to absorb the water from his surprisingly smooth skin.

He stood and let her attend to him, making certain that she dried every centimetre of his flesh. He spread his legs so that she could carefully towel between his thighs, and made her dry his still large erection before, going lower, she dried his feet and between his toes until there wasn't a drop of water left on him.

He then looked at her, naked and wet in front of him, and reached for a second towel. 'Time to dry you off.' He spread the towel on the floor, laid her on her back on it, then fetched another towel and leaning over her body began to dab at it. Lift your arms up above your head once I've dried them and keep your legs spread,' he murmured. 'I want to make sure every crevice is dry, at least from the Jacuzzi water!'

With agonising slowness he began to rub her body with the soft towel. He stroked it over her neck and shoulders, then down her arms so that she could raise them above her head. This left her breasts thrusting up towards him, and as he towelled them more vigorously, the nipples rose and tiny pieces of fluff were left round them when he moved down to absorb the moisture from the lower half of her round globes.

He teased at the soft flesh of her underarms, patting and dabbing with tiny movements that had her flesh jumping. Then he put the towel across the whole of the front of her, moving it up and down in a rubbing motion that had her stomach tensing and caused her legs to move restlessly.

When he came to the creases between her thighs he was extra attentive, and she found that the light touch of the towel so near to her vulva and yet still far away from the vital nerve endings, caused her to long for a more intimate caress. She was shamed by her own need after such a brief respite from sexual satisfaction.

Edmund watched her body's movements and guessed that Tanya had done her work well the previous day. Fiona was now more than ready for sexual gratification, and her body was pressing her to demand it, but as her master he could delay the gratification or allow it as he wished. The realisation was highly exciting.

When he'd dried her legs and feet for as long as possible he moved the towel between her legs and up to the top of her thighs until it brushed against her straining mound. He heard her quickly silenced intake of breath and decided that all he would do was pat at her dark pubic curls and the outer sex-lips.

For Fiona, who could feel a smouldering fire beginning to ignite deep within her, his refusal to touch her more intimately was torture but she lay quite still knowing that she could not voice her own need.

'Finished,' he said thickly. 'Here, put this on.' As he pulled on his jeans he handed her a short garment. Made of pure white silk it was fashioned after the Roman togas but with a plunging neckline and gathered waist, while the armholes were cut wide so that hands could easily be insinuated between her flesh and the material to touch her naked skin.

In length however it was nothing like the Roman togas of old. It had a high thigh-line while the front pleats only reached half-way down her inner thighs. She felt more undressed with it on than when she was naked. Finally Edmund handed her a pair of white stiletto heels. 'Perfect, that's my idea of a female slave!'

Beneath the skimpy hanging folds of the toga's skirt, Fiona was entirely naked and she walked as upright as she could so that nothing was revealed. Once back in the bedroom, Edmund went straight to the huge bed and pulled the curtains aside for her to climb up. 'Lie face down,' he instructed her, then went to his door and called for Marcus.

Lying down on the softness of the goosefeather-filled duvet, with her shoes still on and knowing that her buttocks were exposed, Fiona waited for the second man to join them with what she was appalled to realise was more excitement than fear.

Once Marcus was in the room he too was brought inside the curtained bed and then the two men knelt on either side of Fiona while she lay on her face with her head turned facing her master.

'Isn't she delicious?' he asked Marcus, who nodded and waited to see what he would be allowed to do. 'First of all I want to make sure that you're as satisfied at the end of today as you were yesterday,' Edmund told Fiona, with a laugh in his voice. 'I think your breasts had a great deal of attention then, which means I shall concentrate on other more intimate areas today.'

As he was speaking he was tipping some liquid into his right hand and spreading the oily slick along all his fingers. Then he moved to Fiona and began massaging the calves of her legs, gradually working his way higher across the thin skin at the back of her knees and up into the creases of her buttocks.

Once again he felt her tighten in resistance as he approached the clenched opening; he slapped her lightly on the tensed buttocks. 'No resistance, Fiona. It isn't allowed.' She closed her eyes, feeling his slippery finger inserting itself into her narrow opening, dilating her slowly until he could push two fingers in. Now Marcus had moved round and he was sliding a hand in beneath her right arm and his short, firm fingers were kneading at her breast, the roughness of his skin a startling contrast to Tanya's touch the day before but all the more arousing as a result.

Fiona's breast expanded in the palm of his hand and she pressed down against him so that the nipple could also feel the rough touch of his flesh. Pleased that Marcus was doing so well, Edmund took the opportunity to take out two round love balls joined by a piece of silk cord, and as he withdrew his fingers from Fiona's back entrance he swiftly inserted the first of the balls before her rectum could tighten again.

Fiona felt the heavy intruder and gave a cry of alarm, but Marcus continued to stimulate her breast and Edmund quickly kissed the hollow cleft at the base of her spine, sucking at the flesh and drawing it up in his mouth. Delicious darts of excitement ran through Fiona, and as she relaxed with the pleasure, Edmund pushed the second love ball inside her and then left the end of the cord protruding from the swiftly tightening opening.

Now that both the balls were inside her rectum, Fiona could no longer ignore the full sensation they were causing and her bowels began to cramp at the invasion. Edmund signalled for Marcus to stop stroking her breasts and turned her onto her back. The movement made the balls change position, and they brushed against the inner walls of her rectum making the nerve endings leap.

'I can't keep them in!' gasped Fiona.' 'Please, it feels horrible.'

'Nonsense, it will feel superb once you're used to them. Every time you have an orgasm you'll tighten around them and double your own pleasure. Besides, you don't have any choice. Now, get off the bed and walk around the room. I want to watch you walk with them in place.'

Fiona gingerly eased herself off the bed, pushing aside the curtains that had held her in such claustrophobic confinement with the two men. Then, balancing on the unusually high heels of the shoes she'd been given, she walked around the deeply piled carpet, struggling to keep her balance and ignore the heavy, dull throbbings of initial arousal that were coming from within her rectum.

Edmund laughed. 'Sensational! Marcus, go down on all fours and Fiona can lean back over you. I want her buttocks to be pressing against your body and her vulva exposed to me.'

Marcus quickly dropped to his hands and knees and

Edmund helped Fiona lower herself backwards along the length of the bodyguard's spine with her knees bent and her feet on the floor. He then pushed her knees wider apart and her feet backwards which had the desired effect of opening her up to him. Once she was in position he rang a bell and Chrissie, came into the room. She was carrying a bowl of grapes and under Edmund's gaze she held Fiona's outer sex-lips apart and carefully slipped them into her vagina. All the time she worked, Edmund kept rotating the pad of his thumb along the side of Fiona's clitoris which had the effect of making her juices flow and allowed the grapes to slide in without effort.

For Fiona it seemed as though every possible part of her was being stimulated. The love balls were pressed tightly against the walls of her back passage by the pressure of Marcus's spine, her engorged breasts were being caressed by the silk pleats of the tunic and between her thighs Edmund was causing red-hot swirls of ecstasy to flow through her. Every now and again he would bend his head and tongue at her upthrust abdomen until she felt like an overstretched piece of elastic that might snap at any moment.

Chrissie continued until grapes were visible through the stretched entrance to Fiona's vagina, and then she withdrew, wishing that she could be allowed to stay and take part in what was happening. 'Now I'm going to eat every grape that's in you,' Edmund whispered. 'I shall only use my mouth and tongue, so it might take a long time, but you have to wait for your orgasm until you're empty.'

Fiona's hips moved urgently and he could see moisture covering her entire body in a fine film. 'I can't wait,' she cried. 'You've done too much to me already.'

'I'd hate to have to get annoyed with you,' said Edmund, and then he nipped at the flesh of her stomach more sharply than before. A flash of pain sent a message of warning to her brain, but then tumbled over into sweetness instead and she groaned loudly, needing and wanting release.

'Tanya can do it,' he told her. 'Surely you have as much self-control as she does?'

Beneath her straining body, Marcus was beginning to tremble himself with physical strain and erotic stimulation at the scene being played out in the room. He knew as well as Edmund did that Fiona wouldn't be able to control herself and knew too what would happen when she couldn't.

Slowly, Edmund sucked at the entrance to Fiona's vagina, and the first grape slid smoothly and easily out into his mouth. She felt it leaving her body and as he sucked it between his teeth he sucked at her flesh as well nearly triggering her final spasm. With a superhuman effort she managed to control her throbbing flesh.

Edmund bit into the grape and swallowed it, then returned his head between Fiona's thighs, this time swirling his tongue into her opening in order to bring out another tiny round green fruit. The softness of his tongue combined with the movement of the remaining grapes were arousing enough, but to Fiona's horror Edmund was still moving the pad of this thumb with extraordinary delicacy along the shaft of her clitoris and despite straining with every ounce of self-control Fiona's nerve endings could bear no more and suddenly Edmund found his head gripped tightly between Fiona's thighs as her whole body went rigid, her arms moving down to grab his hair without her knowledge and then she was tumbling into racking sexual release while within her back passage the ivory love balls rolled against the thin inner walls prolonging the spasms almost beyond the point of satisfaction.

Edmund pulled Fiona to her feet before her final contractions were over. 'You failed to obey me,' he said with a thin smile. 'I shall have to let others share in the feast between your thighs.'

169

Fiona, still dazed by the force of the orgasm, shook her head. 'No!'

He didn't answer, but simply pushed her towards his bed and then she was being manhandled onto a pile of bolsters, the men doubled her legs backwards and she heard the door opening as Chrissie returned.

Chrissie managed to extract three grapes from Fiona before her body was racked by another orgasm, then the curtains were opened, Chrissie departed and Craig took her place, closing the curtains about him as he bent his head between the straining, moisture-soaked thighs. This time Fiona climaxed even more quickly, and Edmund realised that she had now reached a level where she would be capable of several orgasms in quick succession. He was delighted.

Fiona continued to lie with her body stretched tightly over the cushions, her breasts stimulated by Marcus's hands and mouth while between her thighs various members of the household came and sucked grapes from her increasingly sensitive opening and Edmund moved his diabolically clever thumb around the entire area of her inner sex-lips, thus ensuring that every orgasm peaked at a higher level of intensity.

When the last grape had been withdrawn, Edmund sat up against the headboard and pulled the limp Fiona onto his lap, lifting her above his erection for a second before pulling her down sharply. Then he continued to move her with his hands until at last his own orgasm was triggered and she felt the warmth of him flooding into her causing his juices to mingle with hers.

There was no climax for Fiona this time though. Her body was exhausted and after Edmund had finished she only hoped he wouldn't hand her over to Marcus. Edmund didn't. 'Time for a rest, I think,' he gasped, letting his hand travel up beneath the hem of her toga and along her spine. 'After we've eaten and regained some strength, Craig and Amy can join us. Amy has a very light touch!' he added with a laugh, and Marcus laughed with him.

Two hours later, Fiona was taken out into the garden for only the second time since her capture. She was still wearing her silk toga with nothing beneath it, and on her feet the white stiletto heels that Edmund found so erotic.

This time she was taken to a secluded lawn, screened on all sides by high privet hedges. Edmund was now wearing pale blue shorts. Although his body was as tanned and muscular as Alessandro's, Fiona realised that she didn't find him nearly so attractive. He lacked the strength that drew her unwillingly towards his older brother, and despite his great enthusiasm for all their sexual activity, she sensed that he wasn't capable of any deep feelings. At times she felt certain that Alessandro knew her better as a person than any man had known her before. Edmund saw only her body, and was interested in nothing but the sexual pleasure they could obtain together.

As she stood passively at his side, Marcus and Grant, the most rarely seen of the inner circle of bodyguards, came along the path, each carrying a large pole. These they slotted into ready-made holes in the ground before withdrawing.

Edmund turned towards the house, looking impatient. 'Where's Amy got to?' he muttered. As he spoke, Craig and Amy appeared from the direction of the house. Between them Fiona saw the figure of Bethany.

Amy was wearing a bikini of red and yellow flowers, the top half scarcely containing her breasts and the bottom half only just covering her pubic hair. Craig had nothing on but a brief red posing pouch, while Bethany was entirely naked.

For the first time since their arrival in Norfolk, Bethany looked far from happy. She cast a sullen glance at Fiona and then Amy pushed her gently towards one of the poles. Fiona realised that Bethany's hands were fastened and watched in silence as her one-time friend was placed with her back against the pole, then secured with a narrow silver chain that ran round her waist and the back of the pole. Once that had been fastened her hands were released, only to be stretched above her head and clipped into rings. Her full breasts hung heavily against her rib cage and her red hair fell about her face which she lowered towards her chest.

'Bethany complained that Craig was too rough with her this morning,' explained Edmund with his most charming smile. 'We've decided to make it up to her, and as you're my slave today you can assist me.'

Still Fiona kept silent, waiting to learn exactly what kind of wickedly erotic teasing they were planning for both her and Bethany. She didn't have to wait long to find out. To her initial surprise, Craig was now fastened to the other pole, but the chain round his waist was loose and he was able to move forward a few feet, until finally the limit of the chain brought him up short as he brushed against Bethany's naked body. After testing how far he could advance, Craig went back to the wooden pole and waited.

Amy, who had gone back into the house, reappeared carrying an assortment of what looked like feather dusters. However, when they were placed at Fiona's feet she saw that they were actually a collection of sprays of ostrich feathers on thin bamboo canes, and some single pointed goose feathers.

'Pick up one of the plumes,' Edmund ordered Fiona. She bent to obey, and at once he slid a hand round her exposed buttocks, squeezing them together so that she could feel the love balls he'd inserted earlier move and brush against her sensitive anal walls. She caught her breath and he laughed before releasing her. 'Good, I see you're still capable of arousal!'

Amy stood beside Fiona. 'You have to brush your friend from neck to toe with regular sweeping movements until Edmund tells you to stop. Don't vary the pace or the pressure, just keep brushing her.'

Fiona hesitated, and Edmund gave her a push in the small of her back. 'It's what I want Fiona. Now do it. Bethany won't find anything to complain about this time. The plumes are extremely soft.'

'Lift your head, Bethany,' Craig called from where he was standing fastened to the other pole. Slowly she lifted her chin and at once Fiona lifted the head of the plume of downy feathers and began to brush against the creamy skin of the red-head's body. She let the feathers sweep down across the breasts, over the rounded stomach and then across the front of her thighs and on down to the ankles. Then she reversed the action and swept back up, realising that this time some of the feathers crept between Bethany's thighs and for a brief second tickled against her vulva before going up over her stomach again.

Fiona continued with the movements for over five minutes and all the time she worked, Bethany's body burgeoned and swelled in front of her. Her breasts thrust upwards and her abodomen grew tight with desire while her thighs slackened, and on every upsweep she tried to force herself against the insinuating caress of the feathers.

'Brush the hollows beneath her arms,' Amy said at one point, and after she'd added this to the movements Fiona found that Bethany's breathing grew yet more rapid and she would give little cries of pleasure that turned to moans of frustration when the plume was never allowed to remain in any one place for more than a brief second.

After five minutes of this gentle stimulation Bethany's eyes were pleading with the onlookers and her body was straining against the silver chain round her waist, the curve of which Fiona was careful to include in every sweep of the plume.

For Bethany the sensation was delicious torture.

Every time the plumes brushed any of her multitude of erogenous zones her flesh would leap with desire, but it was a desire that was never allowed to build in one place, although gradually her entire body expanded until the pleasure utterly consumed her and blood drummed in her ears as the pressure mounted.

'Stop now,' said Edmund suddenly. Fiona quickly dropped the plume and stood looking at Bethany. The red-head's parted lips and flushed face told their own story of arousal, an arousal she was struggling to bring to fruition and for a moment Fiona wished that she could continue to prolong the relentless, fruitless stimulation of the white skin.

Amy turned to look at her husband. His face was contorted as his bulging erection was constrained within his posing pouch but when, at a signal for Edmund, she went over to him they smiled at each other and kissed deeply.

'Fiona, take off Craig's pouch,' Edmund ordered her. She had to kneel beside the kissing couple and ease the pouch down his legs, and his purple-headed shaft sprang free immediately. Bethany was watching too, and between her thighs moisture began to seep from her secret opening as the area between her thighs burned with a fierce sexual hunger.

Edmund laughed. 'I hope this is all gentle enough for you, Bethany! Fiona, pick up the small brush there and take this pot of honey. I want you to paint it over Bethany's nipples and around her inner sex-lips, then we'll see if Craig can get near enough to lick it off.'

Fiona found that she was becoming incredibly aroused by this slow pleasuring of Bethany's flesh; a pleasuring that was so prolonged it was driving Bethany mad with thwarted need. For the first time since she'd learned of her friend's treachery, Fiona was actually in a position to take a kind of revenge, and to her own shame she was enjoying it. As she dipped the tiny brush into the honey pot, Bethany murmured, 'Don't, Fiona, please. I shall explode soon.'

'I'm a slave, I have to obey,' Fiona replied shortly and then she stood up and began to paint the clear sticky honey over the large blood-filled nipples, and the tips grew even harder beneath the insidious touch of the brush. Bethany closed her eyes, trying to trigger an orgasm by imagining it was one of the Trimarchi brothers touching her so skilfully.

'Open your eyes, Bethany!' Edmund ordered sharply. 'You have to watch Fiona.'

Without being told, Fiona decided that before she spread the honey between Bethany's thighs she would let the brush swirl into her navel, and as she did so Bethany's whole body leapt and her honey-coated aureoles glistened in the sunlight as they strained forward for some kind of further contact.

Edmund saw what Fiona had done and smiled. 'You learn quickly!' he applauded her, and going across he slid a hand into the gap beneath her arm, cupping one of her breasts while tweaking the nipple between his fingers. Fiona was already aroused by watching Bethany's responses. Edmund's touch simply increased her excitement and she closed her eyes and let him knead her breast tenderly, feeling how she swelled in his grasp while above her Bethany was forced to watch and her own naked, stimulated breasts screamed for similar attention.

Then, Edmund released Fiona and spread Bethany's ankles. Amy came across to hold Bethany's outer sex-lips apart between her tiny fingers, and Bethany felt certain that now her pleasure would spill over into release, but Amy was far too clever for that and deliberately kept her touch too light to allow the chained red-head her climax.

'Brush carefully,' said Edmund. 'Don't touch the clitoris, it will trigger her orgasm. Just spread the honey around the inner lips so that Craig can lick it off.'

Carefully, with intense concentration, Fiona obeyed. She watched Bethany's soft pink flesh pulsating with need and was careful only to move the brush with the most delicate of touches. Her reward was to see Bethany's entire vulva swell while lubrication flowed from her opening, but still her ultimate satisfaction was withheld.

When Fiona was finished, Bethany's ankles were moved together again, and her sex-lips stuck to each other. She groaned with frustration, having expected Craig, whose erection she could see only too clearly, to immediately start removing the sweet honey.

It wasn't yet time though. Instead Edmund handed Fiona one of the long, pointed goose feathers. 'Use that on her. Do as you wish, but don't precipitate the final release or you'll be held responsible and punished.'

Fiona hardly heard the last part of the sentence. Instead she took the feather with what Bethany could tell was genuine pleasure, and for the first time the red-head sincerely regretted ever having slept with Duncan. But for that, Fiona would never have taken delight in participating in a sex scene like this, and would probably have allowed Bethany to climax. There was no hope of that now.

Fiona stood up and smiled at Bethany. 'Is this the kind of thing you and Duncan used to do?' she asked softly, then stroked the feather down behind Bethany's ear before letting the tip swirl along the lobe and finally into the aperture itself, the gentle tickling caress driving Bethany frantic with increasing desire.

She moaned, and Fiona smiled again. 'I suppose Duncan liked to hear you groan with passion. He never let me reach those dizzy heights, but I suppose that wasn't your fault. Just the same, I can't help blaming you a little.' With that she drew the feather down the side of Bethany's body, tracing the inward curve of her waist, and the soft swell of her hips before drawing it over her straining stomach muscles.

'Be careful!' cautioned Edmund while Craig's erection

throbbed and he started to move forward on his chain. Amy tenderly used the plumes on his spine and the back of his shoulders so that he remained ready for Bethany when Fiona was called off her.

Hearing Edmund's caution, Fiona decided to leave the area between Bethany's thighs alone. Instead she knelt down and rotated the tip of the feather round the back of the red-head's knees. Sparks of pleasure shot upwards and Bethany felt her own juices mingling with the honey that was still keeping her sex lips sealed together, while beads of perspiration joined with the honey on her breasts.

Finally, Fiona concentrated on Bethany's feet and let the feather flick through the gap between each of her toes before encircling the tips of the toes themselves and ending with the lightest of touches on the underside of her arches.

'Enough!' Edmund commanded. Reluctantly Fiona ceased her ministrations. She obediently dropped the feather on the ground and then withdrew to Edmund's side. Now she stood in front of him and he slipped both hands inside her tunic, sliding them down her rib cage and spreading his fingers wide until they were splayed across the surface of her taut stomach. Then, as she watched Craig approaching Bethany across the lawn, he began to move his hands in small circles pressing down against the flesh leaping beneath her skin.

Bethany watched Craig approaching and tried to pull towards him, but her chain wouldn't let her. He was able to reach her though, and immediately he began to suck and lick at the honey on her inflamed breasts, lapping at its sugary sweetness with enthusiasm while Bethany's body tightened and her aching flesh was drawn into his mouth.

He licked her until all the honey had gone, and then bent his knees until he drew level with her navel. For a moment Bethany's stomach lurched. That area wasn't always a trigger for her pleasure. Sometimes the sharp

177

sensations that stimulation there caused, made her need a bathroom rather than a climax but she couldn't stop him and when she felt his rough tongue plunge into the dip her bladder immediately responded by seeming to fill and her hips wriggled helplessly.

Craig knew what was happening and as he moved lower he let his head press above her pubic bone increasing the pressure on the walls of her bladder, knowing that this would increase the intensity of her climax when it finally came, but for a brief moment all Bethany could feel was discomfort and she tried to move to ease the pressure.

'Keep still,' said Edmund, 'otherwise Duncan might not get you back when he pays the money.'

Bethany immediately stopped wriggling. Now Craig moved lower and the pressure eased, becoming more bearable. But when he tried to lick between her thighs her lips were still firmly stuck together and his chain didn't allow him much room for manoeuvre, while his hands had been fastened behind him which meant he had nothing to use except his mouth.

For a dreadful moment Bethany thought that he wasn't going to be able to reach her screaming flesh, but driven on by his own need Craig used the bridge of his nose to ease her outer sex-lips apart, and then at last he was able to start drawing the honey into his mouth, sucking greedily at the liquid that was thinner than that on her breasts because it had been joined by her own secretions. He moved his mouth over her flesh, sucking it in to draw every drop of nectar between his lips, and as he sucked behind Bethany's throbbing clitoris her pleasure grew into a dense mass of aching need.

All at once Amy pushed him away, kept Bethany's outer labia apart with the fingers of one hand and with the other drew a feather up the deliciously tortured flesh of the inner channels until it reached the shrinking clitoris.

Then she stopped, and Bethany held her breath as

her whole body waited in tense expectation. Amy delayed further and Bethany stifled a moan, guessing that would only prolong the bitter-sweet game yet further. Finally, as Edmund's hands moved down Fiona's stomach and began massaging her pubic hair, his fingers straying down to tug on Fiona's flesh-hood, Amy drew the hand holding Bethany's flesh-lips upwards, drawing the red-head's flesh-hood up with the movement and then she drew the tip of the feather with excruciating lightness across the stem of the exposed clitoris.

Immediately, Bethany's body exploded into orgasm. Bursts of ecstasy rolled over her, and her hips pushed forward as her contracting inner muscles yearned for something to fill her. It was now that the full extent of Edmund's cunning became obvious. Craig could just touch her desperate entrance with the tip of his erection, but he was not able to plunge into her. No matter how much he strained or how hard Bethany tried to help him, all he could do was nudge at the round circle of muscle and Bethany screamed at both the intensity of the orgasm and the frustration of his inability to enter her.

Watching Bethany's body rippling with sexual release, Fiona grew damp between her thighs and Edmund's fingers drummed softly against the side of her clitoris so that despite her exhaustion she doubled up with a fiercely sharp climax, the intensity of which took her by surprise.

Finally, as she sank to the grass with Edmund's arms still round her, Amy released Craig who quickly pushed his wife to the ground and mounted her, thrusting furiously into her welcoming entrance as she wrapped her legs round his bare back and held him tight. As Craig shouted his pleasure aloud, Bethany stared down at them, her body slack and her eyes heavy. Despite her satisfaction, she had been deprived of Craig 's thrusting hardness and she hated them all for not letting her climax be totally complete in the way she liked best.

When Craig finally rolled off Amy, Edmund glanced at his watch. 'Nearly six. Time to get those love balls out of you, Fiona. Then you can have a shower and go back to your room. You've done very well today, and I shall tell Alessandro how pleased I am. I hope you've enjoyed some of it too?'

Fiona shivered and stood up. She knew that it was clear to them all how much she'd enjoyed the things she'd been made to do. She felt shamed, both by her own responses and by her growing need for this kind of sexual stimulation. She might have been Edmund's slave, but he hadn't forced her to feel the pleasure and excitement she'd drawn from this scene in the garden. One thing was very clear to her now. She wasn't at all the kind of person she'd once believed herself to be.

Chapter Eleven

Once Bethany and Fiona had been returned to their room, Fiona felt distinctly uncomfortable. She was aware that Bethany had sensed her enjoyment of the afternoon's activities, and knowing there was no way she could justify herself she kept silent. Bethany didn't.

'You're certainly a dark horse,' she said with an edge to her voice. 'I remember the way you carried on when Duncan brought you into my bedroom. You were crying as though having me present was too much for your pure little soul to bear, but today you'd have liked them to let you keep working on me until I screamed for mercy, wouldn't you?'

'Shut up!' exlaimed Fiona. 'I don't have to justify myself to you of all people.'

'Wait until Duncan hears about this new you,' continued Bethany, ignoring the interruption. 'He'll probably be keener to get you back as you've grown up. Maybe he'll invite a few of his more sophisitcated friends round to join the pair of us. Why not? It seems anything goes with you now. Or is it only the Trimarchi brothers who interest you?'

'When do you go?' Fiona asked shortly.

Bethany smirked. 'Tonight, if the money arrives on

time. Craig told me that Duncan was sending it by special messenger. I should be safely in his arms before morning!'

'Good, then I won't have to listen to you any more,' replied Fiona.

'No, and you'll have Alessandro to yourself, which is what you really want. Except there's always Georgina to consider. She told me you were getting in her way, so don't expect much consideration from her when she's got you as her slave for a day.'

Fiona looked carefully at Bethany. 'You love trying to frighten me, don't you? First of all it was a game you and Duncan played, now you're doing it on your own. Well, I'm not so easily frightened any more, and whatever Georgina might think she still has to answer to Alessandro.'

'Who won't let you be hurt? Is that what you mean? How touching!'

'I find it reassuring.'

Bethany shrugged. 'Believe what you like, at the end of the day he's not much different from Duncan.'

'He's nothing like Duncan!' protested Fiona.

Bethany looked startled. 'You're not falling in love with him, are you? Honestly, Fiona you must be out of your mind! Alessandro Trimarchi doesn't fall in love, he enjoys women that's all; lots of them, in varying shapes and sizes. I admit he seems fascinated by you, but that's because you're different. Once he's made you the same as his other women he'll lose interest. What were you thinking of – wedding bells after a divorce from Duncan?' A burst of laughter escaped her lips but before Fiona could reply the door to their room opened and Alessandro himself walked in. He had a small case in one hand which he placed beside Bethany's bed. 'Get dressed,' he ordered her. 'We have half the money, it's time for you to go.'

Suddenly, to Fiona's astonishment, she found that she wanted to cry. It wasn't that she wanted to see

Duncan, it was the realisation that Bethany would now be leaving her alone in the house and that there wasn't anyone truly interested in what became of her. She assumed Duncan would repay the rest of the money in the end, but their marriage could never continue after he had chosen Bethany above her, so what would she be left with when she was released?

Alessandro watched her out of the corner of his eye. He was only too aware of how she must be feeling, and anxious to get Duncan's auburn-haired mistress out of the house as quickly as possible.

As Bethany pulled on the dress that Duncan had sent for her, Alessandro sat next to Fiona, blocking Bethany from her view. 'Edmund tells me that you had a good day with him. Is that right?'

Fiona blinked back the treacherous tears, feeling the comfort of his warm fingers as they closed around hers. 'Some of it was enjoyable,' she admitted.

'She enjoyed it all!' Bethany announced sitting down to pull on her stockings.

'Shut up!' Alessandro said fiercely. 'If you're not dressed in two more minutes you can get in the car naked.'

Fiona looked into his eyes. 'Will he ever repay the rest of the debt?' she whispered.

Alessandro nodded. 'Of course! Within ten days or so it should be possible.'

'He's lying,' Bethany said, walking towards the door. 'Duncan won't ever be able to repay all the money, and the Trimarchi brothers intend to take over his companies instead. I know that's true because Craig told me.'

While Fiona stared blankly at Bethany, Alessandro rose to his feet. 'Craig is nothing more than a hired bodyguard who hasn't got a brain in his head. I would no more dream of discussing my financial affairs with him than I would of asking my accountant for advice on my skiing. Now get out. Duncan Sheldon is more than welcome to you.'

On the far side of the door, Craig was waiting to escort Bethany to the waiting car, and as her footsteps died away Fiona was left sitting on the bed staring blankly out of the small window at the far end of the room.

Alessandro tried to think of something he could say to cheer her up, but for once his quick mind failed him. There was nothing that could possibly ease the pain of a double betrayal, it was something she must somehow come to terms with on her own and it would be insulting to offer platitudes in an effort to comfort such grief.

'Why did you marry him?' he asked suddenly.

Fiona's mind was instantly diverted from the present as she thought back to the first few times she and Duncan had gone out together. 'He seemed safe,' she said slowly. 'My father had lost all his money and my mother had only ever known what it was like to be rich. Duncan was rich, and I believed he was kind. He also claimed to be madly in love with me.'

'And you with him?' asked Alessandro.

'No, not in love, but I liked him and when he said he'd employ my father again, put him on the board of two of his companies and give him back his self-respect, I thought that was wonderful.'

'But he would only do it if you married him, is that right?'

Fiona nodded. 'He didn't make it sound like that, as though he was buying me, he just said that once we were married he'd be able to place his father-in-law in good positions and everything fell into place. I knew my mother would be happy again, I believed Duncan and I would make a good couple, and that was that.'

'What about in bed? Did he ever please you there?' enquired Alessandro.

Fiona nodded. 'Before we married he was consider-

184

ate, but he didn't seem particularly passionate. I mean, it wasn't as though he was forever taking me to bed. It was never more than once every couple of weeks. Later I found out that he was being kept busy by a long-term mistress, but at the time I imagined that was the way he was.'

Alessandro nodded. 'And you didn't mind this lack of passion?'

Fiona lifted her head and stared at him. 'Of course not! I thought that I was the same.'

'But now?' he pressed her.

She lowered her eyes. 'Now I know differently.'

'Does the knowledge please you?'

Fiona shook her head. 'Not at all, because I don't think it's going to be of any benefit to me once I'm free. I shan't return to Duncan, and I can't imagine I'm going to be uninhibited enough to rush around London seeking what they call a "like-minded male companion", can you?'

For the first time his harsh features softened into a smile. 'No, I can't, but a solution may present itself. This, I've found, is often the way in life.'

'In your life perhaps, but not in mine.'

'Tomorrow I shall be here for the day,' Alessandro told her. 'This means it will be possible for me to take my turn as your master. I look forward to it with keen anticipation, and hope that perhaps you do as well?'

Fiona wasn't at all sure, but he had succeeded in taking her mind off Bethany's departure and she slept surprisingly well that night.

Alessandro woke her at six. She turned over sleepily and he put his hands beneath her bare shoulders. 'Come along, Fiona, time to enjoy ourselves! Pull on this towelling robe, I want to start my day by having you bathe me.'

Alessandro's bathroom was tiled in a Roman style with mosaic patterns on the floor and walls. The sunken tub was long and deep, and when Fiona turned on the taps hot water gushed from the mixer faucet. She adjusted the cold tap slightly then let the tub fill before pouring in some liquid from a bottle he'd given her.

By the time Alessandro came through to get into the water, it was full of bubbles and the air was scented with pine. He sniffed appreciatively. 'A perfect start to the day! You can use that hand mitt to scrub my skin, use the roughened side first and start with my back.'

Fiona quickly pulled on the glove and worked the bubbles of soap over his golden-brown skin, scrubbing vigorously until it turned a gentle shade of red. Then she turned her hand over and sluiced him down with water using the soft side of the glove.

After that he lifted each of his legs in turn, and this time she used her hands on him, cleaning carefully between his toes and rubbing her hands slowly up the long length of his legs. Then it was the turn of his chest, arms and neck before he finally stood up and spread his legs for her.

His manhood was hanging down between his legs, his testicles round and heavy but loose, the skin shrivelled and curiously vulnerable. Very gently, Fiona began to soap each of them in turn, letting her hand slide along the delicate skin below them. The testicles expanded and the surrounding skin grew tighter.

Alessandro's erection was beginning now and Fiona touched it, delicately at first but with increasing firmness, letting the suds assist her hands to slide up and down his shaft until he was fully erect. Once that had happened he pushed her hands away and sat down again, letting the water remove the bubbles.

'I'll dry myself,' he told her shortly, amazed at the difficulty he'd had in controlling himself. 'There's fruit and yoghurt in the bedroom. We can eat together once I'm through here.'

After they'd eaten, Fiona poured them both cups of strong steaming coffee from a silver jug and for the first time in days found that she was beginning to relax. Her surroundings were luxurious, and she was in the company of a man she found more attractive than anyone she'd ever met before. Only the bizarre circumstances surrounding her presence in the house spoilt it for her, and she tried to push this thought away.

When he'd drunk his coffee, Alessandro took off the bath robe he'd pulled on in order to eat and went to lie down on his bed, taking Fiona with him. Once they were side by side he slid her robe off her and tenderly ran his hands over her body.

'Did your parents ever know what Duncan was really like?' he asked idly, nibbling at the soft skin beneath her ear.

Fiona shivered at the touch of his mouth and found that her own hands were moving over his hips. 'No,' she murmured. 'I couldn't possibly tell them, not when they were so happy again. Besides, I was ashamed when it all started to go wrong. I thought it must be my fault that I couldn't please Duncan in any ordinary way and so he had to humiliate me in order to gain satisfaction.'

'Just as we've humiliated you,' he said thoughtfully, licking at the hollow at the base of her throat.

'No!' said Fiona quickly. 'It wasn't the same at all. Duncan really hurt me. I was always having to try and hide the bruises he caused, and once I had to see a gynaecologist he hurt me so much.'

Alessandro drew in his breath. 'He deserves everything that happens to him,' he said tightly.

Now he was licking at each of her breasts in turn, licking them so slowly that she wanted to tell him to hurry and yet, perversely, she wanted it to go on longer as well. Pulling her closer to him he thrust a leg between her thighs, allowing the top of his thigh to press against her vulva so that she could stimulate herself by moving against it. To his delight she did this without even being asked, and he soon felt slicks of moisture on his skin marking the places where she touched him.

'Where to they live?' he whispered as Fiona moved in her own rhythm.

She could hardly think who he meant, so great was her rising excitement at this tender lovemaking, but with an effort realised he was still discussing her parents. 'Cornwall,' she gasped as the heat between her thighs began to rise.

Alessandro filed the information away in his brain before giving himself up to his lovemaking. He licked and nibbled on her stomach and hips, then turned her onto her stomach. Beginning at the base of her neck he sucked on every vertebrae of her spine as he travelled down to the cleft between the cheeks of her bottom.

There he swirled his tongue around, and saw her torso lift off the bed at the bolt of delight that coursed through her. Carefully he pressed her back into the mattress, letting his fingers massage her scalp through her long hair so that she understood the gesture was one of affection and not force.

Everywhere his mouth travelled he left the skin warm and moist and then as the air dried his saliva the flesh cooled and heat and cold seemed to beat a kind of tattoo across her body until Fiona trembled all over.

When he reached her feet, Alessandro got Fiona to turn onto her back again. Then he took one foot in his hands, rested the heel in the palm of his left hand and gripped the rest of her foot with his right. Once he had immobilised the foot he let his mouth roam over the toes.

He licked delicately across the top of each, allowing his tongue to plunder the amazingly sensitive skin in the gaps between each one before going on to the next. Then, as Fiona wriggled in stunned delight on the bed, he took the top of her smallest toe in his mouth and sucked strongly.

The pressure on the fleshy pad of her toe seemed to be reciprocated deep within Fiona and she wondered how it was that such a simple action could result in the incredibly intense contractions that she was experiencing deep in her abdomen. Without realising what she was doing, her hands went to her breasts and she began to caress her thrusting nipples with the tips of her fingers until jolts of sexual excitement shot down from her breasts to join the pulsations from her toes at one focal point somewhere deep within the core of her.

Alessandro refused to be hurried. He worked slowly on each toe, and then he released her foot and began the whole process again on the other foot while Fiona tossed restlessly on the bed, her eyes flecked with green and bright with desire, her hands gripping her breasts more and more firmly.

When he'd finally finished he lowered her leg to the bed and then spread himself on top of her, taking his weight on his elbows and brushing his body up and down against her, making sure that his pubic bone was positioned in such a way that every time he moved, her clitoris was stimulated.

Fiona felt this new stimulation and gave a cry of excitement. Now her whole body was gathering itself together and she felt the increasing throb of the pulse behind her clitoris that heralded her orgasms.

'Are you near?' whispered Alessandro.

'Yes, yes!' responded Fiona, grinding her pelvis against him yet more firmly,

At this he stopped moving his body over her and instead inserted his hand between her thighs, sliding two fingers deep inside her, hooking one slightly so that it massaged her G-spot.

For a moment Fiona thought that this would trigger her orgasm, but although the sensations peaked higher she still didn't tumble over the edge into release, and her hips continued to move frantically as her body sought relief.

Alessandro withdrew his fingers and then moved them, damp with her own moisture, along the slippery channels of her inner labia and up to the place beneath her urethra where he knew she was highly sensitive. There they stopped and for a moment Fiona stared into his eyes, awaiting the final touch that would bring her fulfilment. He didn't keep her waiting long, but stared deep into her eyes as the tips of his fingers moved gently against the thin membrane and her whole body started off the bed as though she'd been electrocuted.

She cried out with the joy of it all, the sweetness of the loving and the ease with which he'd brought her to such a climax and then as she shuddered against him he finally let himself plunge into her. Her inner muscles were still contracting from the waves of her orgasm and they gripped him more fiercely than he was expecting.

Alessandro had longed for this moment, fully intending to plunge in and out of her glorious body for as long as possible, but the excitement she'd aroused in him and the fierce clutching of her muscles meant that all he could do was thrust smoothly and quickly four times before he too exploded in a climax that was shattering in its intensity.

Fiona, lying beneath him, watched his eyes close and his teeth clench as he reached the peak of his orgasm. She saw the red flush of sexual excitement spreading across his chest and neck and felt a moment's power at the realisation that it was her body that had brought this about but then to her astonishment his shuddering within her triggered her body into a second orgasm that followed so hard on the heels of the first that it seemed almost to be one and she screamed as yet again her body went rigid in the throes of a climax she hadn't even realised was coming.

Alessandro felt her body gather itself together again below his and he too felt a surge of satisfaction at what he'd accomplished. He watched her from beneath hooded lids as her head thrashed from side to side and the tendons of her neck went tight exposing her tender neck.

When she was at last still he let himself slump on top

of her, nuzzling at her neck and sucking delicately on her skin in such a way as to mark her as his for the next few days. He was heavy, but Fiona didn't mind. She liked the feel of his muscular body against her. Duncan had always turned away from her the moment he'd finished, this was much nicer. She wasn't alone, but sharing in his pleasure as much as revellng in her own, and even better was the tender way he finally rolled off her but cradled her against him so that she didn't feel he had deserted her.

His hands moved in a sexless caress over her back. 'I wanted it to last longer,' he confessed. 'We need more practice!'

'I thought it was never going to end,' Fiona murmured shyly.

He brushed the damp hair back off her face. 'Rest now,' he murmured. 'Edmund can wait a little longer.'

Fiona's eyes widened. 'Edmund?' She would have sat up, but Alessandro's encircling arms prevented her.

'He's my brother. I think it's only fair that I let him share you for a little of the day.'

'I've already been his!' protested Fiona, wondering if her feelings of closeness had been an illusion.

'Don't you see, this is what I want,' Alessandro explained. 'Together, we can make you twice as happy.'

'But it isn't the same with him,' Fiona struggled to explain. 'He only . . .'

Alessandro put a finger across her mouth. 'You're mine, remember? I'm not saying it's the same, just that it will please me to have him here with me for a time. I promise you, you'll enjoy yourself.'

Fiona had no doubt that she would, but the brief magic moment between them had vanished. She didn't know that Alessandro had deliberately made it vanish, because he'd been frightened by the depth of his own feelings for her.

Half an hour later, Alessandro handed Fiona a peach-coloured satin teddy, then once she'd put it on he produced the white high-heels that she already knew Edmund liked and got her to parade around the room for him while he dressed. Before they left the bedroom, he slipped a double strand of pearls around her neck. They hung low, so that the lower strand disappeared into the gap between her breasts.

'You look exactly as Edmund would want you to look!' he said with a smile.

'Is it how you want me to look as well?' asked Fiona.

He shook his head. 'I like to see you lying in bed, your eyes languid and your body limp with exhausted passion, but that's not a very practical way to walk around the house!'

She felt herself grow warm at the realisation of how she must have looked after their earlier lovemaking, but then he was leading her down the stairs and her thoughts turned instead to what lay ahead of her. Her pulse began to race, and she knew that it was as much with excitement as fear.

She was taken into a large drawing room she had never been in before. Again all the windows had heavy velvet curtains, this time in dark blue, and there was a pale blue, wool carpet on the floor. The furniture, a two-seater settee and three huge cream leather arm-chairs, had been pushed back to the sides of the room and all that was left was an inflated mattress the size of a double bed. A soft Egyptian scatter rug had been thrown over it and in the middle of the mattress there was a well-plumped body bolster. Edmund was waiting for them in the room.

'It's nice and warm,' said Alessandro approvingly. 'I don't think you need to keep your clothes on any longer, Fiona. Perhaps you would walk round the perimeter of the room once, for us to admire you, and then you can strip for us. A nice slow striptease, please, and take the shoes off last.'

Feeling agonisingly self-conscious, Fiona walked round the room. She made sure she kept her head high and her shoulders well back, giving Alessandro no opportunity to complain about her deportment. However self-conscious she might feel she was determined not to let the two brothers realise it. After circling the room she stopped at the foot of the makeshift bed and slipped the slim straps of her underwear off her shoulders, letting them fall to her elbows while bending forward a little to make sure the brothers could glimpse the swell of her breasts.

To her surprise she found that she was suddenly enjoying herself. It was fun to have two pairs of dark eyes fixed on her as she very gradually divested herself of the teddy, and she knew from the total silence in the room that she had their full attention.

Spreading her legs slightly apart she slid her right hand palm down along her satin-covered stomach. She then parted her fingers until they covered the area where her pubic hair was hidden beneath the teddy, and let them linger there for a moment before sliding her hand on down to the press-studs that fastened the garment between her thighs.

The brothers kept their eyes on her, Edmund longing for the moment when he could touch her again and Alessandro marvelling at the change they'd wrought in her. Even he had never guessed the extent of the sensuality that lay hidden beneath her cool exterior, and despite having possessed her earlier his mouth went dry at the prospect of taking her again.

Fiona felt as though she was living in a different world. Nothing mattered but this moment of power when she had two men totally absorbed in her every move. She allowed her fingers to move gently across the tightly stretched crotch of the luxurious garment and felt her own flesh respond. Then, very slowly, she unfastened one of the press-studs and heard Edmund release his breath.

Lifting her head, Fiona smiled up at him, before finally unfastening the last three press-studs and drawing the front flap of material upwards. She then stood straight in her high heels, letting the men revel in her exposed mound.

Alessandro wanted to shout at her to hurry and take it off, but he knew that she was obeying his instructions and her skill at tantalising them amazed him. With tiny movements, Fiona wriggled her hips, easing the material upwards, feeling it brush against the delicate undersides of her breasts as she finally raised her arms above her head and peeled the garment off, leaving herself nude except for the pearls and high heels.

'I'll take the shoes off!' Edmund exclaimed.

Alessandro glanced at him coldly. 'You'll do what I let you do, and nothing more.'

Edmund bit on his lip. For a moment, lost in the glories of Fiona's naked body and her unexpected skill in displaying it, he'd forgotten that she was no longer his slave but his brother's. 'Sorry,' he murmured.

'Sit on the foot of the bed, Fiona,' instructed Alessandro.

Obediently, Fiona lowered herself to the mattress, still keeping her shoulders back and enjoying the sensation of the cool pearls against her warm skin. Alessandro nodded at his younger brother. 'You can take off the shoes now.'

Edmund quickly lifted Fiona's right leg, staring down the length of it at her vulva, the outer lips still closed so that he was forced to imagine her inner glories, and then he slipped one of the shoes off her foot and ran his teeth over the fleshy pad at the base of her big toe. Fiona's leg tensed and his hands massaged her tight calf muscle for a moment before he let her leg fall and repeated the whole process with the left leg.

Once the shoes had been removed, Fiona waited. Alessandro crossed the room to a sideboard, opened a drawer and removed an object which he then brought across to her. 'Stand up a moment.' She stood, feeling short without her heels. He proceeded to fasten a leather belt about her waist, a belt with two short straps set close together hanging down both in front of her and behind. He then expanded the straps to their fullest extent before allowing Edmund to insert something between her thighs.

It looked to Fiona like a large plastic pad, but once it was clipped onto the straps, and the straps were released she understood more precisely what the brothers intended because it lay snugly against her vulva, pulled up tight against her most sensitive areas by the pull on the straps and she could feel rows of tiny upraised plastic circles insinuating their way into the fleshy folds of her vulva.

'It's a butterfly vibrator,' Alessandro explained. 'It runs off the mains. There's a wire from the back that we can connect up. Lie on your stomach on the bolster and we'll give you a demonstration.'

A great deal of Fiona's confidence drained away. It was one thing to flaunt herself in front of them for fun, but another to realise that soon her wanton body, so carefully tutored by the brothers and their friends, would again be writhing spasmodically with a pleasure that was out of her control.

She hesitated. 'Lie down, Fiona,' Alessandro said firmly. Slowly she obeyed him. 'Now press your breasts against the bolster and wrap your arms round the top of it. When the vibrator starts to move you'll probably find you want to stimulate yourself by moving your breasts around.'

The very thought of the tight pad vibrating against her was enough to conjure up erotic visions in Fiona's mind and she felt her nipples swelling against the bolster. Then, so gradually that she was scarcely aware of it to begin with, the butterfly vibrator began to move. It was like a very gentle soothing current passing through her, and she felt her outer labia spreading beneath the stimulation.

Alessandro and Edmund sat on each side of her and

watched her press her upper torso more firmly into the bolster. They smiled at each other over her back. Then Alessandro pressed the control switch on the box beside him and the speed of the vibrations increased. Now Fiona's tender inner tissue was being swamped by tiny jolts of excitement and she felt herself swelling between her legs as her pelvic area began to fill with the blood that was coursing through her veins.

Unknown to her, Fiona's hips started to twitch frantically and her legs moved helplessly around on each side of the body bolster. Edmund put a hand on the top of the backs of her thighs to keep her spread apart and he could feel the tremors running through her as her arousal began to mount towards a climax.

Alessandro saw this and lowered the speed again. As the blissfully stimulating charges of excitement decreased in intensity Fiona felt like crying out with disappointment. Her hips moved more quickly and she ground herself against the bolster trying to rekindle the previous level of excitement but without the aid of the control box she couldn't and instead had to settle for the steady pulsations of the lower speed.

Alessandro now took a tiny pen-shaped vibrator and applied it to the base of her skull, just below the roots of her hair at the back of her head. He moved it around the area for a minute or two and then started to glide it down one side of her spine.

Fiona's body was assailed by different sensations. Between her legs the butterfly throbbed softly, tickling but not allowing the excitement to mount, while all along her back sharp sparks were being generated from the touch of the light vibrator so near her spinal cord and some of the sparks lanced through to her breasts while others seemed to shoot in jagged lines straight to her abdomen which was tightening with the pleasure and the pressure of the bolster.

When Alessandro stopped between the cheeks of her bottom she was relieved, but then he started to move the vibrator all the way back up on the other side of her spine while at the same time increasing the speed of the vibrator between her legs.

Now her body was spinning out of control. She moaned and pushed her throbbing breasts desperately against the bolster, wishing one of the men would put a hand round one of her straining globes, but Edmund was more interested in the globes that surrounded her back entrance and he was gripping those tightly, enjoying their spasmodic clenching and unclenching caused by the vibrators.

Fiona's face felt hot and she knew that her back was damp with perspiration. She longed for a climax but couldn't quite reach it as the skilled Alessandro played on her nerve endings with wicked precision, allowing her so much excitement but no more.

Both the brothers could feel their erections pressing hard inside their jeans, but they knew that they had plenty of time to use them later. This was only the beginning. Together they watched Fiona's body as it bore down into the feathery softness of the duvet, and they smiled at the frantic motions of her hips and the trembling of her parted legs.

Finally Alessandro handed the small hand-held vibrator to his brother who quickly dipped it into a jar of lubricating jelly and then he was allowed to spread the delicious curves of Fiona's buttocks apart and he inserted the tip of the vibrator into her puckered opening.

Fiona screamed as yet another series of shocks assailed her tormented body. She gripped the bolster fiercely, knowing from the incredible pressure that was building up behind the core of her that she was close to coming. Encouraged by this, Edmund allowed more of the vibrator to slip inside her suddenly greedy opening.

Once it was inserted more deeply, Edmund nodded at his brother. For the first time Alessandro allowed the butterfly vibrator to reach its top speed and immediately

197

Fiona's orgasm was triggered. She felt the blissful bunching of nerve endings between her hot thighs and then her stimulated flesh exploded into waves of orgasmic pleasure which drowned out every coherent though in her head and all she could do was thrash about wildly on the soft bolster while her internal contractions made the walls of her rectum tighten about the vibrator still being held there. This intensified her pleasure so greatly that she gave a deep groan of incredulous relief.

Immediately her body slackened, the butterfly vibrator was switched off and the other one removed. 'There,' said Alessandro with quiet satisfaction. 'A good start to our time together!'

Chapter Twelve

*F*or several minutes Fiona lay in dazed silence on the bolster as her body slowly came down from the heights of ecstasy and her nerve endings quietened. But far too soon for her liking, Alessandro was pulling her up until she was standing on the carpeted floor.

'Take off the vibrator,' he said with a slow smile. 'I know you enjoyed it, but Edmund and I can give you equal enjoyment, if not better I think!'

Her fingers fumbled with the fastening round her waist, and then she lowered the whole device to the floor, stepping out of it awkwardly, aware that the pad of the butterfly was soaked with her juices.

In the meantime, Edmund had gone to the kitchen. He returned with three bottles of champagne. 'A celebration!' he laughed, handing one chilled bottle to Alessandro.

'What are we celebrating?' asked Fiona. 'Has Duncan paid the second half of his debt?'

Alessandro tilted his head to one side. 'Would that really be something for you to celebrate, Fiona?' he asked softly. 'I don't believe so. No, this is a celebration of your growing sexuality. Kneel upright in the middle of the mattress, we don't seem to have any glasses and will have to drink from you!'

Fiona shivered. Her skin was hot from sexual arousal, the thought of cold champagne on it made her tense, but she obeyed him because she had no choice. Once she was kneeling with her upper legs straight, Edmund positioned himself behind her and Alessandro in front. Then, together, they opened the bottles and as the corks exploded they tipped the necks so that champagne flowed down the length of Fiona's back and front at the same time.

The shock of the cold liquid on her skin made her gasp and arch herself, thrusting out her breasts and taut stomach towards Alessandro while Edmund was able to admire the inward curve of her back.

The brothers both gripped her shoulders and then began to lick at her champagne-streaked body. Alessandro lapped at the hollow at the stem of her throat before moving on to her breasts. He drew the rigid nipples, forced upright by the shock of the ice-cold champagne, into his warm mouth sucking fiercely at the hardness of them before opening his mouth wider and drawing the entire aureole into his mouth.

As he lapped round her breasts, Fiona could feel Edmund's featherlight tongue licking down her spine and along the bottom of her shoulder-blades. This was a spot she had never realised was sensitive before, but as he touched her there, small thrills of excitement began to tease at her again.

Now Alessandro was working his way down the sticky trails to her navel, while Edmund was between her buttocks. Frissons of pleasure ran from her lower spine through to her abdomen and she shook in the brothers' firm grip.

Finally, Edmund released her. She was spread flat on her back, the bolser thrown to the floor, so that now both the brothers could concentrate their attention on her stomach and inner thighs, where she had been soaked with the champagne.

The feeling of two tongues working on her in unison was incredible. Fiona heard herself gasping with excitement as they lapped and sucked at her, Alessandro paying particular attention to the creases at the tops of her thighs and his tongue working there made her long for it to move within her swelling outer lips to drink some of the fluid that had crept into her crevice, but he desisted.

Soon, working one from the front and one from the back, they had her gripping frantically at the Egyptian cotton bedspread with her hands as they continued to tantalise her. Only when they had removed all possible champagne traces from the surface of her stomach and thighs did they part her legs. Now Edmund opened the third bottle and Fiona screamed as the bubbles shot out directly onto her exposed vulva. Some of it forced its way past her outer lips and struck her inner labia and clitoris while the rest spread around her thighs and ran down over her hips onto the bed covering beneath.

To her delight they both drank from her most secret places, their tongues working together as a team. One of them would lick along the channels between her inner and outer lips while the other would swirl his tongue around the sticky, engorged clitoris, so suffused with desire that it was standing out proudly from its covering hood.

The waves of pleasure lapped over her in a never-ending stream. Tiny orgasmic spasms made her body ripple unceasingly, and it was an entirely different sensation from the more intense climaxes she'd experienced with them before.

Dimly she wondered how they were able to work on her so well. She realised that it must have taken practice, but didn't know if Georgina or Tanya had ever been the lucky recipient, or whether they had shared other women in the past, women who meant less to them. After a time she ceased to care. It was enough that they were able to give her such mind-blowing pleasure.

When they stopped she felt desolate. She'd wanted the ripples to continue indefinitely because at that level her body felt as though it could go on being pleasured for hours, but the brothers had finished and after giving her a bottle to drink from, so that she too had shared the champagne, they fetched warm damp flannels and wiped her sticky flesh until she was clean again.

As she lay supine on her back, the Trimarchi brothers stripped off their jeans and were at last naked above her. There erections were huge, the skin around the stems tight and both their glans were purple with beads of moisture in the slits.

Edmund reached out a hand for Fiona and she obediently stood up, watching as Alessandro sat down on the mattress, his legs spread wide. She was then made to sit facing him, balanced on his upper thighs so that he could slide his hardness into her raised vagina. Once they were joined, Edmund lowered Fiona backwards until her head rested on the mattress. Keeping her hands clasped in his, Alessandro now lay flat as well. They could no longer see each other and their only contact was with their hands and feet. Fiona nearly cried out with the glorious full feeling that she experienced in this position. He was so wide and firm that she was totally filled and an ache that had been pulsing softly deep within her, almost without her knowledge, suddenly stopped, eased by the unusual angle of his erection within her.

Realising that Alessandro couldn't move, Fiona began to move herself up and down his shaft and as she moved she gripped him tightly with her inner muscles, knowing by his sudden intake of breath that this was unbearably arousing to him.

Edmund waited until she was lost in what she was doing to his brother and then climbed onto the mattress with them, positioning himself above Fiona's head, kneeling with his legs on each side of her head before lowering himself so that his erection nudged against her mouth.

Fiona's eyes, which were closed to savour the feeling of Alessandro so deep within her, opened wide with surprise but she knew at once what she was expected to do and obediently her lips parted. Now Edmund could slip the highly sensitive tip of his penis between the moist velvet smoothness of her lips and as she closed her mouth about him, sucking lightly, his stomach muscles had to strain to fight back his climax.

Fiona could scarcely believe what she was doing, but her body took over and she simply obeyed her instincts. She worked her mouth on Edmund's straining penis using every ounce of the skill she'd been taught by Georgina, nibbling at the delicate skin beneath his glans, circling the head with her tongue and sucking steadily from time to time until he was close to orgasm, at which point she'd stop and resume slow delicate licks.

At the same time she was working herself along Alessandro's rigid member. He was pushing upwards as hard as he could, and he used his hands to try to control Fiona's rhythm as she moved on him, but sometimes she would move more quickly than he wanted and then he had to grit his teeth in order to delay his final moment of joy.

She didn't know how long the three of them moved in this sensual dance, all she knew was that she felt wonderful and that to be in control of their pleasure was unbearably erotic. Now she understood why they enjoyed controlling her climaxes so much. She brought them both to the brink of release, time after time, and their testicles ached with the need to release the pressure on them, but always she managed to stop just in time and although at first the brothers didn't want to come, by the end they did and both strained to beat Fiona at her teasing game.

Finally, she was unable to control them. Edmund gripped her head between his hands and moved himself in and out of her mouth in rapid movements that she was helpless to slow, while Alessandro's strong hands gripped Fiona's wrists in such a way that she had to go along with what he wanted or risk hurting herself.

For half a minute or more the Trimarchi brothers thrust in and out of her while Fiona lay in silent wonder at her own excitement and then they both ejaculated within seconds of each other. Fiona felt Edmund shudder above her and then her mouth was full of him. Without hesitation she found herself swallowing, sucking at him to draw more of the fluid from his straining penis and she was so excited by this that she continued to suck at him after he was drained and he had to stop her because his pleasure was being spoilt by pain.

At the same time as she was sucking at Edmund, Alessandro was filling her with his own hot liquid, which had shot into her in sharp bursts that caused him to give a long drawn out groan of relief. Again Fiona tightened around his stem, this time milking him with her inner muscles until his pleasure too became tinged with pain and he pulled out of her.

For a while they all lay in an exhausted tangle of arms and legs on the mattress until finally Alessandro decided it was time to move. 'We'll go and eat now,' he said firmly. 'There's no need for any of us to dress. Fiona, you can choose what we have for lunch, and unlike Tanya I think we'll eat off plates!'

It was colder in the kitchen, but Fiona was grateful since it gave her over-heated flesh a chance to cool down. She was no longer in the least self-conscious about being naked in front of the brothers. After what they had shared together it would have been ridiculous. She stretched up to look in the cupboards, bent down to find various cooking utensils, and all the time she gloried in the knowledge that both Edmund and Alessandro were watching her closely, enjoying the sight of her performing such everyday actions without clothes.

They had scrambled eggs with pieces of smoked salmon added and then finished with fresh fruit and plain yoghurt. At the sight of the yoghurt, Fiona remembered Tanya eating frozen yoghurt off her breasts and she knew that if it were to happen again she would be able to enjoy it more because so many of her inhibitions had now been banished. Finally, they drank some of the rich, strong coffee that the Italians seemed to prefer and then Edmund looked expectantly in his brother's direction. 'What now?'

'I wanted to ask Fiona about her husband's Westminster based company,' said Alessandro.

Edmund stared at him. 'I'm serious!' he said.

'So am I.' said Alessandro. 'It seems that this is the company he's most anxious to protect. Do you know why, Fiona?'

This intrusion of her husband's business affairs into the sensual delights that had made up the first half of the day shocked Fiona as much as Edmund. She shook her head in bewilderment. 'I don't know anything about his business affairs. My father is on the board of one company in Kingston and another one that's based in Cornwall, where he's living. He once told me that the Kingston one was a publishing concern, that's all. Duncan never told me anything.'

Alessandro looked closely at her. 'Would it surprise you to learn that Duncan is so frantic to keep the Westminster company that he's told me he'll forfeit you in exchange for it if he can't raise the rest of the money he owes me?'

'What do you mean, forfeit me?' she asked.

'He'll give you up. I can keep you, or dispose of you and he won't say a word to anyone.'

Edmund went white. 'Alessandro, you shouldn't tell her this. It isn't fair.'

His brother's eyes were hard. 'It may not be fair but it's true. If Fiona does know anything I want her to understand exactly what the picture is. That way she won't feel obliged to keep anything back.'

For the first time since she'd been kidnapped, Fiona couldn't prevent her eyes filling with tears. It was that which satisfied Alessandro she was telling the truth when she finally managed to speak again. 'There's nothing I can tell you, nothing. He never did think I was of much importance, certainly not important enough to confide in.'

The Italian leant forward and brushed away a tear that was falling down her face with a surprisingly gentle finger. 'Perhaps it's as well that you didn't know. You may have been safer in ignorance.'

'Duncan really said he didn't care if I was killed?' asked Fiona, her voice breaking.

'I don't remember anyone mentioning death. He simply believed that I might pass you on to friends once I'd tired of you. However, if he can raise the money I assure you he wants you back.'

Edmund continued to stare at his brother in astonishment. 'After what you've told her, how can she possibly go back?'

Alessandro smiled. 'Quite!'

Fiona shook her head. 'Then what will become of me?'

'According to Bethany, you were looking forward to taking control of your own life once you were set free. You'll still be able to do that. Duncan won't be able to force you to stay with him. Now, enough business talk, let's turn our minds back to pleasure. Edmund, how about some nursery games?'

Fiona scarcely heard him. She was trying to imagine what her life would be like out in the world on her own. How could she ever live normally after what the Trimarchi brothers had done to her, she wondered. The sexuality they'd unleashed in her didn't seem as though it would disappear just because she no longer had them around to satisfy it.

'*Will* he raise the money?' she asked abruptly.

Alessandro turned to her. 'I doubt it.'

'Which means you'll decide what happens to me?'

'Yes, but as you've probably been told I'm easily bored. At the moment I find you fascinating. In a few weeks time I might not.'

Fiona felt her cheeks flame. 'Don't worry about that. The last thing I want is to stay here for the rest of my life. I only wondered what you were likely to do with me. I mean, will you let me go free?'

His coal-black eyes clicked over her. 'I might.'

'I'd always look after you,' Edmund said quickly.

Alessandro turned on his brother. 'I don't think you were asked for your opinion, Edmund. If you'd been more successful on your fact-finding mission, we'd know all about Westminster and this conversation wouldn't have been necessary.'

'I went too late,' protested Edmund. 'Bethany knew, but she was gone from here before I learnt that.'

'You mean, Duncan told Bethany about his work!' Fiona couldn't believe it.

'I wouldn't take that as an insult,' said Alessandro slowly. 'It's more likely that he thought she'd accept whatever goes on there more easily than you would have done. Shall we go up to the nursery now?

Fiona got off her chair and walked towards the door. 'I don't understand you,' she said as she drew level with him. 'Sometimes you can be really kind, and at other times . . .'

'Don't try to understand me,' he said shortly. 'I don't even understand myself. Georgina knows that it's best to simply accept me.'

Fiona shook her head. 'I did that with Duncan. I'd never do it again.'

'Certainly if you ever come to choose a second husband you should be much more careful,' agreed Alessandro as he left the room.

The nursery was on the very top floor, next to the bedroom where Bethany and Fiona had been kept at night. It was a large room, and at the far end the roof sloped down so that light only came in from a small window set close to the floor.

The room was littered with toys, but outsize toys. There was a hammock strung along one side of the room, suspended from heavy rings set in the wall; a thin hip-bath like a giant version of the kind used to wash small children in Victorian times and a huge rocking horse, complete with saddle and bridle, its polished surface gleaming in the thin shaft of light from the window.

There were shelves of books, but when Fiona took one down it was full of pictures of erotic Eastern art and she hastily put it back again. Surfaces seemed at first glance to be littered with toys, but they were adult toys. Dildos, vibrators, anal plugs, nipple rings and leather straps were all there, alongside exotic outfits of lace or leather.

'This is where the grown-ups come to play!' laughed Alessandro. The tension she'd sensed in him in the kitchen had vanished now and he looked happy again. 'Would you like to try the rocking horse? It has a very soothing motion, the girls tells me.'

Fiona looked at the horse and nodded. She thought it would be fun to sit on its wide back and feel it moving beneath her. Alessandro nodded in satisfaction. 'Good! First we must get you properly dressed for riding. Edmund, fetch the riding gear.'

Edmund opened a cupboard door and drew out some tight leather boots and what looked like a black leather bra. He also held a small riding crop.

'Bend over and touch your toes,' said Alessandro softly, pressing the palm of his hand against her spine. Fiona bent, and then tried to draw away as she felt him parting her buttocks and remembered what Edmund had done to her when she'd been his slave.

Alessandro simply gripped her tightly round the waist and then Edmund dilated her rectum with lubricated fingers before slipping the now familiar ivory balls inside her, but this time he slid them both in quickly and her muscles immediately tried to expel the invaders in an uncontrollable reflex action. 'Tighten your muscles,' said Alessandro, in a voice that made it clear he expected instant obedience. Fiona struggled to keep the balls inside her, wishing that her body didn't always go into a painful spasm at this kind of intrusion. Finally, the muscles calmed down and she was able to breathe easily again.

'You'll find them most exciting during the ride,' Alessandro assured her. Fiona could imagine only too well that he was telling her the truth. Next the men pulled the boots on her. They were made of leather and gripped her tightly all the way up to the top of her thighs, stopping just an inch below her outer labia. She'd never had her legs tightly encased before and compared with the rest of her nakedness it felt very strange.

The Trimarchi brothers obviously liked it because they kept her standing by the rocking horse and stripped off their clothes, revealing that they were both highly aroused by what they were seeing. Edmund was totally erect, but Alessandro's erection was as yet incomplete. For some reason Fiona found his slowly expanding penis more exciting than the one that was already erect.

'Now for the top half of your body,' said Alessandro. Edmund held out what Fiona could now see wasn't an ordinary bra but two cones joined together by a narrow strip of rubber. There was no back fastening, but from the side of one cone a bulb dangled from the end of a piece of tubing.

Alessandro stroked Fiona's breasts gently for a

moment and then when he felt them start to swell he bent his head and licked them all over so that they were thoroughly moist. Once the whole surface area was damp, Edmund fitted the cones onto them and she felt them gripping her wet skin tightly.

As she grew used to the tight feeling she realised that there were raised bumps inside the cones and they were pressed tightly against her aureoles and nipples.

Alessandro smiled at her. 'Perfect. Now you can mount the horse.'

Fiona put one long, leather-clad leg across the large wooden rocking horse and lifted herself above the saddle. She started to lower herself, but suddenly Alessandro gripped her by the waist and slightly adjusted her position, at the same time as Edmund licked his middle finger, rubbing it quickly between her outer labial lips.

Fiona jerked in surprise, but Alessandro kept her in the air while Edmund continued to work his finger around her inner lips until she felt the familiar, shaming moisture starting to creep out of her vaginal opening. Once that happened, Edmund removed his finger and Alessandro carefully lowered her into the saddle.

It was only then that she realised that set in the middle of the saddle was a two-inch solid leather stem, like a saddle horn, topped by a round knob, and this knob pressed the entrance to her vagina wide open as it slid inside her until she was impaled on the horn.

The rocking horse was sloping very slightly forward, and this meant that Fiona's torso was pulled forward as well, making her more aware of the tightly enclosed breasts and the bumps that were massaging her nipples every time she moved.

The knob of the saddle-horn pressed deeply inside her vagina until she thought that it must brush her cervix, so great was the penetration. At the same time the love balls in her rectum tantalised the numerous nerve endings within that entrance. Alessandro smiled at her flushed face and spread her long chestnut hair around her naked shoulders. 'You look beautiful,' he murmured, and then started to squeeze the bulb that hung from the rubber cones around her breasts.

Immediately some of the air trapped inside the cones was pumped out, creating the start of a vacuum. Fiona felt her breasts expanding, sucked outwards and swelling as the breast area engorged with blood. This meant that the raised bumps of the rubber massaged the tips of her breasts relentlessly and she tingled with electric shocks of arousal.

'Good,' said Alessandro, sliding a hand smoothly down the rounded sweep of her back. 'Now start to ride. Grip the horse with your legs and rock back and forth. It moves very easily.'

Fiona hesitated. If she began to move, the saddle-horn would stimulate her internally while her breasts would continue to expand and the love balls would roll. She wasn't sure she was ready for such stimulation so soon after the morning's excitement. Behind her, Alessandro raised the tiny riding crop and lightly flicked it across her shoulder-blades.

Fiona winced with the shock. It hadn't hurt, but it had stung and she was totally unprepared. 'Ride,' said Alessandro softly. 'We want to see you moving.'

Frantically, Fiona tightened her legs on the rocking horse and she heaved her body back a little. Immediately the knob on the end of the cunningly situated saddle-horn was pulled back too and moved nearer to the front of her vagina, pressing against the top surface of her moist sheath. At the same time her breasts moved and the rubber gripped her closely making her throw back her head as the sparks of pleasure shot through the burgeoning flesh.

'Faster,' said Alessandro dispassionately, and now Fiona began to ride like someone possessed, terrified of where the crop might fall if she disobeyed and the faster

211

she rocked the greater all the sensations grew until they began to merge together.

Her breasts seemed ready to burst as yet more air was expelled from the cups, her vagina was stroked internally by the horn and the leather of the saddle rubbed against her inner lips as her outer ones parted with her growing excitement, while all the time her rectum clenched itself around the tantalising love balls.

The two brothers watched her as she rocked, her hair flying about her face, her head moving forward and back while her eyes closed in order that she might savour the incredible, if frightening, experience to the full.

They let her rock for a long time until they could see the shining dampness of her secretions on the saddle and witnessed also her thrusting breasts so full they looked ready to burst. She was ready, and they knew it.

'Stop!' Alessandro ordered her. Edmund put out a hand to still the rocking horse. As Fiona waited to be helped off, her head hanging down towards the horse's mane, Alessandro took the riding crop, let it hang against the top vertebrae of her spine for a second and then drew it with agonising slowness down the length of her while she shivered and shook from all the frantic pulsations within her. Then, at the base of her spine he lifted the crop and held it above her for one final tortuous second before bringing it down with a whistling sound right between her raised buttocks.

The pulsations ceased. Instead, Fiona's whole body seemed to burst into flames as the pain exploded in her brain and red and white lights danced beneath her closed eyelids while all her muscles contracted in a huge climax that made her legs grip the side of the horse and had her moving shamelessly against the saddle, making the horse move harder and harder within her as she thrust herself down against the pressure of the shiny leather saddle in order to extract the very last ounce of pleasure possible from her clitoris.

The brothers watched her clasping the horse's neck, straining against its back and moaning to herself and they both wanted desperately to take her immediately, there and then on the floor of their 'nursery'. But Edmund couldn't because she wasn't his slave, and Alessandro wanted to wait until she'd been shown the delights of the hammock, and so they both had to restrain themselves and take their pleasure from her abandonment.

Fiona was so lost in the total surrender of her body to unadulterated sexual rapture that she scarcely felt Alessandro lifting her off the joy-inducing saddle-horn. It was only when her feet touched the ground that she realised the ride was over.

'Time for a bath,' Alessandro murmured in her ear, then he lifted her in his arms and carried her down the short flight of stairs to his bathroom. Once there, Edmund filled the tub with steaming hot water, and his brother lowered her into it. 'We let slaves wash themselves!' he said with a laugh. 'Watching is less tiring!'

Still hazy with satisfaction, Fiona indolently soaped herself all over with the bubbles that filled the bath, and then stood up ready to step out and take a towel from the heated rail.

'Wait,' Alessandro said suddenly. She stopped, one foot raised to the edge of the bath. He smiled at her, but she didn't totally trust the smile. 'Step back into the middle of the tub but keep standing up,' he ordered. Fiona complied.

Unseen by her, Edmund had lifted the shower-head from the wall at one end of the bath, and now he pointed it at her unsuspecting back and all at once she was stunned by a fierce spray of freezing cold water cascading along her spine.

As Fiona gasped, Alessandro moved forward and twisted her around so that now it was her breasts and stomach that were beneath the cold water. Her warm flesh shrank from the ice-cold needles, her nipples puckering with the shock of the abrupt change of temperature, but as the water continued to pound against her she felt the blood singing in her veins and slowly she began to glow all over.

As abruptly as it had started, the cold shower stopped. Alessandro lifted Fiona out of the tub and wrapped her in a soft bath towel, then the two brothers rubbed her hard, one working on her back and the other her front. They rubbed and rubbed. Safe within the enfolding towel, Fiona's body was stimulated into warmth again and when the towel was finally removed she stood before them glowing a gentle shade of pink.

Alessandro poured cocoa-butter lotion into his hands and massaged it along her arms, neck, and shoulders, while Edmund did the same for her feet, legs and buttocks. They worked briskly and efficiently, Edmund lifting first one leg and then the other while Alessandro's hands ensured that she never lost her balance. When they were done her whole body gleamed and her skin felt soft and silken.

Just before they went upstairs again, Alessandro carefully spread the lotion over her breasts, gently massaging the rounded curves and working his way up to the nipples which he touched with the lightest of dots, so that they stood sharply erect, shining in the gentle glow of the bathroom lighting.

'Back to the nursery,' he said thickly, desire swelling in him. Fiona felt like purring; now she understood why cats enjoyed being stroked. This kind of physical attention was glorious.

Once in the nursery again, she was led straight to the hammock she'd noticed earlier. It was like a large, strong net with two ropes at each end, both fastened into metal rings set securely in the wall.

'Climb in,' said Alessandro invitingly. 'I think you'll

214

like the rocking motion. Less violent than the horse, but very pleasurable!'

Fiona found this was easier said than done. Every time she tried to scramble in, the net twisted and turned, threatening to hurl her straight out again. In the end, Alessandro lifted her up and laid her flat on her back, the nylon ropes pressing into her spine.

'The secret is to keep still,' he explained. 'If you move around, wriggle or twist, then you'll fall out. Once we start playing, the game keeps going for as long as you stay in the hammock. Once you fall out, it's over!'

Fiona looked up at him, standing naked above her with his erection clearly in evidence. 'What if I want the game to end?'

'Fall out, but I doubt if you'll be in a hurry to finish it.'

Edmund laughed, then told her to lift her head a little. She couldn't look round to see what he was going to do and as soon as her head was raised he slipped the black velet mask over her eyes. 'Just for a short time,' said Alessandro, calmly. 'It will heighten the early sensations.'

One of the brothers pushed the hammock lightly, and Fiona felt it start to sway slowly from side to side. With her eyes covered it was an extraordinary sensation, swaying in pitch blackness with only the feel of the netting against her back and the movement of air across the front of her body.

The two brothers glanced at each other in satisfaction, and Edmund's erection strained tightly upwards, as some of the clear pre-ejaculatory liquid ran from the tip of his glans. Alessandro raised an eyebrow at this lack of control, then went to a nearby cupboard and drew out one of the long ostrich plumes that Fiona had used on Bethany the day the red-head was freed.

As the downy feathers fluttered against her breasts and swept on down the inward curve of her stomach, Fiona gasped and her body automatically jerked, causing the hammock to rock violently. 'Keep still!' Alessandro urged her. She tried to obey but it was difficult to keep from thrusting her hips upwards towards the gorgeous softness of the plumes.

Alessandro swept them up and down her body relentlessly. Her flesh, so quick now to seek satisfaction, began to throb and expand and between her tightly closed legs she felt the familiar sweet throbbing begin. The ripples of gratification ebbed and flowed along her body as she felt herself expanding within her skin until her whole body was tight with longing.

When her breasts were hard and her nipples rigid with sexual tension, Alessandro stopped moving the plume and Edmund removed Fiona's mask. Her mouth was slightly open and she could hear herself panting with desire for some further touch on her tantalised and yearning flesh.

Alessandro looked down, carefully took her knees between his strong hands and spread her legs so that they were hanging over the sides of the hammock. It swung dangerously and she gripped the sides in panic lest she fall out and the game was over too soon.

'You'll be safe as long as you keep absolutely still now,' Alessandro assured her.

'Not that keeping still will be easy,' laughed Edmund, and Fiona wondered what they had in store for her.

Edmund had put some lubricating jelly on the fingers of his right hand, and in full sight of Fiona, he went to the foot of the hammock and reached between her outspread thighs. Fiona couldn't move, couldn't attempt to close her legs because of the danger of the gently swaying net.

Delicately, Edmund let his fingers part Fiona's outer sex lips until the very core of her was exposed to him. Then he spread the jelly all around her fleshy folds, gliding a finger around the crevices and up to the base of her already hardening clitoris. Tenderly he eased back the protective fold of flesh while Fiona held her

216

breath as sharp darts of excitement radiated outwards from where his finger was touching her. She longed to move, to writhe in hedonistic abandonment, but the hammock, chosen so diabolically by Alessandro, prevented her from indulging herself and instead she had to keep perfectly still, only the sudden stiffening of her spine betraying her inward battle.

Edmund loved the feel of her opening flesh. He wished that he could spend longer there, inserting a finger into her opening and titillating the nerve endings but Alessandro was watching him and he was only allowed to do what they had agreed beforehand.

When his fingers withdrew, Fiona's flesh was throbbing and exposed to the air but she couldn't even tighten her thighs to ease the ache he'd caused. Briefly, she tightened her internal muscles, and was rewarded with a flash of searing excitement that made her gasp, and the hammock tipped.

Alessandro guessed what she'd done and tweaked one of her engorged nipples. 'Leave the pleasuring to us!' he said sternly. At the flash of pain, Fiona gave a tiny cry, startled to realise that it had nearly precipitated her climax and she fought to quell her straining abdominal muscles as they began to gather themselves for a blissful spasm of satisfaction.

At last she managed to control herself and the hammock was still again. Now it was Alessandro's turn to stand close to her. He was level with her waist and bent towards her parted thighs, taking care not to touch her leg, which was hanging naked over the side.

In his hand he held a tiny piece of silk cord. He drew it with infinite tenderness down her abdomen, letting it trail softly over her gleaming skin and then Fiona realised that he was going to keep it moving until it touched the pulsating flesh of her inner lips and swollen clitoris and she tensed in readiness for the sensations her fevered imagination was already conjuring up.

Alessandro smiled at the awareness in her eyes and

then he lifted his hand and let the tip of the cord hang between her outspread thighs for a moment, delighting in the look of straining anticipation on her face. At last his hand began to descend, and then the soft end of the cord teased its way over the flesh, so well lubricated by Edmund, and Fiona knew that the game was nearly over.

She fought to contain herself as the cord teased and tantalised her. It brushed the stem of her clitoris, moved lower along the channels of her inner lips and even tormented the entrance to her vagina, swirling round in tiny circles and then up again towards the still expanding clitoris.

Fiona had never felt such intense sensations of approaching ecstasy. Her hips seemed to have a mind of their own, refusing to be stilled and jerking in tiny uncontrollable movements despite her efforts to keep motionless. Electric currents were being triggered by every caress of the cord, currents of almost unbearable pleasure that lanced through her whole body, seeming to tug at her swollen nipples and drawing her stomach yet further in.

Alessandro let the cord dance over her most sensitive areas and he heard her despairing moans as she felt the inexorable rise towards her climax, but he knew that she longed to extend her release as long as possible. He enjoyed watching her voluptuous delight in her body's responses, and drew the cord along the side of her clitoris making Fiona scream with excitement, although she still remained motionless.

Edmund swallowed hard. He hadn't expected her to last so long and his testicles were aching with a need for release, but still Fiona fought to keep her arousal at this high level, which was almost driving her out of her mind with excitement.

Finally Alessandro's own need to possess her made him take the final step to topple her into orgasm. He already knew from their times together that she was

218

acutely sensitive around the opening of her urethra and he let the cord trail over the flesh beneath then drew it so near the opening that tiny fragments of the silk actually touched the tiny entrance and immediately Fiona was lost.

Her body gathered itself together in a frantic bunching of overwrought nerve endings. Then she felt as though a rocket had exploded within her as a cascade of contractions swamped her entire body and her over-engorged pelvic area and vulva finally gained their long-sought release.

There was nothing Fiona could do to control her body's frantic spasms and as her hips heaved and she twisted from side to side the hammock spun out of control, trapped her for a moment and then tipped her unceremoniously onto the nursery floor where she lay gasping and jerking as the incredible sensations died slowly away.

Alessandro didn't wait for her final contractions to cease. He couldn't. Instead he dragged her up and pushed her over to the old-fashioned chest of drawers close at hand. Almost roughly he pushed at her arms until they were resting on the top and she was bent at the waist, then he drove into her like a man possessed, thrusting at her still pulsating body, his hands round her waist so that he could move her as he wished.

Edmund, who had been expecting to share her, was forced to watch his brother thrusting in and out of Fiona, his eyes closed and his mouth set in a tight line as he surged towards his climax.

Fiona, who had come down from her own orgasm, found her body being pounded by Alessandro's thick, hard rod and it was almost too much to feel herself filled by him after such extended stimulation, but she was his slave and had no choice.

This time Alessandro was managing to last as long as he'd always wanted to last and he continued to thrust in and out of her warm, moist vagina as he ascended towards his own peak. 'Tighten your muscles round me,' he whispered against her ear, and the exhausted Fiona tried her hardest to do as he asked.

Her contractions were weak and spasmodic, but the very fact that she was doing as he asked and that he could feel her trying to milk him triggered Alessandro's ejaculation. With a low moan he finally spurted his fluid into her, his hips now twitching as uncontrollably as hers had done earlier, until finally he too was finished.

Edmund watched Alessandro slump against Fiona's back. 'What about me?' he asked hoarsely.

'You'll have to wait for Tanya to get back,' said Alessandro.

'That's not fair!' protested Edmund.

'She's mine,' muttered Alessandro and his look was so uncompromising that Edmund, who knew his brother well, didn't attempt to argue any more but instead left the room hoping desperately that Tanya's flight wouldn't be delayed.

For a long time Alessandro remained slumped against Fiona, and then he took her in his arms and turned her so that they were pressed against each other, face to face. He kissed the tip of her nose. 'We must play that again some time,' he whispered and for the first time, Fiona put her arms around him and hugged him, totally forgetting that she was his prisoner as she was overcome by a wave of pure love.

Chapter Thirteen

When Fiona was dressed and back in her own room that evening, Alessandro brought her dinner on a tray. She looked at him shyly, wondering why it was that she suddenly felt different about him. She realised that at some point in the day she had totally given herself over to him, trusting him to make sure she enjoyed herself and letting him show her the extent to which it was possible to go in pursuit of pleasure.

She had never felt anything like this for Duncan. There had been awkwardness between them on their wedding night, because she'd been so anxious to please him, but she'd never felt shy. The shyness was simply a result of her increasing depth of feeling for Alessandro, a feeling of which she was too ashamed to confess. In any case, she didn't think he would be interested in the way she felt. He enjoyed making love to her, and she knew that her responses delighted him, but emotionally she doubted if she had touched him any more than his other women had done.

Alessandro watched her and wondered if he could bear to let her go. He had never been so obsessed with a woman before. Georgina excited him, and could still give him pleasure in ways that he doubted Fiona would

221

ever come to learn, but she had never seemed vulnerable. Duncan's wife, by trusting him so totally, had made herself vulnerable, and now he wanted to keep her safe and perhaps later lead her a little further along paths of sensuality as yet unexplored. At this moment though, he simply wanted to hold her, and he was badly shaken by his feelings.

'I've got a letter for you,' he said abruptly, aware that his voice sounded harsh and trying to soften it. 'Your husband sent it with the money.'

Fiona glanced at him. 'The money that freed Bethany you mean?' Alessandro nodded. 'Why didn't you give it to me before?'

'I thought it might upset you.'

'And now?' she asked.

'Now I think you're probably strong enough to cope with it.'

'I take it you know the contents?' Fiona asked.

Alessandro nodded. 'I read it, in case it was some kind of escape plan for you.'

Fiona laughed bitterly. 'I don't think Duncan's that anxious to get me back, do you?' Then she opened the envelope and saw the familiar writing. Her eyes scanned the page before she let the note drop to the floor. Her eyes were blank, Alessandro could learn nothing from them. He picked up the note and re-read it.

'My dear Fiona,
As you now know, Bethany is very important to me, but she can never take your place as my wife. She is simply the perfect mistress. As soon as I can raise the rest of the money you will be freed. After your ordeal at the hands of the Trimarchi brothers you may well feel more able to be the kind of wife I need, and then Bethany can live with us permanently. This would be the ideal arrangement as far as I'm concerned. I've told your parents you're abroad on holiday so they have not been

222

alarmed by your absence. I regret what has happened,
but if you had done as I asked on the night of the dinner
party I am sure Alessandro Trimarchi would have come
to an agreement with me that would not have entailed
such unpleasantness.

Be patient.

Duncan.'

'What does he mean about the dinner party?' Alessandro asked.

Fiona sighed. 'That night you came to our house, I was meant to seduce you. Duncan believed that then you wouldn't call in the money.'

The corners of Alessandro's mouth lifted. 'I don't remember you attempting even a small seduction scene!'

'No, well I was going to try, it wasn't the first time I'd had to do such a thing and you were better looking than any of the others had been. Unfortunately, I arrived too late. You were already busy with Georgina, in Duncan's study.'

Now Alessandro laughed. 'So that's what you were doing there! You came to offer up your all for Duncan's sake and instead stayed to watch me with Georgina!'

'I didn't stay until the end. I'd never seen anyone behaving the way you were that night, and I couldn't seem to move. It was incredibly embarrassing, and it also made me realise how inadequate I was.'

'Inadequate?' queried Alessandro.

Fiona nodded. 'I could see that Georgina was having a wonderful time. You were giving her such pleasure, even if it was on my husband's desk top, and I'd never been able to let my body surrender to sexual excitement in that way. I realised you wouldn't be interested in someone like me at any time, let alone straight after a scene like that.'

'I'd have needed a short break,' agreed Alessandro, still smiling.

223

Fiona's eyes grew cold. 'Duncan was furious. That night he dragged me off to Bethany's room and made me take part in what I thought was a threesome designed purely for his pleasure. It was only after we were brought here that I realised she was in on it too.'

'I know. Bethany told us all about that. I'm sorry if I caused it to happen. Had I known you were going to try and seduce me, I think I'd have let Georgina wait a little longer!'

Fiona lifted her chin and looked challengingly at him. 'I'd never have succeeded in seducing you, would I? Be honest. I wasn't your type.'

'I don't have a type,' said Alessandro slowly. 'I find that there are a lot of women I want to make love to, but they don't have anything in common as far as I'm aware.'

'How about sophistication?' suggested Fiona. 'Wasn't that an important qualification?'

Alessandro hesitated. 'Perhaps it was once. It isn't any more. Now I realise how exciting it is to introduce someone to new pleasures.'

Fiona didn't know what to say. 'Have you heard from my husband again?' she asked at last.

'No.'

'Then what happens to me?'

'In the short-term, you sleep well tonight and tomorrow you spend the day with Georgina.' Alessandro saw Fiona's face turn pale. 'I know you aren't looking forward to that, but Georgina is an experienced sensualist. You will find unexpected enjoyment in the course of the day.'

'I hope you're right,' said Fiona dryly. 'I have a feeling that there might be other less pleasant surprises in store as well.'

Alessandro shrugged. 'I've no idea. I shall check Georgina's programme with her of course, but providing it's not too extreme it's up to her how she uses you.'

'Who has me after Georgina?'

Alessandro glanced away from her to look out of the tiny window at the slowly darkening night sky. 'No one. She's the last slave-owner. After that we have to decide your fate.'

At his words Fiona felt a fresh shiver of fear. 'You mean, Duncan will have run out of time?'

'Yes.'

She looked at his dark features, half hidden now. 'The decision will be yours, really, won't it?'

'I suppose it will. There's no point in discussing it further tonight. Once tomorrow has passed it will be time enough. Try and eat your meal. I'm sure you'll sleep well. Today hasn't been too much of an ordeal, has it?'

Now he was looking directly at her again, and she felt a surge of desire for the feel of his body close to hers and the brief comfort of his embrace. 'No,' she whispered. 'Today was very special.'

His hard features relaxed and he nodded in satisfaction. 'I'm please to hear it. Goodnight.'

The door had closed behind him before Fiona gained enough control of her voice to respond.

Georgina didn't have to wake Fiona the next morning. She had been sleepless most of the night, certain that the day which lay ahead of her would not be as pleasurable as the one that had just passed.

'I hope this prompt awakening means you're full of energy,' remarked Georgina, unfastening Fiona from the bed. 'There's no need to dress. I've got different things for you to wear in the bedroom.'

Fiona looked at Alessandro's long-time mistress. Today she was wearing a pair of black and red shorts, cut high on the thigh, and a skimpy yellow T-shirt with thin shoulder straps. There was no trace of the smart business woman in the clothes she was wearing, but her legs were tanned and Fiona realised that even this outfit looked right on Georgina. She was one of those women who could wear anything and get away with it.

'Admiring my figure?' asked Georgina with a laugh. 'Don't worry, you'll see it more closely before the day's out. We should have an interesting girls's day together. So much more fun when the men are out I always think!' She laughed, and Fiona's heart sank. If both Alesssandro and Edmund were away then Georgina could do exactly as she pleased without fear of interruption.

'You don't like me, do you?' Fiona said boldly.

Georgina was clearly taken by surprise. 'I hardly know you, Fiona.'

'That's no answer.'

Georgina ran her fingers through her short, sleeked back hair. 'I suppose it isn't. Let's just say, I'll be happier when you've gone.'

'I didn't ask to come here.'

'Nor to be my slave! Enough talking. Follow me. No, wait, I'll lead you upstairs.' With a smile, Georgina reached into the pockets of her shorts and drew out a thin gold chain with a ring on each end. Then she leant towards Fiona and slowly putting out her tongue began to lick at the other woman's breasts.

Fiona was taken by surprise and tried to draw back. 'Stay still,' ordered Georgina angrily, her tongue encircling each of the nipples in turn. As they came to erection she slid the rings around them, fastening them so tightly that Fiona winced. Now her nipples were firmly imprisoned and between them hung the fine gold chain.

'You respond quickly,' Georgina remarked. 'How well everyone's done their work. Come along then, off we go.' With that she reached out and tugged on the slender chain. Fiona's nipples stabbed with darts of pain and her breasts tensed as she hurriedly followed Georgina out of the room.

All the way up the stairs Georgina had the chain pulled as tight as she could without breaking it and

Fiona's nipples were kept fully extended. The heavy tugging sensation, so painful at first, began to feel strangely pleasurable after a short time and to her shame Fiona could feel her breasts swelling with the stimulation.

Once in the bedroom, Georgina glanced at Fiona with satisfaction. 'It seems you're not averse to a little discomfort. How very interesting. That was something Alessandro didn't tell me about you.'

'I don't like pain,' said Fiona quickly.

'I said discomfort. Not that pain is very far away from that, but we'll have to see how the day goes. Now, I want you to put these clothes on.'

Fiona looked towards a pile of black garments lying in a pile on the stool in front of Georgina's dressing table. 'Hurry up,' said Georgina impatiently, and at the same time she unfastened the nipple rings and drew off the leading chain. 'This will get in the way right now. We'll play with it again later if necessary.'

Fiona began to pick up the clothes. There was a thick leather choker with metal eyelets from which interlocked double rings were suspended, a black leather halter-top bra with a strap which went across the top of the breasts, with very low cut sides, and a pair of tight black leather pants studded with metal round the waistband. She struggled into the bra and when Georgina fastened it behind her she saw that her breasts were almost fully exposed except for the nipples.

The choker also fastened at the back, and this gripped Fiona firmly round the throat while the metal rings hung down to where the cross-bar of the strange halter-type top was fastened over her flesh. They felt cold and she shuddered when they first touched her.

'Now for the panties,' murmured Georgina. 'First though, lie on your back on the bed. There's something that goes inside them. Something you'll like a lot, to begin with.'

Fiona stretched herself nervously on the bed and felt

Georgina's hands easing her ankles apart. 'I do know what I'm doing,' she assured her trembling slave. 'Even if you don't believe this, I happen to be a very good lover and if you'll only give yourself over to me you'll have an exciting day. If you resist, it won't be quite as enjoyable for you.'

'What's that?' asked Fiona as she felt Georgina pressing something round between the tops of her thighs.

'It's a very special vibrator. It fits over your mound and I control it from this little switch that's attached to the wire. Not only does it vibrate, it also gets warm and there are feathers all round the rim of the device which will tickle your outer labia and the creases of your thighs. Delicious, don't you think?'

Fiona didn't know. 'Do I hold it in place?' she asked apprehensively.

'Of course not! It fits inside the leather panties. They hold it firmly against you whether you want it there or not, and it's up to me how hard it vibrates and how warm it gets. There, it seems to be covering you nicely. Now I'll pull the panties up.'

Fiona felt the leather panties being eased up her legs and she raised her hips so that Georgina could pull them up to her waist. Once they were in position she ordered Fiona to stand. Then Georgina was in front of Fiona, holding the small white control box in her hand, one finger poised above a red button. She smiled coldly at the shaking Fiona. 'I expect you'd like to be warmed up first, wouldn't you?' Fiona knew she wasn't expected to answer. Instead she remained standing in front of her mistress for the day and waited. Georgina let her finger press on the button, and almost at once a warm glow began to suffuse Fiona's entire pubic mound. It was soothing and made her legs relax while at the very outer edges of her vulva the feathers began to move slowly, tickling softly in the tender creases.

Georgina watched at Fiona's face gradually grew warm with excited pleasure. When she judged that the other woman had relaxed into the sensations, she pressed the second button and the gadget began to vibrate inside the tight pants. Now the warmth was diffused and as her flesh-lips were moved by the vibrations the feathers started to tickle more intimate areas of Fiona's inner labia. She twitched restlessly and at once Georgina reached out and tugged hard on one of the metal rings suspended from the choker round her neck.

This harsh movement brought Fiona's head down with a jerk and made the back of her neck ache. 'You are not to move without permission,' said Georgina softly. 'Every time you do I shall punish you, either like that or with this.' She picked up a tiny whip that was lying on the stool behind her. 'Have you ever been whipped?' she added casually.

Fiona shook her head, and at once the metal rings banged heavily against her skin again, reminding her of her servitude. 'Good, that will be another fresh experience for you. Now, how do you like my little toy?'

As she asked the question, Georgina increased both the intensity of the heat and the speed of the vibrations so that suddenly the sensations were all doubled and Fiona's legs felt as though they'd cramp with the effort of keeping still as her thighs longed to move and alter the position of the fiendish device so inexorably stimulating her.

'How do you like it?' repeated Georgina, her own nipples sticking out through the fabric of her T-shirt in her excitement at the other woman's growing arousal.

'It's too intense!' Fiona gasped. 'It isn't nice any more, it's painful.'

'Nonsense,' it's simply different. You must be enjoying it, your breasts are swelling.'

Fiona could feel that they were. The black leather cups, so carefully designed, ensured that as her breasts swelled they thrust upwards and she could feel her nipples, already inflamed by the nipple rings earlier, brushing against the leather that was trapping them.

With her free hand that still held the whip, Georgina reached out and stroked across the top of the soft flesh of the round globes. Her touch was startlingly delicate and Fiona's breasts responded, filling the tight cups yet more fully and the ends of her breasts began to tremble which set the rings from her collar moving again.

'Naughty!' reproved Georgina, and all at once she drew back her hand and flicked the whip across the flesh of the upper breasts where she had just been stroking. Fiona gasped at the red-hot flash of pain and when she did so, Georgina tugged at the rings again, bringing her head down hard. 'Be silent!' Fiona closed her lips against another cry, but she could see the thin red line across her tender skin.

'You may lift your head again,' murmured Georgina. Fiona did, and then Georgina turned down the heat and the vibrations of the pad, which was still pressing relentlessly against Fiona's pubic hair and this time the ripples of excitement and the tickling provocation of the feathers joined with the soft heat of the pad to provide an irrresistible combination.

Without any warning at all Fiona's orgasm was triggered and her whole body shuddered as waves of excitement rolled up her, while Georgina watched the heaving flesh and saw Fiona's terrified eyes as she shook helplessly in the grips of undesired sexual passion.

When the orgasm was over, Georgina turned off the vibrator. 'I don't remember saying you could have a climax yet,' she said casually. 'Get yourself undressed at once. You'll have to be punished. You can only have pleasure when I say so.'

With shaking hands, Fiona managed to unclasp the leather halter, and it only took her a couple of minutes to step out of the panties and remove the vibrator pad with its circles of feathers. She put the clothes back on the stool, but couldn't remove the collar herself.

Georgina glanced at it. 'You can leave that on. It

marks you as a slave, and I find it erotic to look at.'
Fiona stood silently waiting for whatever her punishment was to be.

'Lie across the stool,' said Georgina. 'Face downwards of course. I'm going to attend to the one area I've been neglecting.'

Fiona tensed her buttocks and immediately felt the sting of the whip across them. She cried out again, her legs jerking helplessly. This time the pain was brief, quickly melting into a deliciously warm feeling that was distinctly pleasurable, so that without realising it she squirmed against the stool. Georgina saw and smiled to herself.

Then Fiona's buttocks were parted by the other woman's slim fingers and something cold was spread between them. The cold made the rim of her rectum contract and as it contracted, Georgina pushed at it with the tapered end of an anal vibrator. It was covered with flesh-like latex and had a T-shaped base to ensure it stayed in place.

'Push down as though having a bowel motion,' she said coolly. Fiona ignored her, and Georgina began to get impatient. 'If you don't it will hurt. There's no point in trying to be a martyr. You'll enjoy this if you do as I say.'

Fiona doubted it, but feeling utterly humiliated she bore down, and at once the head of the object slid inside her back opening, slowly easing its way in until she could feel its increasing thickness as it was drawn inside her.

Just when she felt she couldn't possibly take any more, the T-shaped base came to rest against her flesh and she knew that it was all inside. Now Georgina switched it on and it started to vibrate softly inside Fiona. Her highly sensitive inner walls once again caused her to cramp internally, but Georgina was already sitting beneath Fiona's hanging breasts and she took each of them in her mouth in turn, nipping at the

231

reddened points with her sharp teeth and then salving them with her tongue. The sensations were delicious, and combined with the pulsations of the anal vibrator Fiona's body quickly began to gather itself together for more gratification.

Georgina moved to the side of the stool, leaving Fiona's damp breasts to cool in the air. She slid a hand beneath her slave's stomach and pressed on it, feeling the throbbing flesh beneath her. 'Do you want to come?' she asked softly. 'Does it feel as though you'll explode soon? Tell me how you feel?'

Fiona's voice was low and scarcely audible. 'I feel tight,' she whispered. 'My skin's a size too small and yet I keep expanding. There are tingles deep inside me and I can feel the blood beating in my ears.'

'Very good,' said Georgina with satisfaction. 'Now, tell me how this makes you feel,' and she slid her hand lower, so that her fingers could pull on the skin where Fiona's pubic hair began, and as it moved her clitoral hood was moved as well and the clitoris indirectly stimulated.

Fiona's whole body threatened to burst with pressure. 'Please, let me come!' she begged Georgina.

'First, tell me how it feels,' Georgina replied, her fingers continuing to massage the flesh, and feeling the rippling contractions beneath the heel of her hand she knew that Fiona was poised right on the edge of her climax.

'There's a pulse beating quicker and quicker below your hand,' Fiona cried. 'I can't control it, it's got a life of its own. Please, either keep your hand still or tell me I can come.'

'Do your breasts ache?' asked Georgina, moving her free hand round to grip one of the globes that was straining for some kind of contact.

'Yes, especially the nipples. Please, Georgina, do something!' Fiona was screaming now, knowing that the explosion was about to happen.

232

'I will,' Georgina promised. Her left hand gripped the nipple tightly between her fingers, the heel of her hand pressed hard just above Fiona's pubic bone and her fingers moved even more rapidly around her pubic hair while inside her rectum the anal vibrator continued its ceaseless arousal.

'Now you can come,' whispered Georgina, and immediately Fiona's body was torn by a racking orgasm that ripped through her, leaving her weak with exhaustion. Georgina stared at the perspiration that beaded the other woman's spine and despite her good intentions couldn't resist a moment of fierce hatred.

This was the first woman ever to have threatened her relationship with Alessandro. Over the past few days he'd become increasingly distant, and their sexual couplings, while wild and streaked with the dark pain she adored, had seemed almost mechanical. There had been little joy on Alessandro's face during their times together, simply the look of a man taking pleasure because it was available. Somehow, Fiona must be banished, but she had no idea how to do it.

She stripped off her own clothes, then the two women went to the bed where Georgina lay back with her arms at her sides and her legs apart. 'Bring me to orgasm with your mouth alone,' she said languidly.

Fiona stared down at the woman she considered, ridiculously she knew, to be her rival. She was aching all over, her labia felt hot and uncomfortable from the vibrator, her breasts burned from the treatment they'd been receiving and her rectum could still feel phantom vibrations although the pulsating device had been removed.

All her exhausted body wanted was rest, and yet she knew that she had to do as she was bid, and do it well because everyone who used her reported back to Alessandro and she was determined that none of them would defeat her.

Slowly, she began to lick at the highly sensitive flesh

beneath Georgina's arms. She worked on this for some time, until the other woman's breasts were hard and tight, the tiny almost child-like nipples pointing upwards to the ceiling and then she moved to them, trailing the tip of her tongue across them in a leisurely fashion refusing to hurry even when Georgina's flesh quivered.

Georgina was amazed at how skilfully Fiona worked on her. She travelled down her stomach, teased at the curves of her waist, lingered above her pubic hair, then sucked and bit around her knees and thighs for unendurable minutes before finally touching the edges of her outer sex-lips.

Fiona took Georgina's instructions literally and didn't even use her hands to part her labia, instead she darted between them with the tip of her tongue, roaming up and down the narrow band of moist inner flesh until the larger lips flattened outwards with arousal leaving Georgina totally exposed at last.

Now Fiona was merciless. She jabbed and flicked alternately; never keeping the pressure the same and never remaining in one spot long enough to trigger Georgina's climax while her mistress sobbed with ecstasy at what was happening to her.

No one, not even Alessandro, had ever been able to keep her at this level of arousal for so long and she squirmed and pressed upwards in a frenzy of excitement while Fiona's tongue moved with her, refusing to be forced into anything.

Georgina felt the tongue invade her vagina, pushing in hard and then flicking against her inner walls. She loved it, but she needed it to touch her clitoris in order to finally come and this movement Fiona delayed. She only moved upwards when Georgina in despair at her own weakness, reached down and tugged on her slave's collar.

At this reminder of her subservience, Fiona moved to the swollen but covered button that could finally release

Georgina's pent-up passion. She remembered what she enjoyed herself and drew her tongue down one side of the stem of the clitoris. She was rewarded by the helpless jerking of Georgina's hips as her climax drew nearer.

Fiona waited a second, lifting her head to draw out the suspense, and then she lowered it again and let the end of her tongue drum in rapid movements against the base of the clitoris making all of Georgina's nerve endings leap at this controlled display of sensual knowledge until she at last spiralled upwards towards the glorious moment when everything burst. Her entire body went rigid as the backs of her heels and head pressed against the bed while her body arched in a bow and she took her final pleasure in silent ecstasy.

When the orgasm was over, Georgina's body fell flat on the bed again and Fiona waited kneeling between her legs. At last, Georgina propped herself up on her elbows. 'You did that well,' she admitted grudgingly. 'Come and lie here in my place. I want to see how you feel between your legs.'

Fiona knew how she felt; burning hot, over-stimulated and yet again sticky with her own lubrications because arousing Georgina had aroused her too. Georgina examined her between her legs almost dispassionately, like a gynaecologist, then let Fiona's hot outer flesh-lips close again and ran her hands over the rest of her body, turning her on her side to enable her to slip a finger between Fiona's buttocks and test her flesh there as well.

'You need treatment,' she said, a gurgle of laughter in her voice, then disappeared into the adjoining dressing room. There she filled a bucket with cubes of ice and then brought them back into the bedroom. Fiona was now propped up and watching her.

'This should cool you down,' said Georgina. 'I think you'll like that, don't you?'

Fiona had no idea, but her throbbing flesh certainly

wanted something to ease the heat. Carefully Georgina took an ice-cube in her mouth and then she slid a cushion beneath Fiona's hips and parted her raised labia. 'Bear down again,' she instructed Fiona. 'I want your vaginal entrance to open.'

Fiona pressed down, but this didn't seem to satisfy Georgina who reached for her whip and flicked at the inner thighs of her slave, leaving another red line to burn and melt into a strange pleasure-pain that was new to the other woman.

'Not good enough. Never mind, I'll do it myself.' Now her hands were opening up Fiona's love channel, and once she was holding it wide open she lowered her head and transferred the ice cube from her mouth into Fiona's vagina, pushing it deep within her with her tongue.

Fiona gasped at the sudden coolness within her, but Georgina had only just begun and soon there were four ice cubes within Fiona, all melting slowly with the heat of her front passage and the water mingled with her juices as it seeped slowly out of the now closed entrance.

After that, Fiona was turned on her side and her knees drawn up to her chest so that Georgina could insert ice cubes into her rectum. This was something that Fiona felt she could hardly bear, the ice cold intrusion into such a tender and abused spot, and yet once the cubes were inside her their coolness gave her some moments of respite from the burning she'd been experiencing until the cold caused her bowels to cramp painfully and she tried to expel the cubes.

'You can't do that!' laughed Georgina. 'You have to wait for them to melt. Just relax. In a moment it will feel good again.'

Fiona waited, hoping against hope that Georgina was telling the truth, and finally her bowels settled and the cool pleasure was there again, combining with the cool trickling sensation within her front passage.

Now she was put on her back once more, and then Georgina sucked on an ice cube, removed it from her mouth and closed her ice-cold lips and tongue around Fiona's burning breasts, drawing each aureole into her mouth in turn and enjoying the instinctive contracting of the flesh that always followed.

Fiona had never imagined experiencing such contrasting feelings as the heat of her earlier arousal and now this cold dampness of the ice treatment, but it was undeniably luxurious and she found that she was relishing this incredible form of arousal.

After a time, Georgina made her stand sideways in front of a full-length mirror, and watch as water seeped from both her front and back passages while Georgina continued to suck on her breasts with an ice-cold mouth.

Only when the ice-cubes had melted away did Georgina allow Fiona to move, and suddenly the expression on her face was less than kind. 'Are you cold now?' she asked agreeably.

Fiona nodded.

'Then I must warm you up. Stand with your back to one of the bedposts and slip your hands into the rings near the top. They're there for when Alessandro and I play this game.'

Fiona obeyed, wondering what was about to happen. Georgina walked to her dressing table and drew out what looked like a leather strap with a split end. 'This is a tawse,' she explained. 'When it strikes your flesh it makes a very loud cracking sound, but it doesn't hurt as much as you might expect. It also has a very warm effect on the skin, which is why I think you were right to ask for it.'

'I didn't!' gasped Fiona. 'I only agreed that I was cold.'

'Really? I could have sworn you asked me to warm you up. That's what I shall tell Alessandro if he asks, and I advise you to agree. That's if you don't enjoy the experience, but I have a feeling that, despite yourself, you will.'

She drew the tawse up from between Fiona's legs, circled her breasts caressingly with it and then lifted it in the air and struck her across the abdomen. The cracking sound made Fiona scream with fright even before her body had time to register the blow. When it did she felt as though she'd been burned and tried to twist away from the next blow, which meant that it fell across her right hip where there was little flesh to protect her.

'Keep still,' Georgina said pleasantly. 'I'm accurate and you won't get damaged if you stand in one place.' Then she began to strike Fiona a number of light but stinging blows across her breasts, thighs and finally between her legs leaving a pattern of cross-crossed scarlet lines all over Fiona's body.

At first there was nothing but pain, but as the tawse went on falling against her, Fione knew that once more the pain was turning to excited hot arousal and she began to burn with a sexual fever she would never have imagined possible so that when she moved her hips it was not from the pain but from her burgeoning excitement.

Georgina knew the difference the moment it occurred. She sensed the exact instant when the pain turned to pleasure and she felt like screaming with frustration. This was something Alessandro liked, something that she'd felt sure Fiona would hate unless introduced to it gradually and only by him. To find that she was already so highly tuned that it had been possible for her to learn the joys of pain so easily was totally disheartening and there was nothing left for Georgina to do.

Reluctantly, she threw the tawse down, then moved her hand between Fiona's thighs, her fingers quickly locating the tight bud of pleasure and as she moved her fingers in rapid circles Fiona's body was racked by yet another climax and she shuddered, her wrists straining against the rings that held her until at last she slumped against the bedpost, her eyes closed.

It was then that Georgina was struck by a brilliant idea. She reached up, undid the rings and pulled Fiona into the middle of the room. 'Listen to me,' she said urgently. 'You don't want to stay here. Think what's happening to you. If you could have seen yourself then you would have been shocked. Is this the way you want to live from now on?'

Fiona stared uncomprehendingly at her. All she wanted right now was sleep.

'You're my slave, yes?' continued Georgina. Fiona nodded. 'And you have to do anything I say?'

'Yes,' murmured Fiona.

Georgina smiled. 'Then I give you your freedom. You can go.'

Fiona blinked. She didn't understand. 'I can do what?'

'You can leave here. I'll find you some clothes and drive you to the nearest station. I can give you enough money to buy a ticket back to London, and then you can go back to your husband or simply vanish without trace. It doesn't matter what you do. You'll be free, and that's what counts, isn't it?'

The two women stared at each other. Georgina, frantic for Fiona to go before Alessandro returned, and Fiona terrified of walking away from the house into an uncertain future without even a chance of seeing Alessandro for one last time.

'I don't know if I want to go,' she said slowly.

Georgina smiled. 'The choice isn't yours to make. You belong to me and I'm setting you free.'

Chapter Fourteen

*L*ess than half an hour after Georgina's command, Fiona was standing fully dressed in her bedroom, waiting for Alessandro's mistress to bring her a bag containing overnight toiletries and money. She wondered where on earth she was going to go. The Mayfair house that she'd shared with Duncan was out of the question. Bethany was almost certainly living there, and in any case she didn't want to set eyes on her husband ever again.

Briefly she considered going to Cornwall. But if she turned up on her parents' doorstep like this, with virtually no luggage and no sign of a tan from her supposed holiday they'd guess that something was very wrong and her father would probably demand an explanation, then go after Duncan himself. He would be no match for the astute businessman, and Fiona couldn't bear to think of bringing another disaster down on her parents at this late stage in their lives.

She racked her brains to think of some friend she could flee to, but there had only ever been Bethany. Once she was married, Duncan had slowly weaned her away from her other girlfriends and she no longer knew whether they were married or single, let alone where they lived.

She had no one. Nowhere to go, and not a single person who would welcome her into their home. The realisation was shattering. She wanted to cry, but with Georgina about to appear again she wouldn't allow herself that luxury. Neither would she think about Alessandro, and how much she needed him. From now on she vowed never to think about him at all. She'd had all the pain she could stand. Thinking about the way she'd felt in his arms, the glorious revelation of her own sexuality that he'd helped her uncover and the moments when she'd been certain that she'd seen love as well as desire in his eyes, would only stop her rebuilding her life. Just the same she wished with all her heart that she could see him once more before she left.

Georgina hurried into the room. 'Here you are. I've put in everything you could possibly need, including a sexy nightie! Come on, I'll bring my car round to the front door.'

'And why would you need to do that?' asked a deep voice from the doorway.

Gerogina's expression changed from excited triumph to shock and she spun round to face her Italian lover. 'What are you doing here? You said you wouldn't be home until eight tonight.'

He glanced at Fiona, fully dressed and clutching the overnight bag. 'I was worried. What's going on here? Has Duncan paid while I've been gone?'

'No,' said Georgina shortly.

'Then why is Fiona leaving?'

'Because I told her to. She's still mine, remember? Mine until six o'clock tonight. If I remember my history lessons correctly, slave owners could grant slaves their freedom if they felt they'd earnt it. Well, Fiona earnt it.'

'What did you do to deserve such an honour?' Alessandro asked the silent Fiona.

She shrugged her shoulders. 'I've no idea.'

'What does it matter?' demanded Georgina. 'She's

241

mine and I can do what I like. Providing she's gone from here by six there's nothing you can do, and that gives me another twenty minutes.'

She went to brush by Alessandro who caught hold of her arm, gripping it tightly until she winced. 'Don't be so ridiculous. Fiona isn't yours! This business of owning her was just a game, another way of teaching her about the joys of sex. You know that as well as I do. How dare you try and set her free behind my back? She's a valuable hostage.'

'No she isn't!' shouted Georgina furiously. 'She's totally useless because Duncan doesn't care if he gets her back or not. He'd rather hang onto his antique manufacturing business for gullible foreigners than pay to have his wife released, so what's the point in keeping her any longer?'

'Are you talking about his Westminster company?' asked Alessandro in a dangerously low voice.

Georgina tried to wrench herself free of his grip but failed. 'Yes, of course I am.'

'I've been trying to find out about that for days. How long have you known what went on there?'

'I heard yesterday. One of his ex-directors applied to the magazine for a job in the home design section and I managed to worm it out of him then.'

'Very commendable. Why didn't you tell me last night?'

'Because you weren't interested in listening to me last night, your head was too full of her!' retorted Georgina, pointing at Fiona who was still standing by the bed.

Alessandro released Georgina's arm, and she rubbed at the place where his fingers had dug into her. 'I see, so that's the real truth of all this. You're jealous of Fiona.'

Georgina's eyes were bright with temper. 'Yes, I am. When she came here she was just Duncan's wife. You wanted your money back, and she was your hostage, but it soon changed. We weren't allowed to upset her

242

feelings by reminding her of how Duncan had been bedding Bethany for over a year. We couldn't hurt her, but we could give her pleasure.

'You should have listened to yourself as the days went by. She became more important to you than the money in the end, didn't she? She wasn't simply a hostage any more; she was yours, your woman.'

Alessandro's dark eyes travelled from Georgina, flushed with anger and cheeks aflame, to Fiona, who was pale and trembling slightly with relief that she'd been able to see him one more time before returning to the unwelcoming world. He didn't know why she was shaking, but again he was stirred by how vulnerable she looked. At that moment he knew Georgina was right. Fiona was far more to him than a hostage, and his mistress's fury was justified.

'Even if you're right,' he said slowly, 'she still wasn't yours to dispose of. Duncan hasn't paid us the money, and until he does, Fiona belongs to me. She's surety for his debt. I loaned her to Edmund, Tanya and you for a day, but that was all. She's been mine all along.'

'Then what's going to become of her?' demanded Georgina, voicing Fiona's fear aloud. 'Since it must be clear even to you that Duncan never is going to pay, preferring to keep his crooked antique business than take her back into his bed, how do you intend to dispose of her?'

'I'd thought she might remain with me,' said Alessandro softly.

This was confirmation of Georgina's deepest fear and she stared at the man who'd been her lover for so long. 'Where would I fit into this new set-up?'

'I don't think there would be room for both of you, do you?' he asked gently.

'She's changed you!' Georgina said angrily. 'You used to be fun. Once everything was a game to you, except for business of course. Sex was exciting and different, and emotions didn't count. What I liked about you was the way you lived on the edge of danger, pushing everything to the limit. Now you sound like some boring English businessman.'

The Italian gazed at her, and the lines down the sides of his face seemed to be etched even more deeply than usual. 'You think I'm afraid to take risks now? That I've lost my appetite for adventure do you? Very well, I'll tell you how we'll decide Fiona's fate. It will be settled by the three of us.

'For the next two days Fiona will rest. She'll read books that I choose and watch videos you choose. No one will touch her, and she most certainly won't be allowed to touch herself.'

'You mean, erotic books and videos?' asked Georgina, intrigued, despite herself.

'Naturally. Once the two days are over, we will have a competition. Fiona will have nothing to do but enjoy herself. You and I will take it in turns to pleasure her. Whoever manages to extract the final orgasm wins the contest and is allowed to decide what happens to her. The loser has to abide by the winner's decision in all things.'

Georgina's eyes narrowed as she thought about what he was suggesting. It was an exciting idea, and she felt certain that towards the end of the game, when Fiona was tiring, it was more likely to be a woman's touch than a man's that would be capable of extracting the final orgasm from her. Women could be so much more gentle in the way they touched, and anyway after today she knew things about Fiona that Alessandro didn't. Armed with that knowledge and her innate skill she felt certain of victory.

'That sounds more like the Alessandro of old,' she said with a laugh. 'I agree.'

'I rather thought you would. Fiona, I'm sorry to talk about you as though you weren't here but I'm sure you understand the need for this to be brought out into the open. How do you feel about the contest?'

Fiona didn't know how she felt. At the moment the mere idea of two days rest was the best thing about it. She would leave what followed to them. Deep down she felt sure that she'd be able to summon up one last orgasm for Alessandro if it meant that she could stay with him, but she also knew that Georgina was a skilful and inventive lover who would make the contest a close one.

'I don't think I really have a choice, do I?' she asked.

He shook his head. 'No, but I promise you one thing. Whatever the outcome, somewhere safe will be found for you to live. You won't have to throw yourself on Duncan's mercy. I have many friends in all parts of the country. We will make it easy for you to begin a new life if you do have to leave.'

Fiona nodded, grateful for the comfort but realising that even Alessandro wasn't entirely confident of the outcome of the contest. She sat down on her bed and ran her hands along the skirt of the silk dress she'd been given in readiness for her departure. 'It doesn't matter,' she said flatly. 'I might as well leave it to you two to decide.'

Alessandro crossed the room and sat next to her, taking her restless hands briefly in his. 'It will be you who decides,' he whispered. 'Sex is seventy-five per cent in the mind. If you want me to win, then I will. Remember that when the contest begins.'

The next morning, having slept in a nightdress for the first time since her arrival, Fiona was handed a pile of books along with her breakfast tray. Once she'd eaten the toast and cereal, Craig came and sat in the room with her while she began to leaf through the top volume.

It was like the book she'd found on the nursery bookshelf, full of Eastern drawings and artwork. Some of it was amazingly erotic and she found herself turning hot at the scenes depicted.

During the morning she worked her way through all the books, and Craig remained with her, his instructions were simply to make sure she didn't try to pleasure herself as a result of the stimulation the books gave her.

After lunch, Tanya took her for a stroll through the garden and as the warm sun beat down on them Tanya talked of how she and Edmund had made love the night before. She described it all in graphic detail, and as she described the way her body felt as orgasm approached, Fiona felt the first finger of desire beginning to stir inside her. Her body, so highly tuned now to the sensual satisfaction it had been receiving, was growing restless.

Noticing her flushed face, Tanya then changed the subject and before long the two women went back indoors. After that, Fiona and Marcus sat in the small drawing room and watched an Italian film on video. It was highly sensuous, and when the heroine was at last stripped of her clothes and her lover began to caress and tongue her body, Fiona felt her whole vulva swelling with reciprocal desire and when the heroine climaxed, Fiona's abdomen and pelvis ached with frustration.

That night she was tied to the bed on her back instead of her front, and her hands and feet were securely fastened, not to stop her running away but to stop her from touching even her breasts.

'You have to wait,' explained Alessandro when he came in to say goodnight. 'This way you'll have far more fun once the game begins.' Fiona hoped he was right, at the moment she was suffering agonies of thwarted desire and she was stunned by her need for sexual pleasure.

The second day they left her lying in bed for longer, and after her late breakfast she was taken to the small room behind the two-way mirror where she had first watched another couple make love. This time she watched Craig and Amy as they engaged in a furious bout of lovemaking.

Amy was the aggressor. She stimulated her own nipples until they rose up from her breasts, red and engorged. Then she played with herself between her thighs, her eyes closed as her stomach rippled with orgasmic pleasure. After that she climbed all over Craig, rubbing her body against his like a cat around its owner's leg and when she finally lowered herself onto him she moved up and down in rapid jerks while between her thighs her hand was once more busy.

Fiona, whose own hands were tied behind her, could feel her body screaming for similar relief. She longed to touch herself, just once. To let her fevered flesh have one orgasm at least before the contest began, but there was no way release could be obtained and she spent her final night over-wrought and awake waiting for the competition to begin.

Alessandro had only seen Fiona from a distance the previous day. He knew how she would be feeling, and was relieved for her because it would mean that her first orgasm would be easy. She should find that at least the first three or four would come without effort. He doubted if she realised quite how many times she would be aroused to the heights of ecstasy when both he and Georgina were using their full knowledge and skill, but hoped that in her last day as his hostage she would learn yet more about herself and her body's responses. He also hoped, deep down, that he wouldn't lose her.

Fiona couldn't eat any breakfast on the morning of the competition. Her whole body was tight with anticipation and she felt as though she'd scream if she was subjected to any more arousal without being touched or caressed.

Edmund collected her, fastening her wrists lightly together before he led her upstairs to the master bedroom where Georgina and Alessandro were waiting.

'It's only to make sure you don't touch yourself,' he explained with a smile.

'There's not much point this morning. I rather think your brother and his mistress will be doing plenty of that for me, don't you?' said Fiona.

'Of course. Tanya is green with envy. You should have a wonderful time.'

'Only if the result is the one I want,' Fiona pointed out.

Edmund sighed. 'I suppose that will make quite a difference, but not during the competition itself. You won't have time to think about anything but the sensations until it's over.'

Fiona didn't know if he was right about that. At that moment the thought of Georgina succeeding in bringing her to her final climax was at the forefront of her mind. She was utterly determined that it would be Alessandro who won, and clung to the words he'd whispered two days earlier. If sex was as much in the mind as he claimed, then he'd win, because that was what she wanted.

To her surprise, both Geogina and Alessandro were fully dressed. Georgina wore a long, cream skirt and a see-through coffee-coloured chiffon blouse. The effect was business-like rather than erotic. Alessandro had on a short-sleeved tan shirt and dark brown slacks. His muscular arms, covered in dark hairs, were resting along the back of the bedroom chair and he watched her approach with a disconcertingly detached expression in his eyes.

Georgina smiled at Fiona. 'Let me take those cuffs off your wrists. No need for them now is there?'

Fiona licked her lips which suddenly felt dry. 'No, I don't imagine so.'

The other woman ran her hands down Fiona's body, feeling her breasts and stroking lightly across her hip bones, noticing the way the skin contracted beneath her fingers. 'How tense you are! Never mind, I'll soon put an end to that. I won the toss you see, so I start first. I've put the bolster on the bed already for you. Would you like to lie on it, on your back with your legs spread on each side?'

Fiona felt her legs shaking with sexual excitement as she obeyed. Her back sank against the down-filled bolster and immediately she remembered the many different times she'd been aroused and satisfied on it and she grew moist at the mere memory.

Georgina bent over her, her chiffon blouse brushing lightly against Fiona's breasts. 'I won't keep you waiting for this first one. It would be too cruel,' she murmured, and then her hand was sliding down the middle of Fiona's body and within seconds her mouth was nuzzling at the swollen nipples while her fingers busied themselves between Fiona's outspread thighs.

'How wet you are,' she whispered, gently parting the outer labia. 'Is that what you've been dreaming of?' and she circled the base of Fiona's clitoris with her fingers. At once the hot throbbing sensation began deep within Fiona's body and her legs moved spasmodically while Georgina's fingers moved away for a moment, sliding up and down the slick channels before returning to the clitoris where she pressed back the flesh-hood and then with the most delicate of touches brushed her fingernail against the very tip of the button that was composed almost entirely of nerve endings.

At once Fiona's body spasmed in release. The tightness dissipated and she let the glorious feelings wash over her, she was finally given release from the frustrations of the previous forty-eight hours.

Georgina climbed off the bed. There was no great sense of achievement in her. Like Alessandro she'd known that the beginning of the competition would be easy. He glanced at his watch. It had been agreed that they would give Fiona five minutes rest between every climax and they were only allowed fifteen minutes to bring each one about. He waited by the chair, watching

Fiona's body, upthrust by the bolster and longing to start tantalising her himself.

At last the five minutes had passed and he went to the bed, removing the bolster from beneath her and helping her upright until she was standing on the end of the bed with her arms extended so that she could hold on to the bedposts. Then he undressed on the bed in front of her, letting her see for herself how aroused he was by her. When he was finally naked he bent his knees and lowered his mouth to her breasts, licking them all over and nipping gently at the flesh with his teeth while his hands clasped her round her buttocks pulling her lower body up against him.

Fiona ground herself against his pubic bone, and when he slid an arm between their bodies so that one hand could explore between her thighs she even pushed against his arms for stimulation. His fingers were invading both her entrances and his mouth grew more demanding on her sensitive breasts.

Fiona's breathing grew increasingly rapid. She could feel his erection nudging against her hip but he clearly wasn't going to penetrate her yet, all he would do was stimulate her manually, one hand probing her between the cheeks of her bottom and the other invading her front entrance, moving two fingers deep inside her. She was tingling all over again, and then he suddenly lifted his head a little and let his early morning stubble graze around her aureoles. It was the first time he'd ever done this and the new rough sensation on such a tender place, together with the darting tremors of pleasure his fingers were causing, was enough to trigger her second climax. As her muscles clenched in an orgasm, Fiona shuddered against Alessandro while her hands gripped the bedposts tightly and she arched her back in joy.

For some time after that it proved easy for Georgina and Alessandro to bring her to climaxes. Some of them were very small, others larger, but after two days of unaccustomed abstinence her body seemed to thrive on the sweetness of satisfaction. Eventually however, even Fiona began to tire. Her body was no longer so frantic for their touch, and her responses slowed. It was now that their skill became important.

Georgina was the first of them to have difficulty in re-arousing Fiona. After the usual five-minute break she'd taken off her own clothes and lain on top of the other woman, moving herself up and down so that their breasts and pubic bones rubbed against each other, but she quickly realised that Fiona wasn't responding.

Climbing off her quiescent rival, Georgina knew that now she must resort to other methods. From her stock of equipment she extracted a 'Jelly' vibrator. Soft and flexible it had a clitoral stimulator at the base and she felt certain that the shock of the entirely different sensation of the vibrator, especially once it was moving inside her, should be sufficient stimulation.

Fiona lifted her head to see what was happening between her thighs but Georgina ordered her to lie back again. 'I want to surprise you,' she explained, gently massaging the outside of Fiona's vulva, making sure that she pressed the outer lips together firmly which she knew would stimulate the inner lips without irritating the possibly over-aroused delicate flesh there.

When she slid a finger inside Fiona's front entrance, she knew by the escaping moisture that she'd been right, and now it was easy for Georgina to slide the strange jelly-like vibrator deep inside the other woman, only stopping when the knob at the base was resting against her clitoris.

Fiona began to squirm. The vibrator felt extraordinary. It seemed to have a life of its own even before it had begun to vibrate, its flexibility making it more like a real penis than a vibrator. She could feel the pressure against her swelling bud as well, and when Georgina switched the vibrator on and it began to move inside her Fiona quickly became aroused again. Her hips twitched, her eyes widened and her stomach started to go rigid as the muscles contracted around the pulsating vibrator.

Slowly but surely her excitement grew and finally Georgina saw the flush of sexual excitement beginning to appear on Fiona's neck and knew that the vibrator had been the right choice. After a few more minutes of internal vibrations Fiona gasped and climaxed sharply, her body jolting with the shock of its intensity.

Fiona was horrified at what was happening. She'd imagined that it would be easy to choose when to climax and when to stop, but it wasn't. She'd thought that she was finished already, yet it had only taken Georgina a few minutes to tease a climax from her. If she could be that wrong about herself, how could she be able to control who won, thought Fiona anxiously.

Alessandro knew that Fiona was reaching a difficult point in the contest. She was certainly tired, but not anywhere near exhausted. It simply meant that her flesh was increasingly reluctant to respond, whatever her mind told her.

After the five-minute break he took her into the bathroom and had her lie in a shallow bath of water with her legs resting up on the side of the bath near the tap. Then he took down the shower-head and let water spray play over her vulva. At first it soothed her over-heated flesh, but when he kept it pointing at her, the drops of water hitting directly on her inner sex-lips, vaginal entrance and retracted clitoris the blissful heat of sexual excitement at last began to build again and to her intense relief he was able to bring about her climax without too much effort.

She dried herself while the other two waited for the interval to pass. Once it was over, Georgina laid Fiona down on the floor of the bathroom, got her to bend her knees and spread them wide, then slid two heavy love balls into her vaginal opening.

Fiona had only ever had them in her rectum before. Now she stood up to go into the bedroom they rolled heavily against her already sensitive vaginal walls and her stomach drew in with the shock. 'Walk round the room' said Georgina. 'Then stop, stand in front of me and rotate your hips until I tell you to stop.'

Fiona did as she was ordered, and the balls pressed yet more steadily against her nerve endings. When she rotated her hips like a striptease artist the sparks of pleasure shot right through her stomach and down her legs so that she fully expected to come, but the climax suddenly died away without ever reaching its pinnacle.

Georgina realised that more was needed. Leaving the balls inside Fiona she drew her over to the stool and made her lie across it. Then she lubricated between the other woman's buttocks and inserted a sturdy, tapered anal plug that she could inflate by squeezing the attached bulb.

Fiona felt her back passage being filled and instinctively pressed down, away from the intrusion. This meant that the pressure of the love balls increased, and frissons of sharp pain-streaked pleasure began to shoot through her pelvic area while her clitoris started to throb.

Georgina squeezed on the bulb and the anal plug expanded deep within Fiona's rectum. Fiona gasped. It felt as though soon the plug and the love balls would meet because everything was expanding until all the sensations from both front and back were running into each other, and finally there was no difference at all. She was just one frantic mass of nerve endings all tightening and bunching together in their climb to a climax which would ease the unbearable pressure.

She didn't want this orgasm. It was too intense and would make the next one, which Alessandro would have to coax from her, all the harder but as Georgina pressed relentlessly on the bulb again and her tortured rectum expanded further she knew that she was lost, and all at once her entire body bucked, her head went from side to side and she shouted in a mixture of ecstatic relief and despair as she climaxed.

Alessandro had to admire Georgina's cunning. Such a fierce orgasm would certainly have exhausted Fiona, and a five-minute break would be too short for her to recover. He decided that it was time to use something from his collection of apparatus.

When Alessandro led Fiona to the bed she felt nothing at all. No hint of excitement, no tingle of arousal. She was utterly sated, and as he piled pillows into a mound her heart sank at the thought of him trying to arouse her exhausted flesh.

The pillows were only beneath her hips which meant that her head hung down low to the bed but her stomach and the area between her thighs were stretched, making stimulation easier. Taut flesh responded more quickly than slack as Alessandro well knew and when he lifted what looked like a rag-mop head above her body Georgina guessed that he might succeed.

From the head, long strips of cord and silk ribbons were suspended. He sat beside Fiona with his shoulders obstructing any possible view she might have had, and then he waited motionless for several minutes. This heightened the tension her belly was already under and at last he saw the skin begin to quake with a fear of the unknown.

At least mentally Fiona was now more in the mood for arousal, and so Alessandro let the alternating strands of ribbon and cord brush over the tight skin of her stomach and hips, fluttering delicately against it, then pausing before reapplying it to the skin at the top of her thighs.

Fiona gasped. She had no idea what he was using on her, but it felt as though dozens of butterflies were skimming across her body, their wings brushing her softly. The image was so clear that for a moment she was convinced she was right, but when the sensation moved on down she knew that it had to be some kind of brush. Her skin trembled, relishing the lightness of the caress, and slowly she opened to him, her outer vaginal lips expanding as he teased at the ridge where they joined with the tips of the ribbons and cords.

Once she was open it was easy for him to let the feelings build. He brushed carefully around the skin between her front and back passages, and her legs twitched as this most sensitive area of her body was touched for the first time. Then, as heat mounted behind her clitoris he drew the tantalising brush up the length of love channel, twirled it against her urethral opening and finally encased her clitoris in its tendrils. With a cry of delight, Fiona climaxed, her upthrust belly rippling and straining with the contractions of bliss.

Georgina decided that it was now time to use the first of the things she'd learnt about Fiona during their day together, and that was the fact that her excitement was always increased when she had to describe the way she was feeling as her climax built.

She decided to combine this with constraint, another inducement to pleasure, and spread-eagled Fiona upright between the bottom bedposts so that she was standing on the floor with her back against the bed, her arms raised and tied in the rings and her ankles spread and fastened in the same way.

Fiona, convinced that Alessandro had won the contest because her flesh no longer felt capable of stimulation, watched indifferently as Georgina picked up a long silk scarf. 'I'm going to rub this along the length of your body, Fiona,' she said huskily 'I'll start on your back and will then come round and work on your front. I think you'll find it an exceptionally delightful experience.'

The very fact that Georgina was telling her what she was going to do caught Fiona's attention and brought her out of the exhausted stupor she'd been in before. Alessandro saw this and acknowledged yet again Georgina's skill. She was playing the less experienced woman like a maestro.

The feel of the long piece of silk rubbing along her body was just as glorious as Georgina had indicated, and Fiona's skin quickly began to warm at the smooth gliding sensation. Her back curved inwards as the silk slid over her spine and then travelled down across her buttocks, coming to rest beneath them and tugging upwards against the firm flesh before resuming its downward journey, tickling against the thin skin of the backs of her knees.

Georgina moved the scarf up and down Fiona's back for a long time, and then she slid the black mask over Fiona's eyes before moving to the front of her. Once again, Fiona had no idea where the scarf would start, and she tensed her abdomen, certain that it would be there, but instead Georgina began right down at floor level, trailing the length of material along the tops of Fiona's feet before progressing up across her kness and the tops of her thighs.

When she reached the pubic mound however, Georgina stopped, removed the scarf and then started again by draping it over Fiona's shoulders, letting the ends dangle onto the tops of her slowly swelling breasts.

Now her entire body was thoroughly alive again to all sensual excitement and Fiona strained against her bonds, inadvertently tightening the flesh that was still to feel the caress of the silk.

Georgina eased the length of material over the rigid stomach and began to talk to Fiona again, her voice insidiously arousing. 'Describe how the silk makes you feel. Does your skin burn, or is it cold? Do you like it here . . .?' and she let it fall over the inward curve of her victim's waist, 'or here . . .?' and for the briefest of seconds an end trailed between Fiona's outspread legs, brushing her thick pubic curls.

Fiona gasped and writhed against the restraints. 'Yes, yes!' she groaned. 'I like it there.'

'Where?' teased Georgina, returning to the bound woman's waist. 'Do you mean here?'

'No! no!' Fiona squirmed and tried to tilt her pelvis upwards. 'There, where you were, please.'

'You mean your breasts?' With another smile to herself, Georgina brought the scarf upwards, keeping it tight between her hands, and this time it lifted the nipples and held them upright, so that the unceasing pressure of the silken bond made Fiona groan.

'Between my thighs, please!'

'Only if you tell me what you're feeling there.'

Fiona had forgotten that this was an orgasm she didn't want, that it was Alessandro who had to give her her final pleasure. All her throbbing body wanted now was satisfaction from the band of silk that was being used so mercilessly on her. 'I'm so tight,' she whispered, shame tinging her voice. 'Everything is drawing in. There's an ache deep inside my belly that won't go away, and I need . . .'

'This?' asked Georgina quietly, and she slipped the silk scarf between the straining young woman's legs and rubbed its silken coolness against her throbbing mound of desire.

The scarf spread Fiona's outer lips effortlessly and as it touched her delicate inner tissue she bore down hard against it, making certain that her clitoris was forced out of its protective hood until it too touched the silk. Immediately she was rewarded with the rippling coils of excitement that at last filled her over-stretched abdomen and then her breasts were shaking with the violence of her contractions as she reached yet another climax.

When it was over, Fiona slumped against her bonds, her legs buckling and her head falling forward. Georgina removed the mask, untied her and smiled sweetly at Alessandro. 'Your turn, I think. She's nearly finished you know.'

He was aware of it. After making sure that the full

257

five minutes had elapsed, he went across to where Fiona was sitting in a dazed heap on the bed and pushed her roughly backwards. He knew that he needed a contrast to the soft caress of the silk, and his body was only too willing to provide it.

Fiona, taken aback by the violence of his hands, fell back and immediately he pushed some cushions beneath her shoulders so that her body was sloping down towards the bottom edge of the bed. He then spread her legs apart, handling her fiercely with a kind of controlled anger that she found intensely stimulating. Now he dropped to his knees and proceeded to use his tongue like a weapon, jabbing hard at her inner flesh-lips, thrusting it into her vagina and flicking at the walls without any restraint, while her hands moved restlessly against the bed covering.

She was aware of the difference in him, the contrast with the way he normally touched her, and this difference only heightened all her senses. When he mercilessly pushed back the folds of flesh that concealed her bud of pleasure and stabbed at the exposed protrusion with urgent hard jabs she stiffened, but although she could feel the sexual tension mounting it was impossible for her to climax and the harder she sought release, the more it seemed to evade her.

Alessandro wasn't surprised, and he only waited a few seconds before standing upright, grabbing her ankles and pulling them up until they rested on his shoulders. Now he supported himself on one knee on the bed and positioned his erection ready for penetration.

Fiona yearned to feel him fill her. She lifted her hips a little to help him and he slipped inside, the angle of penetration deliciously steep. Fresh nerve endings were stimulated within Fiona's body and at last the delicious little pulse began to beat between her thighs again.

Now Alessandro started to move. He had complete control of speed and played her carefully, moving first in long slow strokes but then quickening them before almost totally withdrawing and teasing the opening of her vagina with his swollen glans.

'Rub your breasts,' he murmured. 'Pinch your nipples and feel the blood course through them. I want to see them come erect as I'm taking you.'

Fiona was only too pleased to oblige. Her neglected breasts leapt to life in her hands and now she was full of him, the thrills of electric currents shooting through her faster and faster as he plunged in and out, driving angrily towards his own climax as Fiona's chest and throat became mottled with the pink flush of sexual excitement that he needed to see before he could be certain she'd climax too.

As he approached the point of no return he felt her stiffen on the bed, her spine went rigid and her ankles gripped his ears as she rushed headlong into the oblivion of yet another orgasm just ahead of him.

As Alessandro withdrew he felt certain that she was his. She was clearly sated and he had filled her in a way no woman could, playing what he thought would be his final card. He hoped he'd judged it right.

Georgina was relieved she'd kept one thing back. By the look of Fiona there was very little energy left in her for any kind of sexual response, no matter how skilfull the manipulator of her flesh. No, this would definitely be her last orgasm, and Georgina would be the one to draw it out of her racked body. She would do so with double the normal pleasure because not only would she win, but she would also know how badly Fiona had wanted her to fail.

When Fiona was ordered by Georgina to lie face down on the floor with the bolster spread sideways beneath her hips, Fiona moaned. 'No, I can't do any more. He's won. I just can't come for anyone again.'

'You have to let me try,' said Georgina briskly. 'That's part of the rules. If I fail after fifteen minutes then the game's over, but I'm allowed to have my turn.'

Fiona looked despairingly at Alessandro. 'I can't do it. I want to sleep.'

'If you can't do it then you won't and the game's over. Not much longer, Fiona. Now lie on the floor as Georgina says.'

He wasn't really worried. He was still convinced the game was over, but when he saw Georgina draw out a long leather strap he took a step forward. 'No, she mustn't be hurt. That was agreed.'

Georgina smiled at him. 'She likes it. I used the tawse on her yesterday and she came very quickly.'

'Is that true?' Alessandro asked the prostate Fiona. She nodded, too frightened of what was about to happen to speak but her brief acknowledgement was sufficient and he had to let Georgina go ahead.

Fiona felt the leather strap trailing down her body. It lingered along the backs of her legs, spread the cheeks of her bottom as Georgina turned it sideways and drew it between them, and then it danced its way along her spine making Fiona's hips press down into the bolster and causing her belly to stir.

Suddenly Georgina lifted the strap in the air and then brought it down lightly across Fiona's shoulder-blades. Her breasts were pressed into the carpet and the pain burnt for a moment before dying away, but as it dissipated she felt her nipples brushing against the thick pile of the carpet and realised they were burgeoning again.

Now the strap fell across the back of her waist and as her hips jerked, a warm glow began to spread through her abdomen, increased by the pressure of the carefully placed bolster. Georgina used the leather sparingly and with great care. Every blow was in a stimulating spot that triggered sensations in other areas of Fiona's body until the heat seemed to be everywhere and she wriggled frantically against the floor and the bolster in an attempt to drown out the increasing climax-threatening pressure.

'Turn over,' said Georgina.

Fiona turned, and there were tears of despair on her face. Georgina didn't care. She knew how much pain her victory would cause Fiona and this gave her so much pleasure that she felt close to an orgasm herself. She ran the fingers of one hand between her own flesh-lips and saw Fiona watching in wide-eyed amazement.

It was something new for Fiona, and added to her arousal as well. She didn't want to look but had no choice, and then as Georgina's body began to contract, the leather strap came down one more time, hard, across Fiona's tight and tingling breasts and despite every effort there was nothing Fiona could do to stop the flooding sensation of a damn breaking as another orgasm tore through her body.

Alessandro was appalled. He stared at Fiona as she writhed on the bedroom floor and felt the first hint of possible failure touch him. Frantically, he tried to recall everything he could about her, her every response to him during their times together and all he'd learnt from the others who'd helped tutor her body. When the five-minute break was over he knew what he was going to do, but now he was no longer certain that he would succeed.

Georgina didn't care what he did, she knew in her heart that it was all over. She'd toppled Fiona off the edge into a final orgasm that had not only shattered her body but also her concept of herself. To climax through pain was not something Fiona would ever have permitted herself to consider in such a situation, and her self-respect would be so low that Alessandro would never be able to rearouse her.

Fiona in fact didn't realise he was trying until he lifted her in his arms and placed her on the bed. Then he gently caressed her whole body, stroking her with his hands and murmuring reassuringly in her ear before licking softly along the red line left across her breasts by the leather strap.

Fiona's eyes filled with tears at the realisation of what that blow had done to her. She wondered what kind of a person she'd become, but Alessandro continued to comfort her. 'It's normal,' he murmured. 'Plenty of women love the mixture of pain and pleasure blows like that give. Your senses are so heightened at the moment that any kind of stimulation seems pleasurable. It's nothing to be ashamed of. I've often done it for my women, and enjoyed their enjoyment.'

'I didn't want to come,' Fiona cried. 'Why did I?'

'It doesn't matter. Just relax, let me comfort you.' He was moving his hands all over her as he talked, and when she began to quieten he slipped a hand between her legs and stroked along the creases of her thighs until her legs automatically fell wider apart.

Without alarming her, this allowed him access to her most intimate areas again and although he was aware that her flesh had been far too stimulated that day he also knew that he simply had to bring her to a peak of joy one more time.

As she snuggled against him he lubricated his fingers with jelly and spread it across her inner lips. For the first time Fiona realised that he was playing with her, trying to excite her again, and she made a protesting sound.

'Let me do it,' he said urgently. 'Georgina can't win.'

She shut her eyes. He could try, but she too knew the game was over. Very softly Alessandro continued to stroke her, making sure the jelly was in every possible crevice, and then he began to palpate the flesh beneath his hand, but no matter how skilfully he worked her there was no response and no sign of her own juices joining the jelly to ease him in his task.

There was only one thing left for him to try. Quietly he took a tiny plastic rod from where he'd placed it on the bed, and as one of his hands moved over her breasts and belly in circular motions his other positioned the narrow rod at the entrance to her urethra. The heel of his hand pressed against the base of her vulva, pulling the skin downwards, and then he moved it a fraction releasing the skin and stimulating nerve endings.

A faint spark of feeling tingled deep within Fiona and he felt her stomach muscles move. He repeated the hand movement, while at the same time raising his other hand upwards against the underside of her breasts until he could grasp the nipples one after the other and pinch them tightly. Very reluctantly they began to rise from her slack breasts, while the breast tissue too began to firm up.

Fiona's legs moved a fraction, the first indication of sexual restlessness. Alessandro didn't dare wait any longer. Her arousal might be so fleeting that if he delayed, he'd miss his chance. He knew that she hadn't used the bathroom all the morning, that her bladder must be quite full and the nerve endings under pressure.

With one single deft move he let the plastic rod touch her urethral opening, brushing against the tender place and then pressed it down against the skin beneath, while at the same time whispering, 'I love you,' in Fiona's ear.

For Fiona it was like being electrocuted. Without warning her whole body shot off the bed as an explosion ripped through her making even the tips of her fingers and toes tingle with the secondary shocks. She heard herself scream at this new, almost unendurable sensation and then she was doubled up by a convulsion of muscular spasms that made her fling herself away from Alessandro's restraining hand.

He heard her crying out, 'No! No! No!' as she lost control of herself and the depth of the feelings frightened her into protest, although against what she had no idea, except that she never wanted to experience anything like it again.

When her body was at last still, Alessandro turned her back to face him. Her eyes were closed, and her breathing slow and even. She'd fallen immediately into a deep sleep that he thought was probably close to unconsciousness, and when Georgina, who'd been watching in astonishment from the foot of the bed, saw her rival she knew that the game was truly over and that Alessandro had won.

Chapter Fifteen

*L*ater that day, after Alessandro had settled Fiona in the main guest room and made sure that she was sleeping peacefully, he went looking for Georgina. He found her in the bedroom that they had shared for so long, her vast array of clothes thrown on the bed as she started to pack.

'You don't have to leave immediately,' he said gently.

Georgina turned to look at him. She was pale and her face looked drawn but she managed to smile at him. 'I'd rather go now. It won't help to delay.'

He sat on the dressing-table stool watching her fold her dresses. 'It was good, our time together. You made me very happy.'

'Really?' She turned her back on him and busied herself with her clothes. 'Then why did it end?'

He found it difficult to explain, especially in a language that was not his own. 'There's a time for everthing,' he said at last.

'To everything its season, is that what you mean? A time to lust and a time to love?'

He narrowed his eyes. 'Who mentioned love?'

Georgina slammed the lid of one of the expensive leather suitcases. 'You did, when you managed to drag that last orgasm out of Fiona. I heard you tell her that you loved her. You never once said that to me.'

'It was a contest. Words were just another device, like your leather strap.'

She laughed harshly. 'I hardly think they seemed the same to Fiona! It doesn't matter. I'm realistic enough to accept that it's over. I suppose the biggest surprise is that someone like her should replace me.'

'You were everything I wanted when I met you. I admired your aggression at work and in the bedroom. We both know neither of us have been utterly faithful, but we've had a good run.'

'I don't really want to hear any more,' said Georgina shortly. 'In a minute you'll be saying something ghastly about me soon finding someone else; someone who'll appreciate me more.'

Alessandro laughed. 'I certainly wouldn't say any such thing. No one could appreciate you more than I did.'

'To be frank, you were beginning to get in the way of my work,' Georgina said. 'I was so busy dashing from the office to various dinners in London with you, or else trying to catch your helicopter in time to get to Norfolk for some special occasion that I was losing touch with what was going on in the magazine world. I think I'll try for a magazine editorship that's just come up. Since I'm a free-agent again I can give it my full attention.'

Alessandro respected her attitude. He knew that she was hurting, her competitive approach to the game had shown him exactly how important winning it was to her, but now she'd lost she was keeping her pain to herself.

'I wish you luck then.'

Georgina snapped the locks of her cases closed. 'Ask one of the men to take these down to the car. I'll take what I can and you can send the rest on to me at my London flat.'

'Of course.'

At the door, Georgina paused and turned to look at him one last time. 'You do realise that she'll bore you?'

'I realise that she too will have her season!'

'Goodbye then, Alessandro. I wish you both joy of each other.'

He was relieved she'd gone so quickly. It meant that he could start getting the house cleared in readiness for their move back to Italy. For a few minutes he sat still, remembering his time with Georgina, and then he put it out of his mind and went downstairs to make some telephone calls.

It was nearly tea-time when Fiona came padding into the drawing room on bare feet, a pink towelling robe wrapped round her. She looked sleepy and tousled, and he knew that it would be a long time before he tired of her.

'Where's Georgina?' she asked apprehensively.

'Gone back to London, taking as many cases as her poor car could hold! I take it you slept well?'

She nodded. 'What happens now?'

Alessandro stared at her. 'Why, you stay with me of course.'

'Even if I don't want to?'

Now it was his turn to feel shocked and he gripped the back of the nearest chair. 'No, not if you don't want to. That would be stupid. Duncan's said he can't repay us, we're taking over his companies and he will have to try and start all over again. I understand Bethany's left him. She doesn't like losers. You're not needed as a hostage any more. If you don't want to stay then you're free to leave.'

Her eyes sparkled with amusement. 'I do want to stay. I just wanted to hear you say that I had a choice!'

Alessandro closed his eyes in momentary relief, then went over to her and slid his hands inside the front of her towelling robe. She was quite naked beneath, and he caressed her tenderly.

'We're going back to Italy. I want to make love to you there, in the sun. The climate of Italy is perfect for love. I'll make sure your parents are taken care of.'

Fiona was far wiser now than when she'd first met this charismatic man who'd changed her life and she knew better than to take his words at face value. 'I think you mean the climate's ideal for sensual pleasure, don't you?'

His hands trailed down her spine, the fingers splaying out and his arms tightening until she could hardly breathe. 'Perhaps,' he agreed, his mouth resting against her ear, then his tongue flickered around the earlobe.

'When you said during the contest that you loved me, did you mean it?' she asked, shivering at the feel of his mouth on her ear.

'I meant it then,' he said carefully.

Fiona pressed closer to him, feeling his arousal and seeing his growing need for her by the way his hands were moving more urgently over her body. 'I hoped you did.'

For a moment his hands were still. 'Nothing is forever in my life,' he said slowly, anxious to be honest despite his desire to possess and keep her.

Fiona laughed. 'I never thought it was. That doesn't matter. I'd like to see Italy, and I'm sure that I'll appreciate the climate too!'

He looked down at her. 'I want you, Fiona. I want you now.'

'And I want you now. Who knows, if we're very lucky we may tire of each other at the same time. That way no one will get hurt, will they?'

He stared at her in astonishment, realising that during her time as his hostage she hadn't just matured sexually, but also as a woman. It only increased his arousal and he began to pull the robe off her, then sat on the chair and drew her onto his lap, at the same time unfastening the front of his trousers so that he could pull her onto his erection.

She felt him slide into her, his hands warm on her waist, his breath soft against the nape of her neck and she was utterly content. This was all that mattered. Not the past, and not the future, but this.

She started to move on him, lifting her hips and sliding right to the tip of his erection, then hesitating until his hands tried to pull her back down before lowering herself. She controlled everything; the pace, the rhythm and his mounting desire. She played him like a fish on a line, and his breathing grew jagged, his body trembling with need as he waited for her to allow him his release. When he finally came, thrusting upwards and bucking violently against her, Fiona smiled to herself.

Their roles had changed. At that moment he was held hostage by her sexuality, and she fully intended to keep him prisoner for a very long time.

BLACK
lace

NO LADY
Saskia Hope

30 year-old Kate dumps her boyfriend, walks out of her job and sets off in search of sexual adventure. Set against the rugged terrain of the Pyrenees, the love-making is as rough as the landscape. Only a sense of danger can satisfy her longing for erotic encounters beyond the boundaries of ordinary experience.

ISBN 0 352 32857 6

WEB OF DESIRE
Sophie Danson

High-flying executive Marcie is gradually drawn away from the normality of her married life. Strange messages begin to appear on her computer, summoning her to sinister and fetishistic sexual liaisons with strangers whose identity remains secret. She's given glimpses of the world of The Omega Network, where her every desire is known and fulfilled.

ISBN 0 352 32856 8

BLUE HOTEL
Cherri Pickford

Hotelier Ramon can't understand why best-selling author Floy Pennington has come to stay at his quiet hotel in the rural idyll of the English countryside. Her exhibitionist tendencies are driving him crazy, as are her increasingly wanton encounters with the hotel's other guests.

ISBN 0 352 32858 4

CASSANDRA'S CONFLICT
Fredrica Alleyn

Behind the respectable facade of a house in present-day Hampstead lies a world of decadent indulgence and darkly bizarre eroticism. The sternly attractive Baron and his beautiful but cruel wife are playing games with the young Cassandra, employed as a nanny in their sumptuous household. Games where only the Baron knows the rules, and where there can only be one winner.

ISBN 0 352 32859 2

THE CAPTIVE FLESH
Cleo Cordell

Marietta and Claudine, French aristocrats saved from pirates, learn their invitation to stay at the opulent Algerian mansion of their rescuer, Kasim, requires something in return; their complete surrender to the ecstasy of pleasure in pain. Kasim's decadent orgies also require the services of the handsome blonde slave, Gabriel – perfect in his male beauty. Together in their slavery, they savour delights at the depths of shame.

ISBN 0 352 32872 X

PLEASURE HUNT
Sophie Danson

Sexual adventurer Olympia Deschamps is determined to become a member of the Legion D'Amour – the most exclusive society of French libertines who pride themselves on their capacity for limitless erotic pleasure. Set in Paris – Europe's most romantic city – Olympia's sense of unbridled hedonism finds release in an extraordinary variety of libidinous challenges.

ISBN 0 352 32880 0

ODALISQUE
Fleur Reynolds

A tale of family intrigue and depravity set against the glittering backdrop of the designer set. Auralie and Jeanine are cousins, both young, glamorous and wealthy. Catering to the business classes with their design consultancy and exclusive hotel, this facade of respectability conceals a reality of bitter rivalry and unnatural love.

ISBN 0 352 32887 8

OUTLAW LOVER
Saskia Hope

Fee Cambridge lives in an upper level deluxe pleasuredome of technologically advanced comfort. The pirates live in the harsh outer reaches of the decaying 21st century city where lawlessness abounds in a sexual underworld. Bored with her predictable husband and pampered lifestyle, Fee ventures into the wild side of town, finding an urban outlaw who becomes her lover. Leading a double life of piracy and privilege, will her taste for adventure get her too deep into danger?

ISBN 0 352 32909 2

AVALON NIGHTS
Sophie Danson

On a stormy night in Camelot, a shape-shifting sorceress weaves a potent spell. Enthralled by her magical powers, each knight of the Round Table – King Arthur included – must tell the tale of his most lustful conquest. Virtuous knights, brave and true, recount before the gathering ribald deeds more befitting licentious knaves. Before the evening is done, the sorceress must complete a mystic quest for the grail of ultimate pleasure.

ISBN 0 352 32910 6

THE SENSES BEJEWELLED
Cleo Cordell

Willing captives Marietta and Claudine are settling into an opulent life at Kasim's harem. But 18th century Alergia can be a hostile place. When the women are kidnapped by Kasim's sworn enemy, they face indignities that will test the boundaries of erotic experience. Marietta is reunited with her slave lover Gabriel, whose heart she previously broke. Will Kasim win back his cherished concubines? This is the sequel to *The Captive Flesh*.

ISBN 0 352 32904 1

GEMINI HEAT
Portia Da Costa

As the metropolis sizzles in freak early summer temperatures, twin sisters Deana and Delia find themselves cooking up a heatwave of their own. Jackson de Guile, master of power dynamics and wealthy connoisseur of fine things, draws them both into a web of luxuriously decadent debauchery. Sooner or later, one of them has to make a life-changing decision.

ISBN 0 352 32912 2

VIRTUOSO
Katrina Vincenzi

Mika and Serena, darlings of classical music's jet-set, inhabit a world of secluded passion. The reason? Since Mika's tragic accident which put a stop to his meteoric rise to fame as a solo violinist, he cannot face the world, and together they lead a decadent, reclusive existence. But Serena is determined to change things. The potent force of her ravenous sensuality cannot be ignored, as she rekindles Mika's zest for love and life through unexpected means. But together they share a dark secret.

ISBN 0 352 32912 2

MOON OF DESIRE
Sophie Danson

When Soraya Chilton is posted to the ancient and mysterious city of Ragzburg on a mission for the Foreign Office, strange things begin to happen to her. Wild, sexual urges overwhelm her at the coming of each full moon. Will her boyfriend, Anton, be her saviour – or her victim? What price will she have to pay to lift the curse of unquenchable lust that courses through her veins?

ISBN 0 352 32911 4   *April '94*

FIONA'S FATE
Fredrica Alleyn

When Fiona Sheldon is kidnapped by the infamous Trimarchi brothers, along with her friend Bethany, she finds herself acting in ways her husband Duncan would be shocked by. For it is he who owes the brothers money and is more concerned to free his voluptuous mistress than his shy and quiet wife. Alessandro Trimarchi makes full use of this opportunity to discover the true extent of Fiona's suppressed, but powerful, sexuality.

ISBN 0 352 32913 0   *April '94*

HANDMAIDEN OF PALMYRA
Fleur Reynolds

3rd century Palmyra: a lush oasis in the Syrian desert. The beautiful and fiercely independent Samoya takes her place in the temple of Antioch as an apprentice priestess. Decadent bachelor Prince Alif has other plans for her and sends his scheming sister to bring her to his Bacchanalian wedding feast. Embarking on a journey across the desert, Samoya encounters Marcus, the battle-hardened centurion who will unearth the core of her desires and change the course of her destiny.

ISBN 0 352 32919 X   *May '94*

OUTLAW FANTASY
Saskia Hope

For Fee Cambridge, playing with fire had become a full time job. Helping her pirate lover to escape his lawless lifestyle had its rewards as well as its drawbacks. On the outer reaches of the 21st century metropolis the Amazenes are on the prowl; fierce warrior women who have some unfinished business with Fee's lover. Will she be able to stop him straying back to the wrong side of the tracks? This is the sequel to *Outlaw Lover*.

ISBN 0 352 32920 3   *May '94*

Three special, longer length Black Lace summer sizzlers to be published in June 1994.

THE SILKEN CAGE
Sophie Danson

When University lecturer, Maria Treharne, inherits her aunt's mansion in Cornwall, she finds herself the subject of strange and unexpected attention. Her new dwelling resides on much-prized land; sacred, some would say. Anthony Pendorran has waited a long time for the mistress to arrive at Brackwater Tor. Now she's here, his lust can be quenched as their longing for each other has a hunger beyond the realm of the physical. Using the craft of goddess worship and sexual magnetism, Maria finds allies and foes in this savage and beautiful landscape.

ISBN 0 352 32928 9

RIVER OF SECRETS
Saskia Hope & Georgia Angelis

When intrepid female reporter Sydney Johnson takes over someone else's assignment up the Amazon river, the planned exploration seems straightforward enough. But the crew's photographer seems to be keeping some very shady company and the handsome botanist is proving to be a distraction with a difference. Sydney soon realises this mission to find a lost Inca city has a hidden agenda. Everyone is behaving so strangely, so sexually, and the tropical humidity is reaching fever pitch as if a mysterious force is working its magic over the expedition. Echoing with primeval sounds, the jungle holds both dangers and delights for Sydney in this Indiana Jones-esque story of lust and adventure.

ISBN 0 352 32925 4

VELVET CLAWS
Cleo Cordell

It's the 19th century; a time of exploration and discovery and young, spirited Gwendoline Farnshawe is determined not to be left behind in the parlour when the handsome and celebrated anthropologist, Jonathan Kimberton, is planning his latest expedition to Africa. Rebelling against Victorian society's expectation of a young woman and lured by the mystery and exotic climate of this exciting continent, Gwendoline sets sail with her entourage bound for a land of unknown pleasures.

ISBN 0 352 32926 2

BLACK
lace

WE NEED YOUR HELP . . .
to plan the future of women's erotic fiction –

– and no stamp required!

Yours are the only opinions that matter.
Black Lace is a new and exciting venture: the first series of books devoted to erotic fiction by women for women.

We're going to do our best to provide the brightest, best-written, bonk-filled books you can buy. And we'd like your help in these early stages. Tell us what you want to read.

THE BLACK LACE QUESTIONNAIRE

SECTION ONE: ABOUT YOU

1.1 Sex (*we presume you are female, but so as not to discriminate*)
are you?
Male ☐ Female ☐

1.2 Age
under 21 ☐ 21–30 ☐
31–40 ☐ 41–50 ☐
51–60 ☐ over 60 ☐

1.3 At what age did you leave full-time education?
still in education ☐ 16 or younger ☐
17–19 ☐ 20 or older ☐

1.4 Occupation _____

1.5 Annual household income
        under £10,000   □   £10–£20,000   □
        £20–£30,000   □   £30–£40,000   □
        over £40,000   □

1.6 We are perfectly happy for you to remain anonymous;
but if you would like us to send you a free booklist of
Nexus books for men and Black Lace books for Women,
please insert your name and address

_____

_____

_____

_____

SECTION TWO: ABOUT BUYING BLACK LACE BOOKS

2.1 How did you acquire this copy of *Fiona's Fate*
        I bought it myself   □   My partner bought it □
        I borrowed/found it   □

2.2 How did you find out about Black Lace books?
        I saw them in a shop   □
        I saw them advertised in a magazine   □
        I saw the London Underground posters   □
        I read about them in _____
        Other _____

2.3 Please tick the following statements you agree with:
        I would be less embarrassed about buying Black
        Lace books if the cover pictures were less explicit □
        I think that in general the pictures on Black
        Lace books are about right   □
        I think Black Lace cover pictures should be as
        explicit as possible   □

2.4 Would you read a Black Lace book in a public place – on
a train for instance?
        Yes   □   No   □

SECTION THREE: ABOUT THIS BLACK LACE BOOK

3.1 Do you think the sex content in this book is:
    Too much   ☐   About right   ☐
    Not enough   ☐

3.2 Do you think the writing style in this book is:
    Too unreal/escapist   ☐   About right   ☐
    Too down to earth   ☐

3.3 Do you think the story in this book is:
    Too complicated   ☐   About right   ☐
    Too boring/simple   ☐

3.4 Do you think the cover of this book is:
    Too explicit   ☐   About right   ☐
    Not explicit enough   ☐

Here's a space for any other comments:

SECTION FOUR: ABOUT OTHER BLACK LACE BOOKS

4.1 How many Black Lace books have you read?   ☐

4.2 If more than one, which one did you prefer?

4.3 Why?

SECTION FIVE: ABOUT YOUR IDEAL EROTIC NOVEL

We want to publish the books you want to read – so this is your chance to tell us exactly what your ideal erotic novel would be like.

5.1 Using a scale of 1 to 5 (1 = no interest at all, 5 = your ideal), please rate the following possible settings for an erotic novel:

Medieval/barbarian/sword 'n' sorcery ☐

Renaissance/Elizabethan/Restoration ☐

Victorian/Edwardian ☐

1920s & 1930s – the Jazz Age ☐

Present day ☐

Future/Science Fiction ☐

5.2 Using the same scale of 1 to 5, please rate the following themes you may find in an erotic novel:

Submissive male/dominant female ☐

Submissive female/dominant male ☐

Lesbianism ☐

Bondage/fetishism ☐

Romantic love ☐

Experimental sex e.g. anal/watersports/sex toys ☐

Gay male sex ☐

Group sex ☐

Using the same scale of 1 to 5, please rate the following styles in which an erotic novel could be written:

Realistic, down to earth, set in real life ☐

Escapist fantasy, but just about believable ☐

Completely unreal, impressionistic, dreamlike ☐

5.3 Would you prefer your ideal erotic novel to be written from the viewpoint of the main male characters or the main female characters?

Male ☐   Female ☐

Both ☐

5.4 What would your ideal Black Lace heroine be like? Tick as many as you like:

Dominant	☐	Glamorous	☐
Extroverted	☐	Contemporary	☐
Independent	☐	Bisexual	☐
Adventurous	☐	Naive	☐
Intellectual	☐	Introverted	☐
Professional	☐	Kinky	☐
Submissive	☐	Anything else?	☐
Ordinary	☐	_____	

5.5 What would your ideal male lead character be like? Again, tick as many as you like:

Rugged	☐		
Athletic	☐	Caring	☐
Sophisticated	☐	Cruel	☐
Retiring	☐	Debonair	☐
Outdoor-type	☐	Naive	☐
Executive-type	☐	Intellectual	☐
Ordinary	☐	Professional	☐
Kinky	☐	Romantic	☐
Hunky	☐		
Sexually dominant	☐	Anything else?	☐
Sexually submissive	☐	_____	

5.6 Is there one particular setting or subject matter that your ideal erotic novel would contain?

_____

SECTION SIX: LAST WORDS

6.1 What do you like best about Black Lace books?

_____

6.2 What do you most dislike about Black Lace books?

_____

6.3 In what way, if any, would you like to change Black Lace covers?

_____

6.4   Here's a space for any other comments!

_____

_____

_____

_____

_____

Thank you for completing this questionnaire. Now tear it out of the book – carefully! – put it in an envelope and send it to:

Black Lace
FREEPOST
London
W10 5BR

No stamp is required!